"Mattie," he said, holding out his hand.

"Why, Jed, how are you?" said Mattie, as if they had parted the week before. It had always taken a great deal to disturb Mattie. Whatever happened she was calm. Even an old lover, and the only one she had ever possessed at that, dropping, so to speak, from the skies, after fifteen years' disappearance, did not ruffle her placidity.

"I didn't suppose you'd know me, Mattie," said Jedediah, still holding her hand foolishly.

"I knew you the minute I set eyes on you," returned Mattie. "You're some fatter and older—like myself—but you're Jed still. Where have you been all these years?"

"Pretty near everywhere, Mattie—pretty near everywhere. And ye see what it's come to—here I be driving a tin-wagon for Boone Brothers. Business is business—don't you want to buy some new tinware?"

To himself, Jed thought it was romantic, asking a woman whom he had loved all his life to buy tins on the occasion of their first meeting after fifteen years' separation.

After Many Days
TALES OF TIME PASSED

L. M. MONTGOMERY

edited by Rea Wilmshurst

Sarah Weaver
12/29/92

BANTAM BOOKS
NEW YORK · TORONTO · LONDON · SYDNEY · AUCKLAND

RL 6, age 12 and up

*This edition contains the complete text
of the original hardcover edition.*
NOT ONE WORD HAS BEEN OMITTED

AFTER MANY DAYS

*A Bantam Book / published by arrangement with
McClelland & Stewart Inc.*

PRINTING HISTORY
McClelland & Stewart edition published 1991
Bantam edition / March 1992

*The Starfire logo is a registered trademark of Bantam Books,
a division of Bantam Doubleday Dell Publishing Group, Inc.
Registered in U.S. Patent and Trademark Office and elsewhere.*

ISBN 0-553-29184-X

*Bantam Books are published by Bantam Books, a division of Bantam Doubleday Dell
Publishing Group, Inc. Its trademark, consisting of the words "Bantam Books" and
the portrayal of a rooster, is Registered in U.S. Patent and Trademark Office and in
other countries. Marca Registrada. Bantam Books, 666 Fifth Avenue, New York, New
York 10103.*

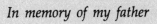

In memory of my father

Contents

Introduction

L. M. Montgomery's own long engagement is a prime example of postponement, the theme of this collection. Because she lived in a small village, and with her elderly grandparents, Montgomery's social life in Cavendish was limited. Indeed, her grandparents were opposed to Montgomery's having any sort of a life outside their home, and made it unpleasant for her to have friends over to visit. But in 1903 she met the Reverend Ewan Macdonald when he was called to Cavendish as the new Presbyterian minister. He later told her that when he first saw her he made up his mind, if she were not already "bespoke," to try his luck and win her heart. For three years he said nothing of his hopes to her, and acquaintance slowly ripened into friendship. She was "intrigued by his smile, and by a certain undeniable . . . physical attraction," but she was not sure that she wanted to be a minister's wife. However, when he announced his plans to go and study in

Scotland for a year in 1906, her indecision vanished: "I felt that I could not let him go out of my life." She accepted his proposal, but told him that they would have to wait to marry until her grandmother died. He agreed, and left her "sitting here with his little diamond solitaire on my left hand!" She was thirty-two. They did not marry until 1911, when she was thirty-seven.

Montgomery's grandfather died in 1898 and left the family farm to his wife for her lifetime only; what Montgomery calls his "absurd will" gave the homestead ultimately to his son John. Montgomery's grandmother was too frail to live alone, but having her granddaughter with her made it possible for her to stay where she was. Montgomery knew that once her grandmother died she would have to find a new home, but love and duty were stronger with her than self-interest; her self-respect could not allow her to let the stern, unloving woman who had raised her be uprooted in her old age, and so she stayed in Cavendish, postponing independence and resolving "to let all attempt at social life go."

Montgomery had had to do much soul-searching before deciding to accept Ewan Macdonald's proposal. If the family farm had been left to her rather than to her Uncle John, it is possible that she might never have married. With an inheritance and a place to live, and with the money she was earning from her writing (these were some of her most productive years as a writer of short stories), spinsterhood would at least have been an option, and she would not have had to leave Cavendish. She said in her journal, "I am not very happy here but I should be wretchedly miserable, I fear, anywhere else." However, she thought marriage might give her, if not "perfect and rapturous happiness," at least "a workaday, bread-and-butter happiness." The "past eight narrow, starved years" had made her, she said, "humble . . . in my demands on life." On the other hand, she still hoped for "a home and companionship; and more than all, to be perfectly candid, I wanted children." As she weighed the pros and cons of a "convenient" marriage, she wrote: "I dreaded unspeakably the *loneliness* of the future when I should be . . . compelled to make a new home alone in some strange place among strangers." And so, in 1906, she had accepted Ewan Macdonald's proposal.

A single woman with property was in much better case than one without, and could serenely and respectably live alone. Indeed, many of Montgomery's short stories and novels contain independent and happy old maids, and they are witnesses that she could see a bright and often humorous side to a life of "single blessedness." But nearly every single woman in this collection is still, plaintively or placidly or busily, waiting for her prince. In those days, both convention and economics decreed that most women, given the opportunity, chose marriage. Many could be the factors keeping them from it, however, and in half of these stories Montgomery rings various changes on the theme of separated lovers, giving us happy endings for them "after many days." Some have been patiently waiting for each other while duties were fulfilled; some were parted (usually by a stern parent), and lacked the confidence to assert themselves; some parted in anger and are later reconciled; some discover that they were separated by a mere misunderstanding, but years have had to pass before the complication could be cleared up. Montgomery believed, in her fiction at least, that love could last for years with no communication, that lovers could remain true to a precious memory, that it was better not to marry at all than to enter into a loveless marriage.

Not all the characters here are lovers, of course. Montgomery pursues other postponement themes: a sudden chance to consummate a life-long desire for revenge; living with a guilty conscience after a crime; the homecoming of errant family members and their reunion and reconciliation with surviving relatives; the return to their native villages of men who left years earlier to make their mark on the world.

Echoing Montgomery's own postponement of marriage for duty, but for a much longer period of time, is "The Story of Uncle Dick." Uncle Dick has waited twenty-five years for his promised bride, Rose. It was not just that his mother needed his care; she had extracted a promise from her son, one of those terrible promises that have figured in other of Montgomery's stories, that he would never marry while she lived. Uncle Dick tells the new schoolmaster, "She didn't think then that she would live long, but she lived for twenty years, Master, and she held me to my promise all the time." His fiancée, Rose, had had to move to California with her father long before Dick's mother died; then, when Dick was free, her father needed her care for five more years. Finally. she was able to come back to him. When the narrator meets her he sees "a small, faded woman of forty-five, gowned in shabby black. . . . bloom and grace were gone." He feels sure that Uncle Dick will be disappointed when he sees her. Can their love possibly be strong enough to survive the passage of time?

Rose has been far away in California, but is one of the few women in these stories to do the travelling. It is more usual that the man has gone to seek his fortune, forget his broken heart—or both. Selwyn Grant went west ten years before the opening of "An Unpremeditated Ceremony," when one of the Graham daughters told him her sister Esme was engaged to another man. He took the child's word for the fact, not even asking Esme if it were true. Another discouraged lover who went west is Jedediah Crane of "The Romance of Jedediah." Mattie Adams's sister broke up their romance years ago because Jedediah was poor, so he left to seek his fortune. Fifteen years later he comes back to see Mattie; he has no thought of marriage, because he has been unsuccessful and is as poor as ever. Miss Hannah's "Prodigal Brother" Ralph Walworth also went west in search of riches. He left home over twenty years ago, and since then Miss Hannah has been planning her future—a new house and trips abroad—to be enjoyed when he returns. The neighbours think that he will not come back at all, or, if he does, that he will be as poor as he was when he left, and are concerned that Miss Hannah's love and confidence in him will be shattered.

Two lovers and a brother gone west for long periods of time, their home-comings affording several questions: Have they found love? If not, will they find it now, on their return? Have they found happiness? If happiness is equated with fortune, have they found riches? If they have, what will they do with their money?

Two tales here contrast nicely two young men who return with the earnings of many years to the towns where they grew up. In the title story, "After Many Days," Ben Butler, the orphaned son of a ne'er-do-well father, comes back after fifteen years out west. No one in town believed that the "young varmint" would prosper in any way, but Ben has made, by whatever means, three thousand dollars. When he returns anonymously to his home town, he overhears in the tavern that Stephen Strong, the man who brought him up, is now bankrupt and will have to leave his farm. It crosses Ben's mind that his savings could help. But can he possibly bring himself to be so generous? He dismisses the idea at first: "Three thousand dollars! I could do it but I reckon I'd be a blamed fool. I ain't a-going to do it." Eventually, however, the better nature that Stephen was always sure Ben had asserts itself, he airily hands over the money as if it were nothing, and goes back west to begin again. This is the only good deed of his life so far, but Montgomery suggests that Stephen's gratitude and faith in him may lead him to better things now. The other young man, Lovell Stevens, has a much more obviously generous nature. As soon as he hears, on his return from the west, that Uncle Tom and Aunt Sally, who raised him, are in the poorhouse, there is no question in his mind at all about spending his money. All his savings are used to buy their house and its furnishings back for them. Uncle Tom and Aunt Sally happily spend their "Golden Wedding" anniversary in their old home.

Lovell's return from the West brings happiness to a long-married couple; Wesley Brooke's decision to leave for the West brings long years of unhappiness to newlyweds in "The Setness of Theodosia." The story begins with the seemingly auspicious marriage of Wesley Brooke and Theodosia Ford, although Old Jim Parmelee states his doubts that things will work out for them; their common great-great-grandfather was "about the settest man you'd ever see or want to see," and Jim fears that Theodosia, at least, has inherited his stubbornness. Theodosia's inheritance is not fully revealed until Wesley announces that he wants to go west. Calmly, quietly, but quite immoveably, she refuses to go with him. But Wesley proves that he is as set as she and leaves her behind. In fifteen years they exchange only three letters, and the village grows used to "the chronic scandal within its decorous borders." Then Montgomery makes a statement that might stand for the kernel of this whole collection: "A life may go on without ripple or disturbance for so many years that it may seem to have settled into a lasting calm; then a sudden wind of passion may sweep over it and leave behind a wake of tempestuous waters." In Theodosia's case the wind of passion comes in the form of news that Wesley is very ill. She and her life are completely unsettled; she goes west immediately, hoping desperately that she will be in time to see Wesley before he dies and to be reconciled with him.

Reconciliation is an important theme in Montgomery's work and is featured in several stories in this collection. "The Bride Roses" is a family tale. Thirty years ago Miss Corona's father and uncle quarrelled bitterly and ordered their two children never to speak to each other again. Miss Corona has spent a lonely life longing for her only relatives, but assumes they still want to continue the feud. However, when the long bloomless "bride" rose-tree in her garden suddenly blossoms, she feels it is an omen of "some rejuvenescence of love and beauty" in her own life. (This rose-tree reminds one of Valancy's rosebush in *The Blue Castle*, which blossoms for the first time when she has emancipated herself and married Barney Snaith.) Miss Corona sends all the roses from the tree for the wedding that day of her niece Juliet, as a token of her desire that the family feud be done with.

Another family is in need of reconciliation in "Elizabeth's Child." Elizabeth Ingelow married James Sheldon "in the face of the most decided opposition on the part of her family," especially her brother Paul. She moved west with her husband, and for seventeen years has not seen her relatives. When James Sheldon dies, Elizabeth's sisters decide that they would like to see their niece, and invite Worth, Elizabeth's daughter, for a visit. She wins them all over to love her, even her stubborn and bitter Uncle Paul, who finally asks Worth to stay east and live with him. She is sorely tempted, and spends a long night "fighting her battle between inclination and duty": on the one hand is her now dearly beloved uncle; on the other her mother, whom she loves no less dearly, and who is struggling alone on the prairie farm with Worth's two young brothers.

Elizabeth's family tried to interfere in her marriage plans and failed; Mattie Adams's sister interfered in Mattie's plans and succeeded. They meant their interference for the best, however. Elizabeth's husband did turn out to be a weak and unsuccessful man; Mattie's Jedediah never did gain the fortune he was seeking. Still, lovers very seldom appreciate interference, even from those who mean well. To be sure, meddling relatives are not the only obstacles that face hopeful lovers in this collection. A woman might care for a man, but what if he would not take the initiative? The conventions of the time forbade her unsought expression of love. Mattie Adams has to face this problem in "The Romance of Jedediah." In "Between the Hill and the Valley" we meet Jeffrey Miller and Sara Stuart. The two were childhood playmates, although her family was considered to be superior to his. He has loved her all his life, bringing her mayflowers every spring (as does Gilbert to Anne), but has persuaded himself that he is content to be only her friend. When Sara's father dies and she has to leave her home, Jeffrey goes to bid her farewell, and in his wretchedness at parting with her, reveals his love. He regrets the revelation immediately, sure that she "would despise him. He had forfeited her friendship for ever." He asks if she is angry, and she is—but not for the reason he expected. She is angry because he has *not* told her of his love, and so for eighteen years she has hidden her own for him.

Many of these stories are told from the man's point of view; two of them contrast men of business. One is Cuthbert Marshall who, after twenty years, returns to his old home: "He had come back to it, heart-sick of his idols of the marketplace. . . . His gods mocked him and he wearied of their service. Were there not better things than these?" He eventually discovers that "the best that God had meant for him had been here" in the home of his youth, "In the Old Valley." The other is Robert Turner, of "Robert Turner's Revenge," who has "the face of a man who never faltered or wavered, who stuck at nothing that might advance his plans and purposes, a face known and dreaded in the business world where he reigned master." Unlike Marshall, Turner has no regrets, and finds nothing lacking in his life in the world of business. But on a trip to his old home, intending to foreclose the mortgage on the farm of an old rival, he discovers that his heart is not totally closed to softer feelings.

Gilroy Gray, a college professor, is the complete antithesis of Robert Turner, the man of the world. Gilroy has finally persuaded Vere Maybee to marry him, but he has had to come to terms with the fact that Vere still loves the memory of Maurice Tisdale, her adolescent sweetheart, who was reported dead out west sixteen years ago. Because her dream of Maurice's perfection has made Vere the ethereal, unworldly woman Gilroy has come to love, he "accepted it all and put it behind him. He would rather have half of her heart than the whole one of any other woman." Later, Gilroy meets Maurice, very much alive, who by chance is visiting their town. Maurice is now rich, married, bald, and fat, and wants to look up Vere, "to put the time in" before he catches a train out of town. For a moment Gilroy hesitates: "If Vere saw him, just as he was," the ghost would be laid; "He would be left without a rival." On the other hand, "If her dream went would it not take with it something that was part of her charm?" Should he prevent their meeting, "For a Dream's Sake"?

The two longer stories in this collection strike a sombre note. In "The Price," Christine North believes she caused the death of her beloved cousin by accidentally giving her the wrong medication. She keeps her terrible mistake a secret, telling neither the nurse nor the doctor, her fiancé; but she decides that "she must atone for it by lifelong penance." She eliminates all pleasure from her life and refuses to marry, eventually even adopting a child, although she dislikes all children, when she begins to feel too comfortable in her austere new life. When the child almost dies from appendicitis, Christine's guilt renews itself and she realizes she can't live with her secret any longer. She must confess her crime and face the consequences.

In "The Man Who Forgot," Montgomery again shows the power of a guilty conscience. Gertrude Stirling loved Anthony Fairweather, but her father, "Old Doc," preferred Gordon Mitchell and ordered her never to marry Anthony. Gertrude "worshipped her father and wouldn't have disobeyed or hurt him, even for Anthony. But she knew time was on her side; she knew her father would come round in due course." Time runs out when Old Doc is killed suddenly in a train accident, and Gertrude feels bound by her promise to him never to marry Anthony. Gordon had been with Old Doc when he was injured and had been given a final message for Gertrude. He keeps secret Old Doc's dying words, but his guilt in so doing leads, at a traumatic moment, to complete memory loss. Although he is able to re-learn his life and business, his heart is left a blank: he has no normal emotions, doesn't love his mother any more, doesn't even love Gertrude. Ten years must pass before the return of his old rival, Anthony Fairweather, can right old wrongs.

Montgomery's theme of postponement comes to life in many ways in these tales, and we see the trials her characters have been through written in their hearts and on their faces. Uncle Dick's long-tested love "glorified his whole inner life with a strange, unfailing radiance"; Joyce (of "In the Old Valley") has a soul that looked out through "splendid steady blue eyes . . . the staunch, brave, sweet soul of the maiden ripened to womanhood." These are not static characters: their experiences in the course of the story can change them. Montgomery describes Robert Turner at first as having "a face that looked as if it might be carved out of granite," but at the end of the tale he is wearing "a smile, whose amusement presently softened to an expression that would have amazed his business cronies." Mrs. March, who "looked hard and revengeful," with "a cruel light" in her eyes when Lou Carroll is first mentioned, not only takes the half-crazed, destitute Lou into her home, but bends over her sleeping guest, "her bright brown eyes softened with tears" ("Mrs. March's Revenge").

Montgomery gives us gentle, wistful lovers and strong-willed, passionate ones. She shows us clear, peaceful souls and turbulent, troubled ones. Her

characters may stay alone in their homes for years
or come back to their homes "after many days"
of wandering; they seek love or rest or sanctuary.
Those who did wrong have discovered their better
selves, and now have more personal happiness.
The passage of time has refined their souls and
spirits.

In *Rilla of Ingleside*, Rilla looks back on the four
years of war and reflects on what she calls her
"soul growth" during that time. In "The Price,"
Montgomery sums up the "soul growth" Christine has gained from her ordeal:

> Later yet again would come a wistful realiza-
> tion that, after all, the years had not been
> wasted. Vanity, selfishness, frivolity had
> been stripped from her soul as a garment.
> Strength, fineness, reserve, dignity, all she
> had lacked had been given unto her in those
> years of penance; even physically they had
> not been barren. In her regular, simple life
> the delicacy of her girlhood had vanished.
> She had become a perfectly healthy woman.
> All this had been bought with a great price,
> but she could never have purchased it in a
> cheaper market.

The happy ending has often been derided in
this day of realistic writing, but many real-life
stories end happily, often because people have
exercised the same virtues that Montgomery's
characters exhibit: patience, trust, forbearance,

and love. There is a satisfaction for the reader in the closings Montgomery provides for these tales. We know, from stories in previous collections, that Montgomery was capable of writing unhappy endings. That she chose to end these tales of postponement happily suggests that she felt her characters had gone through enough trouble during their years of waiting; they had learned self-control, humility, and patience; they deserved their rewards.

After Many Days

The square, bare front room of the Baxter Station Hotel—so called because there was no other house in the place to dispute the title—was filled with men. Some of them were putting up at the hotel while they worked at the new branch line, and some of them had dropped in to exchange news and banter while waiting for the mail train.

Gabe Foley, the proprietor, was playing at checkers with one of the railroad men, but was not too deeply absorbed in the game to take in all that was said around him. The air was dim with tobacco smoke, and the brilliant, scarlet geraniums which Mrs. Foley kept in the bay window looked oddly out of place. Gabe knew all those

1

present except one man—a stranger who had landed at Baxter Station from the afternoon freight. Foley's hotel did not boast of a register, and the stranger did not volunteer any information regarding his name or business. He had put in the afternoon and early evening strolling about the village and talking to the men on the branch line. Now he had come in and ensconced himself in the corner behind the stove, where he preserved a complete silence.

He had a rather rough face and was flashily dressed. Altogether, Gabe hardly liked his looks, but as long as a man paid his bill and did not stir up a row Gabe Foley did not interfere with him.

Three or four farmers from "out Greenvale way" were drawn up by the stove, discussing the cheese factory sales and various Greenvale happenings. The stranger appeared to be listening to them intently, although he took no part in their conversation.

Presently he brought his tilted chair down with a sharp thud. Gabe Foley had paused in his manipulation of a king to hurl a question at the Greenvale men.

"Is it true that old man Strong is to be turned out next week?"

"True enough," answered William Jeffers. "Joe Moore is going to foreclose. Stephen Strong has got three years behind with the interest and Moore is out of patience. It seems hard on old Stephen, but Moore ain't the man to hesitate for that. He'll have his own out of it."

"What will the Strongs do?" asked Gabe.

"That's the question everyone in Greenvale is asking. Lizzie Strong has always been a delicate little girl, but maybe she'll manage to scare up a living. Old Stephen is to be the most pitied. I don't see anything for him but the poorhouse."

"How did Stephen Strong come to get into such a tight place?" the stranger asked suddenly. "When I was in these parts a good many years ago he was considered a well-to-do man."

"Well, so he was," replied William Jeffers. "But he began to get in debt when his wife took sick. He spent no end of money on doctors and medicines for her. And then he seemed to have a streak of bad luck besides—crops failed and cows died and all that sort of thing. He's been going behind ever since. He kind of lost heart when his wife died. And now Moore is going to foreclose. It's my opinion poor old Stephen won't live any time if he's turned out of his home."

"Do you know what the mortgage comes to?"

"Near three thousand, counting overdue interest."

"Well, I'm sorry for old Stephen," said Gabe, returning to his game. "If anybody deserves a peaceful old age he does. He's helped more people than you could count, and he was the best Christian in Greenvale, or out of it."

"He was too good," said a Greenvale man crustily. "He just let himself be imposed upon all his life. There's dozens of people owes him and he's never asked for a cent from them. And he's always had some shiftless critter or other hanging round and devouring his substance."

"D'ye mind that Ben Butler who used to be in Greenvale twenty years ago?" asked a third man. "If ever there was an imp of Satan 'twas him—old Ezra Butler's son from the valley. Old Stephen kept him for three or four years and was as good to him as if he'd been his own son."

"Most people out our way do mind Ben Butler," returned William Jeffers grimly, "even if he ain't been heard tell of for twenty years. He wasn't the kind you could forget in a hurry. Where'd he go? Out to the Kootenay, wasn't it?"

"Somewhere there. He was a reg'lar young villain—up to every kind of mischief. Old Stephen caught him stealing his oats one time and 'stead of giving him a taste of jail for it, as he ought to have done, he just took him right into his family and kept him there for three years. I used to tell him he'd be sorry for it, but he always persisted that Ben wasn't bad at heart and would come out all right some day. No matter what the young varmint did old Stephen would make excuses for him—'his ma was dead,' or he 'hadn't had no bringing-up.' I was thankful when he did finally clear out without doing some penitentiary work."

"If poor old Stephen hadn't been so open-handed to every unfortunate critter he came across," said Gabe, "he'd have had more for himself today."

The whistle of the mail train cut short the discussion of Stephen Strong's case. In a minute the room was vacant, except for the stranger. When left to himself he also rose and walked out. Turning away from the station, he struck briskly into the Greenvale road.

About three miles from the station he halted before a house built close to the road. It was old-fashioned, but large and comfortable-looking, with big barns in the rear and an orchard on the left slope. The house itself was in the shadow of the firs, but the yard lay out in the moonlight and the strange visitor did not elect to cross it. Instead, he turned aside into the shadow of the trees around the garden and, leaning against the old rail fence, gave himself up to contemplation of some kind.

There was a light in the kitchen. The window-blind was not down and he had a fairly good view of the room. The only visible occupant was a grey-haired old man sitting by the table, reading from a large open volume before him. The stranger whistled softly.

"That's old Stephen—reading the Bible same as ever, by all that's holy! He hasn't changed much except that he's got mighty grey. He must be close on to seventy. It's a shame to turn an old man like him out of house and home. But Joe Moore always was a genuine skinflint."

He drew himself softly up and sat on the fence. He saw old Stephen Strong close his book, place his spectacles on it, and kneel down by his chair.

The old man remained on his knees for some time and then, taking up his candle, left the kitchen. The man on the fence still sat there. Truth to tell, he was chuckling to himself as he recalled all the mischief he had done in the old days—the doubtful jokes, tricks, and escapades he had gone through with.

He could not help remembering at the same time how patient old Stephen Strong had always been with him. He recalled the time he had been caught stealing the oats. How frightened and sullen he had been! And how gently the old man had talked to him and pointed out the sin of which he had been guilty!

He had never stolen again, but in other respects he had not mended his ways much. Behind old Stephen's back he laughed at him and his "preaching." But Stephen Strong had never lost faith in him. He had always asserted mildly that "Ben would come out all right by and by." Ben Butler remembered this too, as he sat on the fence.

He had "always liked old Stephen," he told himself. He was sorry he had fallen on such evil times.

"Preaching and praying don't seem to have brought him out clear after all," he said with a chuckle that quickly died away. Somehow, even in his worst days, Ben Butler had never felt easy when he mocked old Stephen. "Three thousand dollars! I could do it but I reckon I'd be a blamed fool. I ain't a-going to do it. Three thousand ain't picked up every day, even in the Kootenay—'specially by chaps like me."

He patted his pocket knowingly. Fifteen years previously he had gone to the Kootenay district with visions of making a fortune that were quickly dispelled by reality. He had squandered his wages as soon as paid, and it was only of late years that he had "pulled up a bit," as he expressed it, and saved his three thousand dollars.

He had brought the money home with him, having some vague notion of buying a farm and "settling down to do the respectable." But he had already given up the idea. This country was too blamed quiet for him, he said. He would go back to the Kootenay, and he knew what he would do with his money. Jake Perkins and Wade Brown, two "pals" of his, were running a flourishing grocery and saloon combined. They would be glad of another partner with some cash. It would suit him to a T.

"I'll clear out tomorrow," he mused as he walked back. "As long as I stay here old Stephen will haunt me, sure as fate. Wonder what he was praying for tonight. He always used to say the Lord would provide, but He don't appear to have done it. Well, I ain't His deputy."

The next afternoon Ben Butler went over to Greenvale and called at Stephen Strong's. He found only the old man at home. Old Stephen did not recognize him at first, but made him heartily welcome when he did.

"Ben, I do declare! Ben Butler! How are you?

How are you? Sit down, Ben—here, take this chair. Where on earth did you come from?"

"Baxter just now—Kootenay on the large scale," answered Ben. "Thought I'd come over and see you again. Didn't expect you'd remember me at all."

"Remember you! Why, of course I do. I haven't ever forgot you, Ben. Many's the time I've wondered where you was and how you was getting on. And you tell me you've been in the Kootenay! Well, well, you have seen a good bit more of the world than I ever have. You've changed a lot, Ben. You ain't a boy no longer. D'ye mind all the pranks you used to play?"

Ben laughed sheepishly.

"I reckon I do. But it ain't myself I come here to talk about—not much to say if I did. It's just been up and down with me. How are you yourself, sir? They were telling me over at Baxter that you were kind of in trouble."

The old man's face clouded over; all the sparkle went out of his kind blue eyes.

"Yes, Ben, yes," he said, with a heavy sigh. "I've kind of gone downhill, that's a fact. The old farm has to go, Ben—I'm sorry for that—I'd have liked to have ended my days here, but it's not to be. I don't want to complain. The Lord does all things well. I haven't a doubt but that it all fits into His wise purposes—not a doubt, Ben, although it may be kind of hard to see it."

Ben was always skittish of "pious talk." He veered around adroitly.

"I dunno as the Lord has had much to do with this, sir. Seems to me as if 'twas the other one as was running it, with Joe Moore for deputy. The main thing, as I look at it, is to get a cinch on him. How much does the mortgage amount to, sir?"

"About three thousand dollars, interest and all."

Old Stephen's voice trembled. The future looked very dark to him in his old age.

Ben put his hand inside his coat and brought out a brand-new, plump pocketbook. He opened it, laid it on his knee, and counted out a number of crisp notes.

"Here, sir," he said, pushing them along the table. "I reckon that'll keep you out of Joe Moore's clutches. There's three thousand there if I ain't made a mistake. That'll set you clear, won't it?"

"Ben!" Old Stephen's voice trembled with amazement. "Ben, I can't take it. It wouldn't be fair—or right. I could never pay you back."

Ben slipped the rubber band around his wallet and replaced it airily.

"I don't want it paid back, sir. It's a little gift, so to speak, just to let you know I ain't ungrateful for all you did for me. If it hadn't been for you I might have been in the penitentiary by now. As for the money, it may seem a pile to you, but we don't think anything more of a thousand or so in the Kootenay than you Greenvale folks do of a fiver—not a bit more. We do things on a big scale out there."

"But, Ben, are you sure you can afford it—that you won't miss it?"

"Pop sure. Don't you worry, I'm all right."

"Bless you—bless you!" The tears were running down old Stephen's face as he gathered up the money with a shaking hand. "I always knew you would do well, Ben—always said it. I knew you'd a good heart. I just can't realize this yet—it seems too good to be true. The old place saved—I can die in peace. Of course, I'll pay you back some of it anyhow if I'm spared a while longer. Bless you, Ben."

Ben would not stay long after that. He said he had to leave on the 4:30 train. He was relieved when he got away from the old man's thanks and questions. Ben did not find it easy to answer some of the latter. When he was out of sight of the house he sat on a fence and counted up his remaining funds.

"Just enough to take me back to the Kootenay— and then begin over again, I s'pose. But 'twas worth the money to see the old fellow's face. He'd thank the Lord and me, he said. How Jake and Wade'd roar to hear them two names in partnership! But I'm going to pull up a bit after this, see if I don't, just to justify the old man's faith in me. 'Twould be too bad to disappoint him if he's believed for so long that I was going to turn out all right yet."

When the 4:30 train went out Ben Butler stood on the rear platform. Gabe Foley watched him abstractedly as he receded.

"Blamed if I know who that fellow was," he remarked to a crony. "He never told his name, but seems to me I've seen him before. He has a kind of hang-dog look, I think. But he paid up square and it is none of my business."

The Bride Roses

Miss Corona awoke that June morning with a sigh, the cause of which she was at first too sleepy to understand. Then it all came over her with a little sickening rush; she had fallen asleep with tear-wet lashes the night before on account of it.

This was Juliet Gordon's wedding day, and she, Miss Corona, could not go to the wedding and was not even invited, all because of the Quarrel, a generation old, and so chronic and bitter and terrible that it always presented itself to Miss Corona's mental vision as spelled with a capital. Well might Miss Corona hate it. It had shut her up into a lonely life for long years. Juliet Gordon and Juliet's father, Meredith Gordon, were the only relations Miss Corona had in the world, and

13

the old family feud divided them by a gulf which now seemed impassable.

Miss Corona turned over on her pillows, lifted one corner of the white window-blind and peeped out. Below her a river of early sunshine was flowing through the garden, and the far-away slopes were translucent green in their splendour of young day, with gauzy, uncertain mists lingering, spiritlike, in their intervales. A bird, his sleek plumage iridescent in the sunlight, was perched on the big chestnut bough that ran squarely across the window, singing as if his heart would burst with melody and the joy of his tiny life. No bride could have wished anything fairer for her day of days, and Miss Corona dropped back on her pillows with another gentle sigh.

"I'm so glad that the dear child has a fine day to be married," she said.

Juliet Gordon was always "dear child" to Miss Corona, although the two had never spoken to each other in their lives.

Miss Corona was a brisk and early riser as a rule, with a genuine horror of lazy people who lay late abed or took over-long to get their eyes well opened, but this morning she made no hurry about rising, even though scurrying footsteps, banging doors, and over-loud tinkling of dishes in the room below betokened that Charlotta was already up and about. And Charlotta, as poor Miss Corona knew only too well, was fatally sure to do something unfortunate if she were not under some careful, overseeing eye. To be sure, Charlotta's intentions were always good.

But Miss Corona was not thinking about Charlotta this morning, and she felt so strong a distaste for her lonely, purposeless life that she was in no haste to go forth to meet another day of it.

Miss Corona felt just the least little bit tired of living, although she feared it was very wicked of her to feel so. She lay there listlessly for half an hour longer, looking through a mist of tears at the portrait of her stern old father hanging on the wall at the foot of the bed, and thinking over the Quarrel.

It had happened thirty years ago, when Miss Corona had been a girl of twenty, living alone with her father at the old Gordon homestead on the hill, with the big black spruce grove behind it on the north and far-reaching slopes of green fields before it on the south. Down in the little northern valley below the spruce grove lived her uncle, Alexis Gordon. His son, Meredith, had seemed to Corona as her own brother. The mothers of both were dead; neither had any other brother or sister. The two children had grown up together, playmates and devoted friends. There had never been any sentiment or lovemaking between them to mar a perfect comradeship. They were only the best of friends, whatever plans the fathers might have cherished for the union of their estates and children, putting the property consideration first, as the Gordons were always prone to do.

But, if Roderick and Alexis Gordon had any such plans, all went by the board when they quar-

relled. Corona shivered yet over the bitterness of
that time. The Gordons never did anything half-
heartedly. The strife between the two brothers
was determined and irreconcilable.

Corona's father forbade her to speak to her
uncle and cousin or to hold any communication
with them. Corona wept and obeyed him. She
had always obeyed her father; it had never entered
into her mind to do anything else. Meredith had
resented her attitude hotly, and from that day
they had never spoken or met, while the years
came and went, each making a little wider and
more hopeless the gulf of coldness and anger and
distrust.

Ten years later Roderick Gordon died, and in
five months Alexis Gordon followed him to the
grave. The two brothers who had hated each
other so unyieldingly in life slept very peaceably
side by side in the old Gordon plot of the country
graveyard, but their rancour still served to embit-
ter the lives of their descendants.

Corona, with a half-guilty sense of disloyalty to
her father, hoped that she and Meredith might
now be friends again. He was married, and had
one little daughter. In her new and intolerable
loneliness Corona's heart yearned after her own
people. But she was too timid to make any
advances, and Meredith never made any. Corona
believed that he hated her, and let slip her last
fluttering hope that the old breach would ever be
healed.

"Oh, dear! oh, dear!" she sobbed softly into her
pillows. It seemed a terrible thing to her that one

of her race and kin was to be married and she
could not be present at the ceremony, she who
had never seen a Gordon bride.

When Miss Corona went downstairs at last, she
found Charlotta sobbing in the kitchen porch. The
small handmaiden was doubled up on the floor,
with her face muffled in her gingham apron and
her long braids of red hair hanging with limp
straightness down her back. When Charlotta was
in good spirits, they always hung perkily over
each shoulder, tied up with enormous bows of
sky-blue ribbon.

"What have you done this time?" asked Miss
Corona, without the slightest intention of being
humorous or sarcastic.

"I've—I've bruk your green and yaller bowl,"
sniffed Charlotta. "Didn't mean to, Miss C'rona.
It jest slipped out so fashion 'fore I c'd grab holt
on it. And it's bruk into forty millyun pieces. Ain't
I the onluckiest girl?"

"You certainly are," sighed Miss Corona. At
any other time she would have been filled with
dismay over the untoward fate of her green and
yellow bowl, which had belonged to her great-
grandmother and had stood on the hall table to
hold flowers as long as she could remember. But
just now her heart was so sore over the Quarrel
that there was no room for other regrets. "Well,
well, crying won't mend it. I suppose it is a judg-
ment on me for staying abed so late. Go and
sweep up the pieces, and do try and be a little
more careful, Charlotte."

"Yes'm," said Charlotta meekly. She dared not

resent being called Charlotte just then. "And I'll
tell you what I'll do, ma'am, to make up, I'll go
and weed the garden. Yes'm, I'll do it beautiful."

"And pull up more flowers than weeds," Miss
Corona reflected mournfully. But it did not matter; nothing mattered. She saw Charlotta sally
forth into the garden with a determined, do-or-
die expression surmounting her freckles, without
feeling interest enough to go and make sure that
she did not root out all the late asters in her tardy
and wilfully postponed warfare on weeds.

This mood lasted until the afternoon. Then Miss
Corona, whose heart and thoughts were still
down in the festive house in the valley, roused
herself enough to go out and see what Charlotta
was doing. After finding out, she wandered idly
about the rambling, old-fashioned place, which
was full of nooks and surprises. At every turn
you might stumble on some clump or tangle of
sweetness, showering elusive fragrance on the
air, that you would never have suspected. Nothing in the garden was planted quite where it
should be, yet withal it was the most delightful
spot imaginable.

Miss Corona pushed her way into the cherry-
tree copse, and followed a tiny, overgrown path
to a sunshiny corner beyond. She had not been
there since last summer; the little path was getting
almost impassable. When she emerged from the
cherry trees, somewhat rumpled and pulled about
in hair and attire, but attended, as if by a benediction, by the aromatic breath of the mint she had

trodden on, she gave a little cry and stood quite
still, gazing at the rosebush that grew in the corner. It was so large and woody that it seemed
more like a tree than a bush, and it was snowed
over with a splendour of large, pure white roses.

"Dear life," whispered Miss Corona tremulously, as she tiptoed towards it. "The bride roses
have bloomed again! How very strange! Why,
there has not been a rose on that tree for twenty
years."

The rosebush had been planted there by Corona's great-grandmother, the lady of the green and
yellow bowl. It was a new variety, brought out
from Scotland by Mary Gordon, and it bore large
white roses which three generations of Gordon
brides had worn on their wedding day. It had
come to be a family tradition among the Gordons
that no luck would attend the bride who did not
carry a white rose from Mary Gordon's rose-tree.

Long years ago the tree had given up blooming,
nor could all the pruning and care given it coax a
single blossom from it. Miss Corona, tinctured
with the superstition apt to wait on a lonely womanhood, believed in her heart that the rosebush
had a secret sympathy with the fortunes of the
Gordon women. She, the last of them on the old
homestead, would never need the bride roses.
Wherefore, then, should the old tree bloom? And
now, after all these years, it had flung all its long-
hoarded sweetness into blossom again. Miss
Corona thrilled at the thought. The rosebush had
bloomed again for a Gordon bride, but Miss

Corona was sure there was another meaning in it too; she believed it foretokened some change in her own life, some rejuvenescence of love and beauty like to that of the ancient rose-tree. She bent over its foam of loveliness almost reverently.

"They have bloomed for Juliet's wedding," she murmured. "A Gordon bride must wear the bride roses, indeed she must. And this—why, it is almost a miracle."

She ran, light-footedly as a girl, to the house for scissors and a basket. She would send Juliet Gordon the bride roses. Her cheeks were pink from excitement as she snipped them off. How lovely they were! How very large and fragrant! It was as if all the grace and perfume and beauty and glory of those twenty lost summers were found here at once in them. When Miss Corona had them ready, she went to the door and called,

"Charlotte! Charlotte!"

Now Charlotta, having atoned to her conscience for the destruction of the green and yellow bowl by faithfully weeding the garden, a task which she hated above all else, was singing a hymn among the sweet peas, and her red braids were over her shoulders. This ought to have warned Miss Corona, but Miss Corona was thinking of other things, and kept on calling patiently, while Charlotta weeded away for dear life, and seemed smitten with treble deafness.

After a time Miss Corona remembered and sighed. She did hate to call the child that foolish name with its foreign sound. Just as if plain

"Charlotte" were not good enough for her, and much more suitable to "Smith" too! Ordinarily Miss Corona would not have given in. But the case was urgent; she could not stand upon her dignity just now.

"Charlotta!" she called entreatingly.

Instantly Charlotta flew to the garden gate and raced up to the door.

"Yes'm," she said meekly. "You want me, Miss C'rona?"

"Take this box down to Miss Juliet Gordon, and ask that it be given to her at once," said Miss Corona. "Don't loiter, Charlotta. Don't stop to pick gum in the grove, or eat sours in the dike, or poke sticks through the bridge, or—"

But Charlotta had gone.

Down in the valley, the other Gordon house was in a hum of excitement. Upstairs Juliet had gone to her invalid mother's room to show herself in her wedding dress to the pale little lady lying on the sofa. She was a tall, stately young girl with the dark grey Gordon eyes and the pure creaminess of colouring, flawless as a lily petal. Her face was a very sweet one, and the simple white dress she wore became her dainty, flowerlike beauty as nothing elaborate could have done.

"I'm not going to put on my veil until the last moment," she said laughingly. "I would feel married right away if I did. And oh, Mother dear, isn't it too bad? My roses haven't come. Father is back from the station, and they were not there. I am so disappointed. Romney ordered pure white roses because I said a Gordon bride must carry nothing else. Come in"—as a knock sounded at the door.

Laura Burton, Juliet's cousin and bridesmaid, entered with a box.

"Juliet dear, the funniest little red-headed girl with the most enormous freckles has just brought this for you. I haven't an idea where she came from; she looked like a messenger from pixy-land."

Juliet opened the box and gave a cry.

"Oh, Mother, look—look! What perfect roses! Who could have sent them? Oh, here's a note from—from—why, Mother, it's from Cousin Corona."

"My dear child," ran the letter in Miss Corona's fine, old-fashioned script. "I am sending you the Gordon bride roses. The rose-tree has bloomed for the first time in twenty years, my dear, and it must surely be in honour of your wedding day. I hope you will wear them for, although I have never known you, I love you very much. I was once a dear friend of your father's. Tell him to let you wear the roses I send for old times' sake. I wish you every happiness, my dear.

"Your affectionate cousin,
"Corona Gordon."

"Oh, how sweet and lovely of her!" said Juliet gently, as she laid the letter down. "And to think she was not even invited! I wanted to send her an invitation, but Father said it would be better not to—she was so hard and bitter against us that she would probably regard it as an insult."

"He must have been mistaken about her attitude," said Mrs. Gordon. "It certainly is a great pity she was not invited, but it is too late now. An invitation sent two hours before the ceremony would be an insult indeed."

"Not if the bride herself took it!" exclaimed Juliet impulsively. "I'll go myself to Cousin Corona, and ask her to come to my wedding."

"Go yourself! Child, you can't do such a thing! In that dress . . ."

"Go I must, Momsie. Why, it's only a three minutes' walk. I'll go up the hill by the old field-path, and no one will see me. Oh, don't say a word—there, I'm gone!"

"That child!" sighed the mother protestingly, as she heard Juliet's flying feet on the stairs. "What a thing for a bride to do!"

Juliet, with her white silken skirts caught up above grasses and dust, ran light-footedly through the green lowland fields and up the hill, treading for the first time the faint old field-path between the two homes, so long disused that it was now barely visible in its fringing grasses and star-dust of buttercups. Where it ran into the spruce grove was a tiny gate which Miss Corona had always kept in good repair, albeit it was never used. Juliet pushed up the rusty hasp and ran through.

Miss Corona was sitting alone in her shadowy parlour, hanging over a few of the bride roses with falling tears, when something tall and beauti-

ful and white came in like a blessing and knelt by
her chair.

"Cousin Corona," said a somewhat breathless
bride, "I have come to thank you for your roses
and ask you to forgive us all for the old quarrel."

"Dear child," said Miss Corona out of her
amazement, "there is nothing to forgive. I've
loved you all and longed for you. Dear child, you
have brought me great happiness."

"And you must come to my wedding," cried
Juliet. "Oh, you must—or I shall think you have
not really forgiven us. You would never refuse
the request of a bride, Cousin Corona. We are
queens on our wedding day, you know."

"Oh, it's not that, dear child—but I'm not
dressed—I—"

"I'll help you dress. And I won't go back without you. The guests and the minister must wait
if necessary—yes, even Romney must wait. Oh, I
want you to meet Romney. Come, dear."

And Miss Corona went. Charlotta and the bride
got her into her grey silk and did her hair, and
in a very short time she and Juliet were hurrying
down the old field-path. In the hollow Meredith
Gordon met them.

"Cousin Meredith," said Miss Corona tremulously.

"Dear Corona."

He took both her hands in his, and kissed her
heartily. "Forgive me for misunderstanding you
so long. I thought you hated us all."

Turning to Juliet, he said with a fatherly smile,

"What a terrible girl it is for having its own way! Who ever heard of a Gordon bride doing such an unconventional thing? There, scamper off to the house before your guests come. Laura has made your roses up into what she calls 'a dream of a bouquet.' I'll take Cousin Corona up more leisurely."

"Oh, I knew that something beautiful was going to happen when the old rose-tree bloomed," murmured Miss Corona happily.

The Romance of Jedediah

Jedediah was not a name that savoured of romance. His last name was Crane, which is little better. And it would be no use to call this story "Mattie Adams's Romance" because Mattie Adams is not a romantic name either. But names have really nothing to do with romance. The most exciting and tragic affair I ever knew was between a man named Silas Putdammer and a woman named Kezia Cullen—which has nothing to do with the present story.

Jedediah, to all outward seeming, did not appear to be any more romantic than his name. He looked distinctly commonplace as he rode comfortably along the winding country road that was dreaming in the haze and sunshine of a midsummer afternoon. He was perched on the seat of a bright red pedlar's wagon, above and behind a dusty, ambling, red pony of that peculiar gait and appearance pertaining to the ponies of country pedlars—a certain placid, unhasting leanness, as of a nag that has encountered troubles of his own and has lived them down by sheer patience and staying power. From the bright red wagon proceeded a certain metallic rumbling and clinking as it bowled along, and two or three nests of tin pans on its flat rope-encircled top flashed back the light so dazzlingly that Jedediah seemed the beaming sun of a little planetary system all his own. A new broom sticking up aggressively at each of the four corners gave the wagon a resemblance to a triumphal chariot.

Jedediah himself had not been in the tin-peddling business long enough to acquire the apologetic, out-at-elbows appearance which distinguishes a tin pedlar from other kinds of pedlars. In fact, this was his maiden venture in this line; hence he still looked plump and self-respecting. He had a round red face under his plug hat, twinkling blue eyes, and a little pursed-up mouth, the shape of which was partly due to nature and partly to much whistling. Jedediah's pudgy body was clothed in a suit of large, light checks, and he wore a bright pink necktie and an amethyst pin. Will I still be believed when I assert that, in spite of all this, Jedediah was full of, and bubbling over with, romance?

Romance cares not for appearances and apparently delights in contradictions. The homely shambling man you pass unnoticed on the street may have, tucked away in his past, a story more exciting and thrilling than anything you have ever read in fiction. So it was, in a measure, with Jedediah; poor, unknown to fame, afflicted with a double chin and bald spot, reduced to driving a tin-wagon for a living, he yet had his romance and he was still romantic.

As Jedediah rode through Amberley he looked about him with interest. He knew it well, although it was fifteen years since he had seen it. He had been born and brought up in Amberley; he had left it at the age of twenty-five to make his fortune. But Amberley was Amberley still. Jedediah found it hard to believe that it or himself was fifteen years older.

"There's the Stanton place," he said. "Charlie has painted the house yellow—it used to be white; and Bob Hollman has cut the trees down behind the blacksmith forge. Bob never had any poetry in his soul—no romance, as you might say. He was what you might call a plodder—you might call him that. Get up, my nag, get up. There's the old Harkness place—seems to be spruced up considerable. Folks used to say if ye wanted to see how the world looked the morning after the flood just go into George Harkness's barn-yard on a rainy day. The pond and the old hills ain't changed any. Get up, my nag, get up. There's the Adams homestead. Do I really behold it again?"

Jedediah thought the moment deliciously romantic. He revelled in it and, to match his exhilarated mood, he touched the pony with his whip and went clinking and glittering down the hill under the poplars at a dashing rate. He had not intended to offer his wares in Amberley that day. He meant to break the ice in Occidental, the village beyond. But he could not pass the Adams place. When he came to the open gate he turned in under the willows and drove down the wide, shady lane, girt on both sides with a trim white paling smothered in lavish sweetbriar bushes that were gay with bloom. Jedediah's heart was beating furiously under his checks.

"What a fool you are, Jed Crane," he told himself. "You used to be a young fool, and now you're an old one. Sad, that! Get up, my nag, get up. It's a poor lookout for a man of your years, Jed. Don't get excited. It ain't the least likely that Mattie Adams is here yet. She's married and gone years ago, no doubt. It's probable there's no Adamses here at all now. But it's romantic, yes, it's romantic. It's splendid. Get up, my nag, get up."

The Adams place itself was not unromantic. The house was a large, old-fashioned white one, with green shutters and a front porch with Grecian columns. These were thought very elegant in Amberley. Mrs. Carmody said they gave a house such a classical air. In this instance the classical effect was somewhat smothered in honeysuckle, which rioted over the whole porch and hung in pale yellow, fragrant festoons over the rows of potted scarlet geraniums that flanked the green steps. Beyond the house a low-boughed orchard covered the slope between it and the main road, and behind it there was a revel of colour betokening a flower garden.

Jedediah climbed down from his lofty seat and walked dubiously to a side door that looked more friendly, despite its prim screen, than the classical front porch. As he drew near he saw a woman sitting behind the screen—a woman who rose as he approached and opened the door. Jedediah's heart had been beating a wild tattoo as he crossed the yard. It now stopped altogether—at least he declared in later years it did.

The woman was Mattie Adams—Mattie Adams fifteen years older than when he had seen her last, plumper, rosier, somewhat broader-faced, but still unmistakably Mattie Adams. Jedediah felt that the situation was delicious.

"Mattie," he said, holding out his hand.

"Why, Jed, how are you?" said Mattie, as if they had parted the week before. It had always taken a great deal to disturb Mattie. Whatever happened she was calm. Even an old lover, and the only one she had ever possessed at that, dropping, so to speak, from the skies, after fifteen years' disappearance, did not ruffle her placidity.

"I didn't suppose you'd know me, Mattie," said Jedediah, still holding her hand foolishly.

"I knew you the minute I set eyes on you," returned Mattie. "You're some fatter and older—

like myself—but you're Jed still. Where have you been all these years?"

"Pretty near everywhere, Mattie—pretty near everywhere. And ye see what it's come to—here I be driving a tin-wagon for Boone Brothers. Business is business—don't you want to buy some new tinware?"

To himself, Jed thought it was romantic, asking a woman whom he had loved all his life to buy tins on the occasion of their first meeting after fifteen years' separation.

"I don't know but I do want a quart measure," said Mattie, in her sweet, unchanged voice, "but all in good time. You must stay and have tea with me, Jed. I'm all alone now—Mother and Father have gone. Unhitch your horse and put him in the third stall in the stable."

Jed hesitated.

"I ought to be getting on, I s'pose," he said wistfully. "I hain't done much today—"

"You must stay to tea," interrupted Mattie. "Why, Jed, there's ever so much to tell and ask. And we can't stand here in the yard and talk. Look at Selena. There she is, watching us from the kitchen window. She'll watch as long as we stand here."

Jed swung himself around. Over the little valley below the Adams homestead was a steep, treeless hill, and on its crest was perched a bare farmhouse with windows stuck lavishly all over it. At one of them a long, pale face was visible.

"Has Selena been pasted up at that window

ever since the last time we stood here and talked, Mattie?" asked Jed, half resentfully, half amusedly. It was characteristic of Mattie to laugh first at the question, and then blush over the memory it revived.

"Most of the time, I guess," she said shortly. "But come—come in. I never could talk under Selena's eyes, even if they were four hundred yards away."

Jed went in and stayed to tea. The old Adams pantry had not failed, nor apparently the Adams skill in cooking. After tea Jed hung around till sunset and drove away with a warm invitation from Mattie to call every time his rounds took him through Amberley. As he went, Selena's face appeared at the window of the house over the valley.

When he had gone Mattie went around to the classical porch and sat herself down under the honeysuckle festoons that dangled above her smooth braids of fawn-coloured hair. She knew Selena would be down posthaste presently, agog with curiosity to find out who the pedlar was whom Mattie had delighted to honour with an invitation to tea. Mattie preferred to meet Selena out of doors. It was easier to thrust and parry there. Meanwhile, she wanted to think over things.

Fifteen years before Jedediah Crane had been Mattie Adams's beau. Jedediah was romantic even then, but, as he was a slim young fellow at the time, with an abundance of fair, curly hair and innocent blue eyes, his romance was rather an attraction than not. At least the then young and pretty Mattie had found it so.

The Adamses looked with no favour on the match. They were a thrifty, well-to-do folk. As for the Cranes—well, they were lazy and shiftless, for the most part. It would be a *mésalliance* for an Adams to marry a Crane. Still, it would doubtless have happened—for Mattie, though a meek-looking damsel, had a mind of her own—had it not been for Selena Ford, Mattie's older sister.

Selena, people said, had married James Ford for no other reason than that his house commanded a view of nearly every dooryard in Amberley. This may or may not have been sheer malice. Certainly nothing that went on in the Adams yard escaped Selena.

She watched Mattie and Jed in the moonlight one night. She saw Jed kiss Mattie. It was the first time he had ever done so—and the last, poor fellow. For Selena swooped down on her parents the next day. Such a storm did she brew up that Mattie was forbidden to speak to Jed again. Selena herself gave Jed a piece of her mind. Jed usually was not afflicted with undue sensitiveness. But he had some slumbering pride at the basis of his character and it was very stubborn when roused. Selena roused it. Jed vowed he would never creep and crawl at the feet of the Adamses, and he went west forthwith, determined, as aforesaid, to make his fortune and hurl Selena's scorn back in her face.

And now he had come home, driving a tin-

wagon. Mattie smiled to think of it. She bore Jed
no ill will for his failure. She felt sorry for him
and inclined to think that fate had used him
hardly—fate and Selena together. Mattie had never
had another beau. People thought she was
engaged to Jed Crane until her time for beaus
went by. Mattie did not mind; she had never liked
anybody so well as Jed. To be sure, she had not
thought of him for years. It was strange he should
come back like this—"romantic," as he said
himself.

Mattie's reverie was interrupted by Selena.
Angular, pale-eyed Mrs. Ford was as unlike the
plump, rosy Mattie as a sister could be. Perhaps
her chronic curiosity, which would not let her
rest, was accountable for her excessive leanness.

"Who was that pedlar that was here this afternoon, Mattie?" she demanded as soon as she
arrived.

Mattie smiled. "Jed Crane," she said. "He's
home from the West and driving a tin-wagon for
the Boones."

Selena gave a little gasp. She sat down on the
lowest step and untied her bonnet strings.

"Mattie Adams! And you kept him hanging
about the whole afternoon."

"Why not?" said Mattie wickedly. She liked to
alarm Selena. "Jed and I were always beaus, you
know."

"Mattie Adams! You don't mean to say you're
going to make a fool of yourself over Jed Crane
again? A woman of your age!"

"Don't get excited, Selena," implored Mattie. In

the old days Selena could cow her, but that time was past. "I never saw the like of you for getting stirred up over nothing."

"I'm not excited. I'm perfectly calm. But I might well be excited over your folly, Mattie Adams. The idea of your taking up again with old Jed Crane!"

"He's fifteen years younger than Jim," said Mattie, giving thrust for thrust.

When Selena had come over Mattie had not the slightest idea of resuming her former relationship with the romantic Jedediah. She had merely shown him kindness for old friendship's sake. But so well did the unconscious Selena work in Jed's behalf that when she flounced off home in a pet Mattie was resolved that she would take Jed back if he wanted to come. She wasn't going to put up with Selena's everlasting interference. She would show her that she was independent.

When a week had passed Jed came again. He sold Mattie a stew-pan and he would not go in to tea this time, but they stood and talked in the yard for the best part of an hour, while Selena glared at them from her kitchen window. Their conversation was most innocent and harmless, being mainly gossip about what had come and gone during Jed's exile. But Mattie knew that Selena thought that she and Jed were making love to each other in this shameless, public fashion. When Jed went, Mattie, more for Selena's benefit than his, broke off some sprays of honeysuckle and pinned them on his coat. The fragrance went

with Jedediah as he drove through Amberley, and
pleasant thoughts were born of it.

"It's romantic," he told the pony. "Blessed if it
ain't romantic! Not that Mattie cares anything
about me now. I know she don't. But it's just her
kind way. She wants to cheer me up and let me
know I've a friend still. Get up, my nag, get up.
I ain't one to persoom on her kindness neither; I
know my place. But still, say what you will, it's
romantic—this sitooation. This is it. Here I be,
loving the ground she walks on, as I've always
done, and I can't let on that I do because I'm a
poor ne'er-do-well as ain't fit to look at her, an
independent woman with property. And she's a-
showing kindness to me for old times' sake, and
piercing my heart all the time, not knowing. Why,
it's romance with a vengeance, that's what it is.
Get up, my nag, get up."

Thereafter Jed called at the Adams place every
week. Generally he stayed to tea. Mattie always
bought something of him to colour an excuse. Her
kitchen fairly glittered with new tinware. She
gave Selena the overflow by way of heaping coals
of fire.

After every visit Jedediah held stern counsel
with himself and decided that he must not call to
see Mattie again—at least, not for a long time;
then he must not stay to tea. He would struggle
with himself all the way down the poplar hill—
not without a comforting sense of the romance of
the struggle—but it always ended the same way.
He turned in under the willows and clinked musi-

cally into Mattie's yard. At least, the rattle of the tin-wagon sounded musically to Mattie.

Meanwhile, Selena watched from her window and raged.

Amberley people shrugged their shoulders when gossip noised the matter abroad. But, being good-humoured in the main, they forebore to do more than say that Mattie Adams was free to make a goose of herself if it pleased her, and that Jed Crane wasn't such a fool as he looked. The Adams farm was one of the best in Amberley, and it had not grown any poorer under Mattie's management.

"If Jed walks in there and hangs up his hat he'll have done well for himself after all."

This was Selena's view of it also, barring the good nature. She was furious at the whole affair, and she did her best to make Mattie's life a burden to her with slurs and thrusts. But they all misjudged Jed. He had no intention of "walking in and hanging up his hat"—or trying to. Romantic as he was, it never occurred to him that Mattie might be as romantic as himself. She did not care for him, and anyhow he, Jed, had a little too much pride to ask her, a rich woman, to marry him, a poor man who had lost all caste he ever possessed by taking up tin-peddling. Jed was determined not to "persoom." And, oh, how deliciously romantic it all was! He hugged himself with sorrowful delight over it.

As the summer waned and the long yellow leaves began to fall thickly from the willows in

the Adams lane Jed began to talk of going out
west again. Tin-peddling was not possible in winter, and he didn't think he would try it another
summer. Mattie listened with dismay in her heart.
All summer she had made much of Jed, by way
of tormenting Selena. But now she realized what
he really meant to her. The old love had wakened
to life in her heart; she could not let Jed go out
of her life again, leaving her to the old loneliness.
If Jed went away everything would be flat, stale,
and unprofitable.

She knew him to be at heart the kindest, most
gentle of human beings, and the mere fact of his
having been unsuccessful, even what some of his
old neighbours might call stupid, did not change
her feelings toward him in the least. He was Jed—
that was sufficient for her, and she had business
capability enough for both, when it came to that.

Mattie began to drop hints. But Jed would not
take them. True, once or twice he thought that
perhaps Mattie did care a little for him yet. But it
would not do for him to take advantage of that.

"No, I just couldn't do that," he told the pony.
"I worship the ground that woman treads on, but
it ain't for the likes of me to tell her so, not now.
Get up, my nag, get up. This has been a mighty
pleasant summer with that visit to look forward
to every week. But it's about over now and you
must tramp, Jed."

Jed sighed. He remembered that it was more
romantic than ever, but all at once this failed to
comfort him. Romance up to a certain point was

food; beyond that it palled, so to speak. Jed's romance failed him just when he needed it most.

Mattie, meanwhile, was forced to the dismal conclusion that her hints were thrown away. Jed was plainly determined not to speak. Mattie felt half angry with him. She did not choose to make a martyr of herself to romance, and surely the man didn't expect her to ask him to marry her.

"I'm sure and certain he's as fond of me as ever he was," she mused. "I suppose he's got some ridiculous notion about being too poor to aspire to me. Jed always had more pride than a Crane could carry. Well, I've done all I can—all I'm going to do. If Jed's determined to go, he must go, I s'pose."

Mattie would not let herself cry, although she felt like it. She went out and picked apples instead.

Mattie might have remained so and Jedediah's romance might never have reached a better ending, if it had not been for Selena, who came over just then to help Mattie pick the golden russets. Fate had evidently destined her as Jed's best helper. All summer she had been fairly goading Mattie into love with Jedediah and now she was moved to add the last spur.

"Jed Crane's going away, I hear," she said maliciously. "Seems to me you're bound to be jilted again, Mattie."

Mattie had no answer ready. Selena went on undauntedly.

"You've made a nice fool of yourself all sum-

mer, I vow. Throwing yourself at Jed's head—
and he doesn't want you, even with all your
property."

"He does want me," said Mattie calmly. Her
lips were very firm and her cheeks scarlet. "He
is not going away. We are to be married about
Christmas, and Jed will take charge of the farm
for me."

"Matilda Adams!" said Selena. It was all she
was capable of saying.

The rest of the golden russets were picked in a
dead silence, Mattie working with an unusually
high colour in her cheeks, while Selena's thin lips
were pressed so closely together as to be little else
than a hair line.

After Selena had gone home, sulking, Mattie
picked on with a very determined face. The die
was cast; she could not bear Selena's slurs and
she would not. And she had not told a lie either.
Her words were true; she would make them true.
All the Adams determination—and that was not
a little—was roused in her.

"If Jed jilts me, he'll do it to my face, clean and
clever," she said viciously.

When Jed came again he was very solemn. He
thought it would be his last visit, but Mattie felt
differently. She had dressed herself with unusual
care and crimped her hair. Her cheeks were scarlet and her eyes bright. Jed thought she looked
younger and prettier than ever. The thought that
this was the last time he would see her for many
a long day to come grew more and more unbear-

able, yet he firmly determined he would let no presuming word pass his lips. Mattie had been so kind to him. It was only honourable of him in return not to let her throw herself away on a poor failure like himself.

"I suppose this is your last round with the wagon," she said. She had taken him out into the garden to say it. The garden was out of view from the Ford place. Propose she must, but she drew the line at proposing under Selena's eyes.

Jed nodded dully. "Yes, and then I must toddle off and look for something else to do. You see, I haven't much of a gift so to speak for business, Mattie, and it takes me so long to get worked into an understanding of a business or trade that I'm generally asked to quit before you might say I've really commenced. It's been a mighty happy summer for me, though I can't say I've done much in the selling line except to you, Mattie. What with your kindness and these little visits you've been good enough to let me make every week, I feel I may say it's been the happiest summer of my life, and I'm never going to forget it, but as I said, it's time for me to be moving on elsewhere and finding something else to do."

"There is something for you to do right here— if you will do it," said Mattie faintly. For a moment she felt as if she could not go on; Jed and the garden and the scarf of late asters whirled around her dizzily. She held by the sweet-pea trellis to steady herself.

"I—I said a terrible thing to Selena the other

day. I—I don't know what I'll do about it if—if—you don't help me out, Jed."

"I'll do anything I can," said Jed, with hearty sympathy. "You know that, Mattie. What is the trouble?"

His kindly voice and the good will and affection beaming in his honest blue eyes gave Mattie renewed courage to go on with her self-imposed and most embarrassing task, although before she ended her voice shook and dwindled away to such a low whisper that Jed had to bend his head close to hers to hear what she was saying.

"I—I said—she goaded me into saying it, Jed—slighting and slurring—jeering at me because you were going away. I just got mad, Jed—and I told her you weren't going—that you and I—that we were to be—married."

"Mattie, did you mean that?" he cried. "If you did, I'm the happiest man alive. I didn't dare persoom—I didn't s'pose you thought anything of me. But if you do—and if you want me—here's all there is of me, heart and soul and body, forever and ever, as I've been all my life."

Thinking over this speech afterwards Jed was dissatisfied with it. He thought he might have made it much more eloquent and romantic than it was. But it served the purpose very well. It was convincing—it came straight from his honest, stupid heart, and Mattie knew it. She held out her hands and Jed gathered her into his arms.

It was certainly a most fortunate circumstance that the garden was well out of the range of Sele-

na's vision, or the sight of her sister and the
remaining member of the despised Crane family
repeating their foolish performance, which many
years previous had resulted in Jed's long banish-
ment, might have caused her to commit almost
any unheard-of act of spite as an outlet for her
jealous anger. But only the few remaining garden
flowers were witness to the lovers' indiscretion,
and they kept their own counsel after the manner
of flowers, so Selena's feelings were mercifully
spared this further outrage.

That evening Jed drove slowly away through
the twilight, mounted for the last time on the tin-
wagon. He was so happy that he bore no grudge
against even Selena Ford. As the pony climbed
the poplar hill Jed drew a long breath and freed
his mind to the surrounding landscape and to his
faithful and slow-plodding steed that had been
one of the main factors in this love affair, having
patiently carried him to and from the abode of
his lady-love throughout the summer just passed.
Jedediah was as brimful of happiness as mortal
man could be, and his rosy thoughts flowed forth
in a kind of triumphant chant which would have
driven Selena stark distracted had she been within
hearing distance. What he said too was but a poor
expression of what he thought, but to the trees
and fields and pony he chanted,

"Well, this *is* romance. What else would you
call it now? Me, poor, scared to speak—and Mattie ups and does it for me, bless her. Yes, I've
been longing for romance all my life, and I've got

it at last. None of your commonplace courtships for me, I always said. Them was my very words. And I guess this has been a little uncommon—I guess it has. Anyhow, I'm uncommon happy. I never felt so romantic before. Get up, my nag, get up."

Elizabeth's Child

The Ingelows, of Ingelow Grange, were not a marrying family. Only one of them, Elizabeth, had married, and perhaps it was her "poor match" that discouraged the others. At any rate, Ellen and Charlotte and George Ingelow at the Grange were single, and so was Paul down at Greenwood Farm.

It was seventeen years since Elizabeth had married James Sheldon in the face of the most decided opposition on the part of her family. Sheldon was a handsome, shiftless ne'er-do-well, without any violent bad habits, but also "without any backbone," as the Ingelows declared. "There is sometimes hope of a man who is actively bad," Charlotte Ingelow had said sententiously, "but who ever heard of reforming a jellyfish?"

47

Elizabeth and her husband had gone west and settled on a prairie farm in Manitoba. She had never been home since. Perhaps her pride kept her away, for she had the Ingelow share of that, and she soon discovered that her family's estimate of James Sheldon had been the true one. There was no active resentment on either side, and once in a long while letters were exchanged. Still, ever since her marriage, Elizabeth had been practically an outsider and an alien. As the years came and went the Ingelows at home remembered only at long intervals that they had a sister on the western prairies.

One of these remembrances came to Charlotte Ingelow on a spring afternoon when the great orchards about the Grange were pink and white with apple and cherry blossoms, and over every hill and field was a delicate, flower-starred green. A soft breeze was blowing loose petals from the August Sweeting through the open door of the wide hall when Charlotte came through it. Ellen and George were standing on the steps outside.

"This kind of a day always makes me think of Elizabeth," said Charlotte dreamily. "It was in apple-blossom time she went away." The Ingelows always spoke of Elizabeth's going away, never of her marrying.

"Seventeen years ago," said Ellen. "Why, Elizabeth's oldest child must be quite a young woman now! I—I—" a sudden idea swept over and left her a little breathless. "I would really like to see her."

"Then why don't you write and ask her to come east and visit us?" asked George, who did not often speak, but who always spoke to some purpose when he did.

Ellen and Charlotte looked at each other. "I would like to see Elizabeth's child," repeated Ellen firmly.

"Do you think she would come?" asked Charlotte. "You know when James Sheldon died five years ago, we wrote to Elizabeth and asked her to come home and live with us, and she seemed almost resentful in the letter she wrote back. I've never said so before, but I've often thought it."

"Yes, she did," said Ellen, who had often thought so too, but never said so.

"Elizabeth was always very independent," remarked George. "Perhaps she thought your letter savoured of charity or pity. No Ingelow would endure that."

"At any rate, you know she refused to come, even for a visit. She said she could not leave the farm. She may refuse to let her child come."

"It won't do any harm to ask her," said George.

In the end, Charlotte wrote to Elizabeth and asked her to let her daughter visit the old homestead. The letter was written and mailed in much perplexity and distrust when once the glow of momentary enthusiasm in the new idea had passed.

"What if Elizabeth's child is like her father?" queried Charlotte in a half-whisper.

"Let us hope she won't be!" cried Ellen fervently. Indeed, she felt that a feminine edition of James Sheldon would be more than she could endure.

"She may not like us, or our ways," sighed Charlotte. "We don't know how she has been brought up. She will seem like a stranger after all. I really long to see Elizabeth's child, but I can't help fearing we have done a rash thing, Ellen."

"Perhaps she may not come," suggested Ellen, wondering whether she hoped it or feared it.

But Worth Sheldon did come. Elizabeth wrote back a prompt acceptance, with no trace of the proud bitterness that had permeated her answer to the former invitation. The Ingelows at the Grange were thrown into a flutter when the letter came. In another week Elizabeth's child would be with them.

"If only she isn't like her father," said Charlotte with foreboding, as she aired and swept the southeast spare room for their expected guest. They had three spare rooms at the Grange, but the aunts had selected the southeast one for their niece because it was done in white, "and white seems the most appropriate for a young girl," Ellen said, as she arranged a pitcher of wild roses on the table.

"I think everything is ready," announced Charlotte. "I put the very finest sheets on the bed, they smell deliciously of lavender, and we had very good luck doing up the muslin curtains. It is pleasant to be expecting a guest, isn't it, Ellen? I have often thought, although I have never said so before, that our lives were too self-centred. We seemed to have no interests outside of ourselves. Even Elizabeth has been really nothing to us, you know. She seemed to have become a stranger. I hope her child will be the means of bringing us nearer together again."

"If she has James Sheldon's round face and big blue eyes and curly yellow hair I shall never really like her, no matter how Ingelowish she may be inside," said Ellen decidedly.

When Worth Sheldon came, each of her aunts drew a long breath of relief. Worth was not in the least like her father in appearance. Neither did she resemble her mother, who had been a sprightly, black-haired and black-eyed girl. Worth was tall and straight, with a long braid of thick, wavy brown hair, large, level-gazing grey eyes, a square jaw, and an excellent chin with a dimple in it.

"She is the very image of Mother's sister, Aunt Alice, who died so long ago," said Charlotte. "You don't remember her, Ellen, but I do very well. She was the sweetest woman that ever drew breath. She was Paul's favourite aunt, too," Charlotte added with a sigh. Paul's antagonistic attitude was the only drawback to the joy of this meeting. How delightful it would have been if he had not refused to be there too, to welcome Elizabeth's child.

Worth came to hearts prepared to love her, but they must have loved her in any case. In a day Aunt Charlotte and Aunt Ellen and shy, quiet

Uncle George had yielded wholly to her charm. She was girlishly bright and merry, frankly delighted with the old homestead and the quaint, old-fashioned, daintily kept rooms. Yet there was no suggestion of gush about her; she did not go into raptures, but her pleasure shone out in eyes and tones. There was so much to tell and ask and remember the first day that it was not until the second morning after her arrival that Worth asked the question her aunts had been dreading. She asked it out in the orchard, in the emerald gloom of a long arcade of stout old trees that Grandfather Ingelow had planted fifty years ago.

"Aunt Charlotte, when is Uncle Paul coming up to see me? I long to see him; Mother has talked so much to me about him. She was his favourite sister, wasn't she?"

Charlotte and Ellen looked at each other. Ellen nodded slyly. It would be better to tell Worth the whole truth at once. She would certainly find it out soon.

"I do not think, my dear," said Aunt Charlotte quietly, "that your Uncle Paul will be up to see you at all."

"Why not?" asked Worth, her serious grey eyes looking straight into Aunt Charlotte's troubled dark ones. Aunt Charlotte understood that Elizabeth had never told Worth anything about her family's resentment of her marriage. It was not a pleasant thing to have to explain it all to Elizabeth's child, but it must be done.

"I think, my dear," she said gently, "that I will

have to tell you a little bit of our family history that may not be very pleasant to hear or tell. Perhaps you don't know that when your mother married we—we—did not exactly approve of her marriage. Perhaps we were mistaken; at any rate it was wrong and foolish to let it come between us and her as we have done. But that is how it was. None of us approved, as I have said, but none of us was so bitter as your Uncle Paul. Your mother was his favourite sister, and he was very deeply attached to her. She was only a year younger than he. When he bought the Greenwood farm she went and kept house for him for three years before her marriage. When she married, Paul was terribly angry. He was always a strange man, very determined and unyielding. He said he would never forgive her, and he never has. He has never married, and he has lived so long alone at Greenwood with only deaf old Mrs. Bree to keep house for him that he has grown odder than ever. One of us wanted to go and keep house for him, but he would not let us. And—I must tell you this although I hate to—he was very angry when he heard we had invited you to visit us, and he said he would not come near the Grange as long as you were here. Oh, you can't realize how bitter and obstinate he is. We pleaded with him, but I think that only made him worse. We have felt so bad over it, your Aunt Ellen and your Uncle George and I, but we can do nothing at all.''

Worth had listened gravely. The story was all

new to her, but she had long thought there must be a something at the root of her mother's indifferent relations with her old home and friends. When Aunt Charlotte, flushed and half-tearful, finished speaking, a little glimmer of fun came into Worth's grey eyes, and her dimple was very pronounced as she said,

"Then, if Uncle Paul will not come to see me, I must go to see him."

"My dear!" cried both her aunts together in dismay. Aunt Ellen got her breath first.

"Oh, my dear child, you must not think of such a thing," she cried nervously. "It would never do. He would—I don't know what he would do—order you off the premises, or say something dreadful. No! No! Wait. Perhaps he will come after all—we will see. You must have patience."

Worth shook her head and the smile in her eyes deepened.

"I don't think he will come," she said. "Mother has told me something about the Ingelow stubbornness. She says I have it in full measure, but I like to call it determination, it sounds so much better. No, the mountain will not come to Mohammed, so Mohammed will go to the mountain. I think I will walk down to Greenwood this afternoon. There, dear aunties, don't look so troubled. Uncle Paul won't run at me with a pitchfork, will he? He can't do worse than order me off his premises, as you say."

Aunt Charlotte shook her head. She understood that no argument would turn the girl from her purpose if she had the Ingelow will, so she said nothing more. In the afternoon Worth set out for Greenwood, a mile away.

"Oh, what will Paul say?" exclaimed the aunts, with dismal forebodings.

Worth met her Uncle Paul at the garden gate. He was standing there when she came up the slope of the long lane, a tall, massive figure of a man, with deep-set black eyes, a long, prematurely white beard, and a hooked nose. Handsome and stubborn enough Paul Ingelow looked. It was not without reason that his neighbours called him the oddest Ingelow of them all.

Behind him was a fine old farmhouse in beautiful grounds. Worth felt almost as much interested in Greenwood as in the Grange. It had been her mother's home for three years, and Elizabeth Ingelow had loved it and talked much to her daughter of it.

Paul Ingelow did not move or speak, although he probably guessed who his visitor was. Worth held out her hand. "How do you do, Uncle Paul?" she said.

Paul ignored the outstretched hand. "Who are you?" he asked gruffly.

"I am Worth Sheldon, your sister Elizabeth's daughter," she answered. "Won't you shake hands with me, Uncle Paul?"

"I have no sister Elizabeth," he answered unbendingly.

Worth folded her hands on the gatepost and met his frowning gaze unshrinkingly. "Oh, yes, you have," she said calmly. "You can't do away with natural ties by simply ignoring them, Uncle Paul. They go on existing. I never knew until this morning that you were at enmity with my mother. She never told me. But she has talked a great deal of you to me. She has told me often how much you and she loved each other and how good you always were to her. She sent her love to you."

"Years ago I had a sister Elizabeth," said Paul Ingelow harshly. "I loved her very tenderly, but she married against my will a shiftless scamp who—"

Worth lifted her hand slightly. "He was my father, Uncle Paul, and he was always kind to me; whatever his faults may have been I cannot listen to a word against him."

"You shouldn't have come here, then," he said, but he said it less harshly. There was even a certain reluctant approval of this composed, independent niece in his eyes. "Didn't they tell you at the Grange that I didn't want to see you?"

"Yes, they told me this morning, but *I* wanted to see you, so I came. Why cannot we be friends, Uncle Paul, not because we are uncle and niece, but simply because you are you and I am I? Let us leave my father and mother out of the question and start fair on our own account."

For a moment Uncle Paul looked at her. She met his gaze frankly and firmly, with a merry smile lurking in her eyes. Then he threw back his head and laughed a hearty laugh that was good to hear. "Very well," he said. "It is a bargain."

He put his hand over the gate and shook hers. Then he opened the gate and invited her into the house. Worth stayed to tea, and Uncle Paul showed her all over Greenwood.

"You are to come here as often as you like," he told her. "When a young lady and I make a compact of friendship I am going to live up to it. But you are not to talk to me about your mother. Remember, we are friends because I am I and you are you, and there is no question of anybody else."

The Grange Ingelows were amazed to see Paul bringing Worth home in his buggy that evening. When Worth had gone into the house Charlotte told him that she was glad to see that he had relented towards Elizabeth's child.

"I have not," he made stern answer. "I don't know whom you mean by Elizabeth's child. That young woman and I have taken a liking for each other which we mean to cultivate on our own account. Don't call her Elizabeth's child to me again."

As the days and weeks went by Worth grew dearer and dearer to the Grange folk. The aunts often wondered to themselves how they had existed before Worth came and, oftener yet, how they could do without her when the time came for her to go home. Meanwhile, the odd friendship between her and Uncle Paul deepened and grew. They read and drove and walked together. Worth spent half her time at Greenwood. Once Uncle Paul said to her, as if speaking half to himself,

"To think that James Sheldon could have a daughter like you!"

Up went Worth's head. Worth's grey eyes flashed. "I thought we were not to speak of my parents?" she said. "You ought not to have been the first to break the compact, Uncle Paul."

"I accept the rebuke and beg your pardon," he said. He liked her all the better for those little flashes of spirit across her girlish composure.

One day in September they were together in the garden at Greenwood. Worth, looking lovingly and regretfully down the sun-flecked avenue of box, said with a sigh, "Next month I must go home. How sorry I shall be to leave the Grange and Greenwood. I have had such a delightful summer, and I have learned to love all the old nooks and corners as well as if I had lived here all my life."

"Stay here!" said Uncle Paul abruptly. "Stay here with me. I want you, Worth. Let Greenwood be your home henceforth and adopt your crusty old bachelor uncle for a father."

"Oh, Uncle Paul," cried Worth, "I don't know—I don't think—oh, you surprise me!"

"I surprise myself, perhaps. But I mean it, Worth. I am a rich, lonely old man and I want to keep this new interest you have brought into my life. Stay with me. I will try to give you a very happy life, my child, and all I have shall be yours."

Seeing her troubled face, he added, "There, I don't ask you to decide right here. I suppose you have other claims to adjust. Take time to think it over."

"Thank you," said Worth. She went back to the

Grange as one in a dream and shut herself up in the white southeast room to think. She knew that she wanted to accept this unexpected offer of Uncle Paul's. Worth's loyal tongue had never betrayed, even to the loving aunts, any discontent in the prairie farm life that had always been hers. But it had been a hard life for the girl, narrow and poverty-bounded. She longed to put forth her hand and take this other life which opened so temptingly before her. She knew, too, that her mother, ambitious for her child, would not be likely to interpose any objections. She had only to go to Uncle Paul and all that she longed for would be given her, together with the faithful, protecting fatherly love and care that in all its strength and sweetness had never been hers.

She must decide for herself. Not even of Aunt Charlotte or Aunt Ellen could she ask advice. She knew they would entreat her to accept, and she needed no such incentive to her own wishes. Far on into the night Worth sat at the white-curtained dormer window, looking at the stars over the apple trees, and fighting her battle between inclination and duty. It was a hard and stubbornly contested battle, but with that square chin and those unfaltering grey eyes it could end in only one way. Next day Worth went down to Greenwood.

"Well, what is it to be?" said Uncle Paul without preface, as he met her in the garden.

"I cannot come, Uncle Paul," said Worth steadily. "I cannot give up my mother."

"I don't ask you to give her up," he said

gruffly. "You can write to her and visit her. I
don't want to come between parent and child."

"That isn't the point exactly, Uncle Paul. I hope
you will not be angry with me for not accepting
your offer. I wanted to—you don't know how
much I wanted to—but I cannot. Mother and I are
so much to each other, Uncle Paul, more, I am
sure, than even most mothers and daughters. You
have never let me speak of her, but I must tell
you this. Mother has often told me that when I
came to her things were going very hard with her
and that I was heaven's own gift to comfort and
encourage her. Then, in the ten years that followed, the three other babies that came to her all
died before they were two years old. And with
each loss Mother said I grew dearer to her. Don't
you see, Uncle Paul, I'm not merely just one child
to her but I'm *all* those children? Six years ago the
twins were born, and they are dear, bright little
lads, but they are very small yet, so Mother has
really nobody but me. I know she would consent
to let me stay here, because she would think it
best for me, but it wouldn't be really best for me;
it couldn't be best for a girl to do what wasn't
right. I love you, Uncle Paul, and I love Greenwood, and I want to stay so much. But I cannot.
I have thought it all over and I must go back to
Mother."

Uncle Paul did not say one word. He turned
his back on Worth and walked the full length of
the box alley twice. Worth watched him wistfully.
Was he very angry? Would he forgive her?

"You are an Ingelow, Worth," he said when he came back. That was all, but Worth understood that her decision was not to cause any estrangement between them.

A month later Worth's last day at the Grange came. She was to leave for the West the next morning. They were all out in Grandfather Ingelow's arcade, Uncle George and Aunt Charlotte and Aunt Ellen and Worth, enjoying the ripe mellow sunshine of the October day, when Paul Ingelow came up the slope. Worth went to meet him with outstretched hands. He took them both in his and looked at her very gravely.

"I have not come to say goodbye, Worth. I will not say it. You are coming back to me."

Worth shook her brown head sadly. "Oh, I cannot, Uncle Paul. You know—I told you—"

"Yes, I know," he interrupted. "I have been thinking it all over every day since. You know yourself what the Ingelow determination is. It's a good thing in a good cause but a bad thing in a bad one. And it is no easy thing to conquer when you've let it rule you for years as I have done. But I have conquered it, or you have conquered it for me. Child, here is a letter. It is to your mother—my sister Elizabeth. In it I have asked her to forgive me, and to forget our long estrangement. I have asked her to come back to me with you and her boys. I want you all—all—at Greenwood and I will do the best I can for you all."

"Oh, Uncle Paul," cried Worth, her face aglow and quivering with smiles and tears and sunshine.

"Do you think she will forgive me and come?"

"I know she will," cried Worth. "I know how she has longed for you and home. Oh, I am so happy, Uncle Paul!"

He smiled at her and put his arm over her shoulder. Together they walked up the golden arcade to tell the others. That night Charlotte and Ellen cried with happiness as they talked it over in the twilight.

"How beautiful!" murmured Charlotte softly. "We shall not lose Worth after all. Ellen, I could not have borne it to see that girl go utterly out of our lives again."

"I always hoped and believed that Elizabeth's child would somehow bring us all together again," said Ellen happily.

In the Old Valley

The man halted on the crest of the hill and looked sombrely down into the long valley below. It was evening, and although the hills around him were still in the light the valley was already filled with kindly, placid shadows. A wind that blew across it from the misty blue sea beyond was making wild music in the rugged firs above his head as he stood in an angle of the weather-grey longer fence, knee-deep in bracken. It had been by these firs he had halted twenty years ago, turning for one last glance at the valley below, the home valley which he had never seen since. But then the firs had been little more than vigorous young saplings; they were tall, gnarled trees now, with lichened trunks, and their lower boughs were

63

dead. But high up their tops were green and caught the saffron light of the west. He remembered that when a boy he had thought there was nothing more beautiful than the evening sunshine falling athwart the dark green fir boughs on the hills.

As he listened to the swish and murmur of the wind, the earth-old tune with the power to carry the soul back to the dawn of time, the years fell away from him and he forgot much, remembering more. He knew now that there had always been a longing in his heart to hear the wind-chant in the firs. He had called that longing by other names, but he knew it now for what it was when, hearing, he was satisfied.

He was a tall man with iron-grey hair and the face of a conqueror—strong, pitiless, unswerving. Eagle eyes, quick to discern and unfaltering to pursue; jaw square and intrepid; mouth formed to keep secrets and cajole men to his will—a face that hid much and revealed little. It told of power and intellect, but the soul of the man was a hidden thing. Not in the arena where he had fought and triumphed, giving fierce blow for blow, was it to be shown; but here, looking down on the homeland, with the strength of the hills about him, it rose dominantly and claimed its own. The old bond held. Yonder below him was home—the old house that had sheltered him, the graves of his kin, the wide fields where his boyhood dreams had been dreamed.

Should he go down to it? This was the question

he asked himself. He had come back to it, heart-sick of his idols of the marketplace. For years they had satisfied him, the buying and selling and getting gain, the pitting of strength and craft against strength and craft, the tireless struggle, the exultation of victory. Then, suddenly, they had failed their worshipper; they ceased to satisfy; the sacrifices he had heaped on their altars availed him nothing in this new need and hunger of his being. His gods mocked him and he wearied of their service. Were there not better things than these, things he had once known and loved and forgotten? Where were the ideals of his youth, the lofty aspirations that had upborne him then? Where was the eagerness and zest of new dawns, the earnestness of well-filled, purposeful hours of labour, the satisfaction of a good day worthily lived, at eventide the unbroken rest of long, starry nights? Where might he find them again? Were they yet to be had for the seeking in the old valley? With the thought came a great yearning for home. He had had many habitations, but he realized now that he had never thought of any of these places as home. That name had all unconsciously been kept sacred to the long, green, sea-ward-looking glen where he had been born.

So he had come back to it, drawn by a longing not to be resisted. But at the last he felt afraid. There had been many changes, of that he felt sure. Would it still be home? And if not, would not the loss be most irreparable and bitter? Would it not be better to go away, having looked at it

from the hill and having heard the saga of the
firs, keeping his memory of it unblurred, than risk
the probable disillusion of a return to the places
that had forgotten him and friends whom the var-
ying years must certainly have changed as he had
changed himself? No, he would not go down. It
had been a foolish whim to come at all—foolish,
because the object of his quest was not to be
found there or elsewhere. He could not enter
again into the heritage of boyhood and the heart
of youth. He could not find there the old dreams
and hopes that had made life sweet. He understood that he could not bring back to the old valley what he had taken from it. He had lost that
intangible, all-real wealth of faith and idealism
and zest; he had bartered it away for the hard,
yellow gold of the marketplace, and he realized
at last how much poorer he was than when he
had left that home valley. His was a name that
stood for millions, but he was beggared of hope
and purpose.

No, he would not go down. There was no one
left there, unchanged and unchanging, to welcome him. He would be a stranger there, even
among his kin. He would stay awhile on the hill,
until the night came down over it, and then he
would go back to his own place.

Down below him, on the crest of a little up-
land, he saw his old home, a weather-grey house,
almost hidden among white birch and apple trees,
with a thick fir grove to the north of it. He had
been born in that old house; his earliest memory

was of standing on its threshold and looking afar
up to the long green hills.

"What is over the hills?" he had asked of his
mother. With a smile she had made answer,

"Many things, laddie. Wonderful things, beautiful things, heart-breaking things."

"Some day I shall go over the hills and find
them all, Mother," he had said stoutly.

She had laughed and sighed and caught him to
her heart. He had no recollection of his father,
who had died soon after his son's birth, but how
well he remembered his mother, his little, brown-
eyed, girlish-faced mother!

He had lived on the homestead until he was
twenty. He had tilled the broad fields and gone
in and out among the people, and their life had
been his life. But his heart was not in his work.
He wanted to go beyond the hills and seek what
he knew must be there. The valley was too narrow, too placid. He longed for conflict and accom-
plishment. He felt power and desire and the lust
of endeavour stirring in him. Oh, to go over the
hills to a world where men lived! Such had been
the goal of all his dreams.

When his mother died he sold the farm to his
cousin, Stephen Marshall. He supposed it still
belonged to him. Stephen had been a good sort
of a fellow, a bit slow and plodding, perhaps,
bovinely content to dwell within the hills, never
hearkening or responding to the lure of the
beyond. Yet it might be he had chosen the better
part, to dwell thus on the land of his fathers, with

a wife won in youth, and children to grow up around him. The childless, wifeless man looking down from the hill wondered if it might have been so with him had he been content to stay in the valley. Perhaps so. There had been Joyce.

He wondered where Joyce was now and whom she had married, for of course she had married. Did she too live somewhere down there in the valley, the matronly, contented mother of lads and lassies? He could see her old home also, not so far from his own, just across a green meadow by way of a footpath and stile and through the firs beyond it. How often he had traversed that path in the old days, knowing that Joyce would be waiting at the end of it among the firs—Joyce, the playmate of childhood, the sweet confidante and companion of youth! They had never been avowed lovers, but he had loved her then, as a boy loves, although he had never said a word of love to her. Joyce alone knew of his longings and his ambitions and his dreams; he had told them all to her freely, sure of the understanding and sympathy no other soul in the valley could give him. How true and strong and womanly and gentle she had always been!

When he left home he had meant to go back to her some day. They had parted without pledge or kiss, yet he knew she loved him and that he loved her. At first they corresponded, then the letters began to grow fewer. It was his fault; he had gradually forgotten. The new, fierce, burning interests that came into his life crowded the old ones out. Boyhood's love was scorched up in that hot flame of ambition and contest. He had not heard from or of Joyce for many years. Now, again, he remembered as he looked down on the homeland fields.

The old places had changed little, whatever he might fear of the people who lived in them. There was the school he had attended, a small, low-eaved, white-washed building set back from the main road among green spruces. Beyond it, amid tall elms, was the old church with its square tower hung with ivy. He felt glad to see it; he had expected to see a new church, offensively spick-and-span and modern, for this church had been old when he was a boy. He recalled the many times he had walked to it on the peaceful Sunday afternoons, sometimes with his mother, sometimes with Joyce.

The sun set far out to sea and sucked down with it all the light out of the winnowed dome of sky. The stars came out singly and crystal clear over the far purple curves of the hills. Suddenly, glancing over his shoulder, he saw through an arch of black fir boughs a young moon swung low in a lake of palely tinted saffron sky. He smiled a little, remembering that in boyhood it had been held a good omen to see the new moon over the right shoulder.

Down in the valley the lights began to twinkle out here and there like earth-stars. He would wait until he saw the kitchen light from the window of his old home. Then he would go. He waited until the whole valley was zoned with a glittering girdle, but no light glimmered out through his native trees. Why was it lacking, that light he had so often hailed at dark, coming home from boyish rambles on the hills? He felt anxious and dissatisfied, as if he could not go away until he had seen it.

When it was quite dark he descended the hill resolutely. He must know why the homelight had failed him. When he found himself in the old garden his heart grew sick and sore with disappointment and a bitter homesickness. It needed but a glance, even in the dimness of the summer night, to see that the old house was deserted and falling to decay. The kitchen door swung open on rusty hinges; the windows were broken and lifeless; weeds grew thickly over the yard and crowded wantonly up to the very threshold through the chinks of the rotten platform.

Cuthbert Marshall sat down on the old red sandstone step of the door and bowed his head in his hands. This was what he had come back to—this ghost and wreck of his past! Oh, bitterness!

From where he sat he saw the new house that Stephen had built beyond the fir grove, with a cheerful light shining from its window. After a long time he went over to it and knocked at the door. Stephen came to it, a stout grizzled farmer, with a chubby boy on his shoulder. He was not much changed; Cuthbert easily recognized him, but to Stephen Marshall no recognition came of this man with whom he had played and worked for years. Cuthbert was obliged to tell who he was. He was made instantly and warmly welcome. Stephen was unfeignedly glad to see him, and Stephen's comely wife, whom he remembered as a slim, fresh-cheeked valley girl, extended a kind and graceful hospitality. The boys and girls, too, soon made friends with him. Yet he felt himself the stranger and the alien, whom the long, swift-passing years had shut forever from his old place.

He and Stephen talked late that night, and in the morning he yielded to their entreaties to stay another day with them. He spent it wandering about the farm and the old haunts of wood and stream. Yet he could not find himself. This valley had his past in its keeping, but it could not give it back to him; he had lost the master word that might have compelled it.

He asked Stephen fully about all his old friends and neighbours with one exception. He could not ask him what had become of Joyce Cameron. The question was on his lips a dozen times, but he shrank from uttering it. He had a vague, secret dread that the answer, whatever it might be, would hurt him.

In the evening he yielded to a whim and went across to the Cameron homestead, by the old footpath which was still kept open. He walked slowly and dreamily, with his eyes on the far hills scarfed in the splendour of sunset. So he had walked in the old days, but he had no dreams now of what

lay beyond the hills, and Joyce would not be waiting among the firs.

The stile he remembered was gone, replaced by
a little rustic gate. As he passed through it he
lifted his eyes and there before him he saw her,
standing tall and gracious among the grey trees,
with the light from the west falling over her face.
So she had stood, so she had looked many an
evening of the long-ago. She had not changed;
he realized that in the first amazed, incredulous
glance. Perhaps there were lines on her face, a
thread or two of silver in the soft brown hair, but
those splendid steady blue eyes were the same,
and the soul of her looked out through them, true
to itself, the staunch, brave, sweet soul of the
maiden ripened to womanhood.

"Joyce!" he said, stupidly, unbelievingly.

She smiled and put out her hand. "I am glad
to see you, Cuthbert," she said simply. "Stephen's Mary told me you had come. And I
thought you would be over to see us this
evening."

She had offered him only one hand but he took
both and held her so, looking hungrily down at
her as a man looks at something he knows must
be his salvation if salvation exists for him.

"Is it possible you are here still, Joyce?" he said
slowly. "And you have not changed at all."

She coloured slightly and pulled away her
hands, laughing. "Oh, indeed I have. I have
grown old. The twilight is so kind it hides that,
but it is true. Come into the house, Cuthbert.
Father and Mother will be glad to see you."

"After a little," he said imploringly. "Let us stay here awhile first, Joyce. I want to make sure that this is no dream. Last night I stood on those hills yonder and looked down, but I meant to go away because I thought there would be no one left to welcome me. If I had known you were here! You have lived here in the old valley all these years?"

"All these years," she said gently, "I suppose you think it must have been a very meagre life?"

"No. I am much wiser now than I was once, Joyce. I have learned wisdom beyond the hills. One learns there—in time—but sometimes the lesson is learned too late. Shall I tell you what I have learned, Joyce? The gist of the lesson is that I left happiness behind me in the old valley when I went away from it, happiness and peace and the joy of living. I did not miss these things for a long while; I did not even know I had lost them. But I have discovered my loss."

"Yet you have been a very successful man," she said wonderingly.

"As the world calls success," he answered bitterly. "I have place and wealth and power. But that is not success, Joyce. I am tired of these things; they are the toys of grown-up children; they do not satisfy the man's soul. I have come back to the old valley seeking for what might satisfy, but I have little hope of finding it, unless—unless—"

He was silent, remembering that he had forfeited all right to her help in the quest. Yet he realized clearly that only she could help him, only she could guide him back to the path he had missed. It seemed to him that she held in her keeping all the good of his life, all the beauty of his past, all the possibilities of his future. Hers was the master word, but how should he dare ask her to utter it?

They walked among the firs until the stars came out, and they talked of many things. She had kept her freshness of soul and her ideals untarnished. In the peace of the old valley she had lived a life, narrow outwardly, wondrously deep and wide in thought and aspiration. Her native hills bounded the vision of her eyes, but the outlook of the soul was far and unhindered. In the quiet places and the green ways she had found what he had failed to find—the secret of happiness and content. He knew that if this woman had walked hand in hand with him through the years, life, even in the glare and tumult of that world beyond the hills, would never have lost its meaning for him. Oh, fool and blind that he had been! While he had sought and toiled afar, the best that God had meant for him had been here in the home of youth. When darkness came down through the firs he told her all this, haltingly, blunderingly, yearningly.

"Joyce, is it too late? Can you forgive my mistake, my long blindness? Can you care for me again—a little?"

She turned her face upward to the sky between the swaying fir tops and he saw the reflection of a star in her eyes. "I have never ceased to care," she said in a low tone. "I never really wanted to cease. It would have left life too empty. If my love means so much to you it is yours, Cuthbert—it always has been yours."

He drew her close into his arms, and as he felt her heart beating against his he understood that he had found the way back to simple happiness and true wisdom, the wisdom of loving and the happiness of being loved.

The Prodigal Brother

Miss Hannah was cutting asters in her garden. It was a very small garden, for nothing would grow beyond the shelter of the little, grey, low-eaved house which alone kept the northeast winds from blighting everything with salt spray; but small as it was, it was a miracle of blossoms and a marvel of neatness. The trim brown paths were swept clean of every leaf or fallen petal, each of the little square beds had its border of big white quahog clamshells, and not even a sweet-pea vine would have dared to straggle from its appointed course under Miss Hannah's eye.

Miss Hannah had always lived in the little grey house down by the shore, so far away from all the other houses in Prospect and so shut away

from them by a circle of hills that it had a seeming
isolation. Not another house could Miss Hannah
see from her own doorstone; she often declared
she could not have borne it if it had not been for
the lighthouse beacon at night flaming over the
northwest hill behind the house like a great
unwinking, friendly star that never failed even on
the darkest night. Behind the house a little tongue
of the St. Lawrence gulf ran up between the
headlands until the wavelets of its tip almost
lapped against Miss Hannah's kitchen doorstep.
Beyond, to the north, was the great crescent of
the gulf, whose murmur had been Miss Hannah's lullaby all her life. When people wondered
to her how she could endure living in such a
lonely place, she retorted that the loneliness was
what she loved it for, and that the lighthouse
star and the far-away call of the gulf had always
been company enough for her and always
would be . . . until Ralph came back. When
Ralph came home, of course, he might like a
livelier place and they might move to town or
up-country as he wished.

"Of course," said Miss Hannah with a proud
smile, "a rich man mightn't fancy living away
down here in a little grey house by the shore.
He'll be for building me a mansion, I expect, and
I'd like it fine. But until he comes I must be contented with things as they are."

People always smiled to each other when Miss
Hannah talked like this. But they took care not to
let her see the smile.

Miss Hannah snipped her white and purple asters off ungrudgingly and sang, as she snipped, an old-fashioned song she had learned long ago in her youth. The day was one of October's rarest, and Miss Hannah loved fine days. The air was clear as golden-hued crystal, and all the slopes around her were mellow and hazy in the autumn sunshine. She knew that beyond those sunny slopes were woods glorying in crimson and gold, and she would have the delight of a walk through them later on when she went to carry the asters to sick Millie Starr at the Bridge. Flowers were all Miss Hannah had to give, for she was very poor, but she gave them with a great wealth of friendliness and goodwill.

Presently a wagon drove down her lane and pulled up outside of her white garden paling. Jacob Delancey was in it, with a pretty young niece of his who was a visitor from the city, and Miss Hannah, her sheaf of asters in her arms, went over to the paling with a sparkle of interest in her faded blue eyes. She had heard a great deal of the beauty of this strange girl. Prospect people had been talking of nothing else for a week, and Miss Hannah was filled with a harmless curiosity concerning her. She always liked to look at pretty people, she said; they did her as much good as her flowers.

"Good afternoon, Miss Hannah," said Jacob Delancey. "Busy with your flowers, as usual, I see."

"Oh, yes," said Miss Hannah, managing to

stare with unobtrusive delight at the girl while
she talked. "The frost will soon be coming now,
you know, so I want to live among them as much
as I can while they're here."

"That's right," assented Jacob, who made a profession of cordial agreement with everybody and
would have said the same words in the same tone
had Miss Hannah announced a predilection for
living in the cellar. "Well, Miss Hannah, it's
flowers I'm after myself just now. We're having a
bit of a party at our house tonight, for the young
folks, and my wife told me to call and ask you if
you could let us have a few for decoration."

"Of course," said Miss Hannah, "you can have
these. I meant them for Millie, but I can cut the
west bed for her."

She opened the gate and carried the asters over
to the buggy. Miss Delancey took them with a
smile that made Miss Hannah remember the date
forever.

"Lovely day," commented Jacob genially.

"Yes," said Miss Hannah dreamily. "It reminds
me of the day Ralph went away twenty years ago.
It doesn't seem so long. Don't you think he'll be
coming back soon, Jacob?"

"Oh, sure," said Jacob, who thought the very
opposite.

"I have a feeling that he's coming very soon,"
said Miss Hannah brightly. "It will be a great day
for me, won't it, Jacob? I've been poor all my life,
but when Ralph comes back everything will be so
different. He will be a rich man and he will give

me everything I've always wanted. He said he would. A fine house and a carriage and a silk dress. Oh, and we will travel and see the world. You don't know how I look forward to it all. I've got it all planned out, all I'm going to do and have. And I believe he will be here very soon. A man ought to be able to make a fortune in twenty years, don't you think, Jacob?"

"Oh, sure," said Jacob. But he said it a little uncomfortably. He did not like the job of throwing cold water, but it seemed to him that he ought not to encourage Miss Hannah's hopes. "Of course, you shouldn't think too much about it, Miss Hannah. He mightn't ever come back, or he might be poor."

"How can you say such things, Jacob?" interrupted Miss Hannah indignantly, with a little crimson spot flaming out in each of her pale cheeks. "You know quite well he will come back. I'm as sure of it as that I'm standing here. And he will be rich, too. People are always trying to hint just as you've done to me, but I don't mind them. I know."

She turned and went back into her garden with her head held high. But her sudden anger floated away in a whiff of sweet-pea perfume that struck her in the face; she waved her hand in farewell to her callers and watched the buggy down the lane with a smile.

"Of course, Jacob doesn't know, and I shouldn't have snapped him up so quick. It'll be my turn to crow when Ralph does come. My, but isn't that girl pretty. I feel as if I'd been looking at some lovely picture. It just makes a good day of this. Something pleasant happens to me most every day and that girl is today's pleasant thing. I just feel real happy and thankful that there are such beautiful creatures in the world and that we can look at them."

"Well, of all the queer delusions!" Jacob Delancey was ejaculating as he and his niece drove down the lane.

"What is it all about?" asked Miss Delancey curiously.

"Well, it's this way, Dorothy. Long ago Miss Hannah had a brother who ran away from home. It was before their father and mother died. Ralph Walworth was as wild a young scamp as ever was in Prospect and a spendthrift in the bargain. Nobody but Hannah had any use for him, and she just worshipped him. I must admit he was real fond of her too, but he and his father couldn't get on at all. So finally he ups and runs away; it was generally supposed he went to the mining country. He left a note for Hannah bidding her goodbye and telling her that he was going to make his fortune and would come back to her a rich man. There's never been a word heard tell of him since, and in my opinion it's doubtful if he's still alive. But Miss Hannah, as you saw, is sure and certain he'll come back yet with gold dropping out of his pockets. She's as sane as anyone everyway else, but there is no doubt she's a little cracked on that p'int. If he never turns up she'll go on hoping quite happy to her death. But if he should turn up and be poor, as is ten times likelier than anything else, I believe it'd most kill Miss Hannah. She's terrible proud for all she's so sweet, and you saw yourself how mad she got when I kind of hinted he mightn't be rich. If he came back poor, after all her boasting about him, I don't fancy he'd get much of a welcome from her. And she'd never hold up her head again, that's certain. So it's to be hoped, say I, that Ralph Walworth never will turn up, unless he comes in a carriage and four, which is about as likely, in my opinion, as that he'll come in a pumpkin drawn by mice."

When October had passed and the grey November days came, the glory of Miss Hannah's garden was over. She was very lonely without her flowers. She missed them more this year than ever. On fine days she paced up and down the walks and looked sadly at the drooping, unsightly stalks and vines. She was there one afternoon when the northeast wind was up and doing, whipping the gulf waters into whitecaps and whistling up the inlet and around the grey eaves. Miss Hannah was mournfully patting a frosted chrysanthemum under its golden chin when she saw a man limping slowly down the lane.

"Now, who can that be?" she murmured. "It isn't any Prospect man, for there's nobody lame around here."

She went to the garden gate to meet him. He came haltingly up the slope and paused before her, gazing at her wistfully. He looked old and bent and broken, and his clothes were poor and worn. Who was he? Miss Hannah felt that she ought to know him, and her memory went groping back amongst all her recollections. Yet she could think of nobody but her father, who had died fifteen years before.

"Don't ye know me, Hannah?" said the man wistfully. "Have I changed so much as all that?"

"Ralph!"

It was between a cry and a laugh. Miss Hannah flew through the gate and caught him in her arms. "Ralph, my own dear brother! Oh, I always knew you'd come back. If you knew how I've looked forward to this day!" She was both laughing and crying now. Her face shone with a soft gladness. Ralph Walworth shook his head sadly.

"It's a poor wreck of a man I am come back to you, Hannah," he said. "I've never accomplished anything and my health's broken and I'm a cripple as ye see. For a time I thought I'd never show my face back here, such a failure as I be, but the longing to see you got too strong. It's naught but a wreck I am, Hannah."

"You're my own dear brother," cried Miss Hannah. "Do you think I care how poor you are? And if your health is poor I'm the one to nurse you up, who else than your only sister, I'd like to know! Come right in. You're shivering in this wind. I'll mix you a good hot currant drink. I knew them black currants didn't bear so plentiful for nothing last summer. Oh, this is a good day and no mistake!"

In twenty-four hours' time everybody in Prospect knew that Ralph Walworth had come home, crippled and poor. Jacob Delancey shook his head as he drove away from the station with Ralph's shabby little trunk standing on end in his buggy. The station master had asked him to take it down to Miss Hannah's, and Jacob did not fancy the errand. He was afraid Miss Hannah would be in a bad way and he did not know what to say to her.

She was in her garden, covering her pansies with seaweed, when he drove up, and she came to the garden gate to meet him, all smiles.

"So you've brought Ralph's trunk, Mr. Delancey. Now, that was real good of you. He was going over to the station to see about it himself, but he had such a cold I persuaded him to wait till tomorrow. He's lying down asleep now. He's just real tired. He brought this seaweed up from the shore for me this morning and it played him out. He ain't strong. But didn't I tell you he was coming back soon? You only laughed at me, but I knew."

"He isn't very rich, though," said Jacob jokingly. He was relieved to find that Miss Hannah did not seem to be worrying over this.

"That doesn't matter," cried Miss Hannah. "Why, he's my brother! Isn't that enough? I'm rich if he isn't, rich in love and happiness. And

I'm better pleased in a way than if he had come back rich. He might have wanted to take me away or build a fine house, and I'm too old to be making changes. And then he wouldn't have needed me. I'd have been of no use to him. As it is, it's just me he needs to look after him and coddle him. Oh, it's fine to have somebody to do things for, somebody that belongs to you. I was just dreading the loneliness of the winter, and now it's going to be such a happy winter. I declare last night Ralph and I sat up till morning talking over everything. He's had a hard life of it. Bad luck and illness right along. And last winter in the lumber woods he got his leg broke. But now he's come home and we're never going to be parted again as long as we live. I could sing for joy, Jacob."

"Oh, sure," assented Jacob cordially. He felt a little dazed. Miss Hannah's nimble change of base was hard for him to follow, and he had an injured sense of having wasted a great deal of commiseration on her when she didn't need it at all. "Only I kind of thought, we all thought, you had such plans."

"Well, they served their turn," interrupted Miss Hannah briskly. "They amused me and kept me interested till something real would come in their place. If I'd had to carry them out I dare say they'd have bothered me a lot. Things are more comfortable as they are. I'm happy as a bird, Jacob."

"Oh, sure," said Jacob. He pondered the business deeply all the way back home, but could make nothing of it.

"But I ain't obliged to," he concluded sensibly. "Miss Hannah's satisfied and happy and it's nobody else's concern. However, I call it a curious thing."

Robert Turner's Revenge

When Robert Turner came to the green, ferny triangle where the station road forked to the right and left under the birches, he hesitated as to which direction he would take. The left led out to the old Turner homestead, where he had spent his boyhood and where his cousin still lived; the right led down to the Cove shore where the Jameson property was situated. Since he had stopped off at Chiswick for the purpose of looking this property over before foreclosing the mortgage on it he concluded that he might as well take the Cove road; he could go around by the shore afterward—he had not forgotten the way even in forty years—and so on up through the old spruce wood in Alec Martin's field—if the spruces were there still and the field still Alec Martin's—to his cousin's place. He would just about have time to make the round before the early country supper hour. Then a brief visit with Tom—Tom had always been a good sort of a fellow although woefully dull and slow-going—and the evening express for Montreal. He swung with a businesslike stride into the Cove road.

As he went on, however, the stride insensibly slackened into an unaccustomed saunter. How well he remembered that old road, although it was forty years since he had last traversed it, a set-lipped boy of fifteen, cast on the world by the indifference of an uncle. The years had made surprisingly little difference in it or in the surrounding scenery. True, the hills and fields and lanes seemed lower and smaller and narrower than he remembered them; there were some new houses along the road, and the belt of woods along the back of the farms had become thinner in most places. But that was all. He had no difficulty in picking out the old familiar spots. There was the big cherry orchard on the Milligan place which had been so famous in his boyhood. It was snow-white with blossoms, as if the trees were possessed of eternal youth; they had been in blossom the last time he had seen them. Well, time had not stood still with him as it had with Luke Milligan's cherry orchard, he reflected grimly. His springtime had long gone by.

The few people he met on the road looked at him curiously, for strangers were not commonplace in Chiswick. He recognized some of the older among them but none of them knew him. He had been an awkward, long-limbed lad with fresh boyish colour and crisp black curls when he had left Chiswick. He returned to it a somewhat portly figure of a man, with close-cropped, grizzled hair, and a face that looked as if it might be carved out of granite, so immobile and unyielding it was—the face of a man who never faltered or wavered, who stuck at nothing that might advance his plans and purposes, a face known and dreaded in the business world where he reigned master. It was a cold, hard, selfish face, but the face of the boy of forty years ago had been neither cold nor hard nor selfish.

Presently the homesteads and orchard lands grew fewer and then ceased altogether. The fields were long and low-lying, sloping down to the misty blue rim of sea. A turn of the road brought him in sudden sight of the Cove, and there below him was the old Jameson homestead, built almost within wave-lap of the pebbly shore and shut away into a lonely grey world of its own by the sea and sands and those long slopes of tenantless fields.

He paused at the sagging gate that opened into the long, deep-rutted lane and, folding his arms on it, looked earnestly and scrutinizingly over the buildings. They were grey and faded, lacking the prosperous appearance that had characterized them once. There was an air of failure about the whole place as if the very land had become disheartened and discouraged.

Long ago, Neil Jameson, senior, had been a
well-to-do man. The big Cove farm had been one
of the best in Chiswick then. As for Neil Jameson,
junior, Robert Turner's face always grew something grimmer when he recalled him—the one
person, boy and man, whom he had really hated
in the world. They had been enemies from childhood, and once in a bout of wrestling at the Chiswick school Neil had thrown him by an unfair
trick and taunted him continually thereafter on
his defeat. Robert had made a compact with himself that some day he would pay Neil Jameson
back. He had not forgotten it—he never forgot
such things—but he had never seen or heard of
Neil Jameson after leaving Chiswick. He might
have been dead for anything Robert Turner knew.
Then, when John Kesley failed and his effects
turned over to his creditors, of whom Robert
Turner was the chief, a mortgage on the Cove
farm at Chiswick, owned by Neil Jameson, had
been found among his assets. Inquiry revealed the
fact that Neil Jameson was dead and that the farm
was run by his widow. Turner felt a pang of disappointment. What satisfaction was there in
wreaking revenge on a dead man? But at least his
wife and children should suffer. That debt of his
to Jameson for an ill-won victory and many a
sneer must be paid in full, if not to him, why,
then to his heirs.

His lawyers reported that Mrs. Jameson was
two years behind with her interest. Turner in-
structed them to foreclose the mortgage promptly.

Then he took it into his head to revisit Chiswick and have a good look at the Cove farm and other places he knew so well. He had a notion that it might be a decent place to spend a summer month or two in. His wife went to seaside and mountain resorts, but he liked something quieter. There was good fishing at the Cove and in Chiswick pond, as he remembered. If he liked the farm as well as his memory promised him he would do, he would bid it in himself. It would make Neil Jameson turn in his grave if the penniless lad he had jeered at came into the possession of his old ancestral property that had been owned by a Jameson for over one hundred years. There was a flavour in such a revenge that pleased Robert Turner. He smiled one of his occasional grim smiles over it. When Robert Turner smiled, weather prophets of the business sky foretold squalls.

Presently he opened the gate and went through. Halfway down the lane forked, one branch going over to the house, the other slanting across the field to the cove. Turner took the latter and soon found himself on the grey shore where the waves were tumbling in creamy foam just as he remembered them long ago. Nothing about the old cove had changed; he walked around a knobby headland, weather-worn with the wind and spray of years, which cut him off from sight of the Jameson house, and sat down on a rock. He thought himself alone and was annoyed to find a boy sitting on the opposite ledge with a book on his knee.

The lad lifted his eyes and looked Turner over
with a clear, direct gaze. He was about twelve
years old, tall for his age, slight, with a delicate,
clear-cut face—a face that was oddly familiar to
Turner, although he was sure he had never seen
it before. The boy had oval cheeks, finely tinted
with colour, big, shy blue eyes quilled about with
long black lashes, and silvery-golden hair lying
over his head in soft ringlets like a girl's. What
girl's? Something far back in Robert Turner's
dreamlike boyhood seemed to call to him like a
note of a forgotten melody, sweet yet stirring
like a pain. The more he looked at the boy the
stronger the impression of a resemblance grew
in every feature but the mouth. That was alien
to his recollection of the face, yet there was
something about it, when taken by itself, that
seemed oddly familiar also—yes, and unpleas-
antly familiar, although the mouth was a good
one—finely cut and possessing more firmness
than was found in all the other features put
together.

"It's a good place for reading, sonny, isn't it?"
he inquired, more genially than he had spoken to
a child for years. In fact, having no children of
his own, he so seldom spoke to a child that his
voice and manner when he did so were generally
awkward and rusty.

The boy nodded a quick little nod. Somehow,
Turner had expected that nod and the glimmer of
a smile that accompanied it.

"What book are you reading?" he asked.

The boy held it out; it was **an** old *Robinson Crusoe*, that classic of boyhood.

"It's splendid," he said. "Billy Martin lent it to me and I have to finish it today because Ned Josephs is to have it next and he's in a hurry for it."

"It's a good while since I read *Robinson Crusoe*," said Turner reflectively. "But when I did it was on this very shore a little further along below the Miller place. There was a Martin and a Josephs in the partnership then too—the fathers, I dare say, of Billy and Ned. What is your name, my boy?"

"Paul Jameson, sir."

The name was a shock to Turner. This boy a Jameson—Neil Jameson's son? Why, yes, he had Neil's mouth. Strange he had nothing else in common with the black-browed, black-haired Jamesons. What business had a Jameson with those blue eyes and silvery-golden curls? It was flagrant forgery on Nature's part to fashion such things and label them Jameson by a mouth.

Hated Neil Jameson's son! Robert Turner's face grew so grey and hard that the boy involuntarily glanced upward to see if a cloud had crossed the sun.

"Your father was Neil Jameson, I suppose?" Turner said abruptly.

Paul nodded. "Yes, but he is dead. He has been dead for eight years. I don't remember him."

"Have you any brothers or sisters?"

"I have a little sister a year younger than I

am. The other four are dead. They died long
ago. I'm the only boy Mother had. Oh, I do so
wish I was bigger and older! If I was I could do
something to save the place—I'm sure I could.
It is breaking Mother's heart to have to leave
it."

"So she has to leave it, has she?" said Turner
grimly, with the old hatred stirring in his heart.

"Yes. There is a mortgage on it and we're to be
sold out very soon—so the lawyers told us.
Mother has tried so hard to make the farm pay
but she couldn't. I could if I was bigger—I know
I could. If they would only wait a few years! But
there is no use hoping for that. Mother cries all
the time about it. She has lived at the Cove farm
for over thirty years and she says she can't live
away from it now. Elsie—that's my sister—and I
do all we can to cheer her up, but we can't do
much. Oh, if I was only a man!"

The lad shut his lips together—how much his
mouth was like his father's—and looked out seaward with troubled blue eyes. Turner smiled
another grim smile. Oh, Neil Jameson, your old
score was being paid now!

Yet something embittered the sweetness of
revenge. That boy's face—he could not hate it as
he had accustomed himself to hate the memory
of Neil Jameson and all connected with him.

"What was your mother's name before she married your father?" he demanded abruptly.

"Lisbeth Miller," answered the boy, still frowning seaward over his secret thoughts.

Turner started again. Lisbeth Miller! He might have known it. What woman in all the world save Lisbeth Miller could have given her son those eyes and curls? So Lisbeth had married Neil Jameson—little Lisbeth Miller, his schoolboy sweetheart. He had forgotten her—or thought he had; certainly he had not thought of her for years. But the memory of her came back now with a rush.

Little Lisbeth—pretty little Lisbeth—merry little Lisbeth! How clearly he remembered her! The old Miller place had adjoined his uncle's farm. Lisbeth and he had played together from babyhood. How he had worshipped her! When they were six years old they had solemnly promised to marry each other when they grew up, and Lisbeth had let him kiss her as earnest of their compact, made under a bloom-white apple tree in the Miller orchard. Yet she would always blush furiously and deny it ever afterwards; it made her angry to be reminded of it.

He saw himself going to school, carrying her books for her, the envied of all the boys. He remembered how he had fought Tony Josephs because Tony had the presumption to bring her spice apples: he had thrashed him too, so soundly that from that time forth none of the schoolboys presumed to rival him in Lisbeth's affections—roguish little Lisbeth! who grew prettier and saucier every year.

He recalled the keen competition of the old days when to be "head of the class" seemed the

highest honour within mortal reach, and was
striven after with might and main. He had seldom
attained to it because he would never "go up
past" Lisbeth. If she missed a word, he, Robert,
missed it too, no matter how well he knew it. It
was sweet to be thought a dunce for her dear sake.
It was all the reward he asked to see her holding
her place at the head of the class, her cheeks
flushed pink and her eyes starry with her pride
of position. And how sweetly she would lecture
him on the way home from school about learning
his spellings better, and wind up her sermon
with the frank avowal, uttered with deliciously
downcast lids, that she liked him better than
any of the other boys after all, even if he
couldn't spell as well as they could. Nothing of
success that he had won since had ever thrilled
him as that admission of little Lisbeth's!

She had been such a sympathetic little sweetheart too, never weary of listening to his dreams
and ambitions, his plans for the future. She had
always assured him that she knew he would
succeed. Well, he had succeeded—and now one
of the uses he was going to make of his success
was to turn Lisbeth and her children out of their
home by way of squaring matters with a dead
man!

Lisbeth had been away from home on a long
visit to an aunt when he had left Chiswick. She
was growing up and the childish intimacy was
fading. Perhaps, under other circumstances, it
might have ripened into fruit, but he had gone

away and forgotten her; the world had claimed him; he had lost all active remembrance of Lisbeth and, before this late return to Chiswick, he had not even known if she were living. And she was Neil Jameson's widow!

He was silent for a long time, while the waves purred about the base of the big red sandstone rock and the boy returned to his *Crusoe*. Finally Robert Turner roused himself from his reverie.

"I used to know your mother long ago when she was a little girl," he said. "I wonder if she remembers me. Ask her when you go home if she remembers Bobby Turner."

"Won't you come up to the house and see her, sir?" asked Paul politely. "Mother is always glad to see her old friends."

"No, I haven't time today." Robert Turner was not going to tell Neil Jameson's son that he did not care to look for the little Lisbeth of long ago in Neil Jameson's widow. The name spoiled her for him, just as the Jameson mouth spoiled her son for him. "But you may tell her something else. The mortgage will not be foreclosed. I was the power behind the lawyers, but I did not know that the present owner of the Cove farm was my little playmate, Lisbeth Miller. You and she shall have all the time you want. Tell her Bobby Turner does this in return for what she gave him under the big sweeting apple tree on her sixth birthday. I think she will remember and understand. As for you, Paul, be a good boy and good to your

mother. I hope you'll succeed in your ambition of
making the farm pay when you are old enough
to take it in hand. At any rate, you'll not be disturbed in your possession of it."

"Oh, sir! oh, sir!" stammered Paul in an
agony of embarrassed gratitude and delight.
"Oh, it seems too good to be true. Do you really
mean that we're not to be sold out? Oh, won't
you come and tell Mother yourself? She'll be so
happy—so grateful. Do come and let her thank
you."

"Not today. I haven't time. Give her my message, that's all. There, run; the sooner she gets
the news the better."

Turner watched the boy as he bounded away,
until the headland hid him from sight.

"There goes my revenge—and a fine bit of
property eminently suited for a summer resi-
dence—all for a bit of old, rusty sentiment," he
said with a shrug. "I didn't suppose I was capable
of such a mood. But then—little Lisbeth. There
never was a sweeter girl. I'm glad I didn't go with
the boy to see her. She's an old woman now—
and Neil Jameson's widow. I prefer to keep my
old memories of her undisturbed—little Lisbeth of
the silvery-golden curls and the roguish blue eyes.
Little Lisbeth of the old time! I'm glad to be able
to have done you the small service of securing
your home to you. It is my thanks to you for
the friendship and affection you gave my lonely
boyhood—my tribute to the memory of my first
sweetheart."

He walked away with a smile, whose amusement presently softened to an expression that would have amazed his business cronies. Later on he hummed the air of an old love song as he climbed the steep spruce road to Tom's.

For a Dream's Sake

"I think I've been a little off my head ever since last night," said Gilroy Gray.

He had hurried up from college as soon as his classes were over to make sure that last night had not been a dream . . . that Vere had really promised to marry him at last . . . after all these years of devotion when he had so little hope of winning her.

And it was true. She had met him in the rose garden and held up her lips to be kissed. Then she had turned again quietly to her occupation of cutting roses for potpourri. Vere still made potpourri every summer. It was a rule with her. None of the younger generation bothered with it. They gathered their roses while they might and flung them aside when faded.

There was a basket at Vere's feet, half tipped, spilling its contents in a little pool of pink and white and crimson sweetness on the grass. She wore some kind of a pale blue dress, quite long. Gilroy was glad that long dresses were coming in again. They suited Vere as short ones had never done. In the shadow of her garden hat the distinction of her slightly lined, slightly sad face impressed him anew. She had a kind of pale, luminous beauty . . . the beauty of the first evening star in the sky or a white mountain peak smitten with dawn. She was not young, but when she came into a room every other woman in it suddenly became common and undistinguished. She was usually calm and fine and a little chill. She did not have many close friends, but those she did have were always unchangeably loyal to her. She had a strange holding power under all her aloofness.

Gilroy did not know just why he loved her or why she was so full of enchantment for him. But it had been so ever since he had first seen her. And now, at last, she was his . . . with reservations.

He had accepted those reservations. He knew— she had told him—that she had only second-hand love to give. He must be content with that. He had known something of it before, but she had told him the whole story the previous evening.

When she was a girl of seventeen she had loved Maurice Tisdale. She did not say a great deal about him, but Gilroy got the impression that Maurice had been a slim, romantic, starry-eyed youth, fonder of reading poetry than of work, although Vere most certainly did not say that. And her father, the irascible old entomologist, had sent him away.

"Father never liked him. He—he—the Maybee pride, you know. And Maurice was poor. I would have gone with him . . . what did I care for the Maybee pride or the Tisdale poverty? But I couldn't leave Mother then. She was so ill. Maurice went west. We corresponded until . . . until the word of his death came. He had gone with a prospecting company into the mountains . . . he got lost . . . he was never found. Life seemed over for me . . . that kind of life anyway. I've never cared since . . . like that . . . and I never can. I do care for you, Gilroy, and if having me will give you happiness, why, take me. Only . . . you know I have to be frank, Gilroy . . . the real me will always belong to Maurice. I can't forsake my dream. It has been a part of my life so long. He—he didn't deserve that I should ever be unfaithful to him. He died loving me."

Gilroy accepted it all and put it behind him. He would rather have half of her heart than the whole one of any other woman.

"All day I've been wondering if I only imagined last night," he said. "Come, darling, never mind the roses . . . I've only an hour and I want you to give me every minute."

"But I can give you only half an hour," said Vere, smiling. "Then I've got to help Father classify some lovely new bugs he's got. He's so excited over them, poor dear. Myself, I can get a little tired of them. I think . . . I really think I'd prefer you."

When the half hour was over and Vere had gone in to help Professor Maybee with his bugs, Gilroy went away, taking the short cut through the little park below the block where the old Maybee place was. He sat down on one of the benches to dream of Vere for a few minutes. He wondered if he would ever win her wholly . . . if there would ever come a time when he would not feel that his wife was the thrall of a dream whose core was another man . . . a dead man, dead in his youth . . . always young, romantic, alluring, in contrast to his—Gilroy's—greying middle age. Gilroy sighed in spite of his happiness. But he had lived long enough to learn that there are very few unspoiled things in this world.

"Hot, ain't it?" sympathetically agreed the man who was sitting on the other end of the bench.

Gilroy started slightly. He had not noticed his coming. He was a stout, rather commonplace man, rather flashily dressed, with a very weird and terrible necktie. He had taken off his hat to mop his forehead, and Gilroy saw that he was bald. His face was red, his eyes bleared and puffy. "I've been looking round this little old burg trying to locate someone I know," said the stranger. "I was born and bred here and it's sixteen years since I left. There doesn't seem to be any of my old pals in the place."

"That is . . . sad," said Gilroy idiotically. He did not want to talk to this man.

"It would have been a bit of a shock to them if I had found them," said the man, with a grin. He paused to light a cigarette, a huge diamond shining like a small sun on his little finger . . . the nail of which was not impeccable. "You see, everybody in this town thinks I'm dead."

"Indeed?"

"Yes. After I'd been west awhile I went out with a prospecting party and got lost. Had a dickens of a time finding my way back to civilization. Found everybody thought I was a goner, so I let 'em think so. I had my reasons. There was a skirt . . . well, you know. Lit out for another town and went into the real estate business. I've done well . . . you bet I ain't the poverty-stricken kid I was when I left here. It used to be a saying that all the Tisdales had holes in their pockets. But you bet I sewed up mine."

Gilroy sat as if stunned. He could not have spoken if his life had depended on it. This was Maurice Tisdale . . . this!

"I'm taking the wife and kids east to visit her people. She wanted to stop off in Trentville to see an old chum, so I thought I'd come on here and she could pick me up on the 6:15 train. But I'm blessed if I don't wish I hadn't bothered. Can't find anyone who ever knew me and there isn't even a place where a fellow could wet his whistle."

Still Gilroy said nothing. What was there to say? Maurice Tisdale mopped his face again.

"Say, when I used to live here there was an old bug-hunter on that street up there . . . old

Professor Maybee. Maybee, he was some guy.
Went off his chump watching bugs. He had a
daughter, though. There was some class to her . . .
a bit skinny . . . no more figger than an umbrella.
We were quite sweet on each other in those days.
Not that I meant anything much, but her face was
easy to look at and a fellow had to kill time. We
read miles of poetry together . . . say, she used
to write some herself, 'pon my word, and read it
to me. Then the bug-man got his dander up . . .
the Maybees had a rotten pride. He packed me
off . . . if you could have seen him"—Maurice
paused to give an imitation of Professor Maybee
in the act of dismissal. It was so well done that
even the frozen Gilroy almost smiled. The creature could mimic.

"I pretended to be a bit cut up—just to let Vere
down easy—but I was glad enough to snap out
of it. We wrote for a while after I went west, but
when I found I was so conveniently dead . . .
well, that suited me too. D'ye happen to know
what became of Vere? I suppose she's been married for years and put on weight like myself."

"No, she is not married," Gilroy found himself
able to say.

"Whew! I'm surprised . . . and yet I'm not. 'Taint
everybody that would interest her. Well, she's no
chicken now. Must be pretty definitely on the
shelf. Do they still live up there?"

"Yes."

"Then I believe I'll toddle up and see her. It'll
help to put the time in. I suppose since I'm safely

married old Maybee won't be scared of my running off with his lady daughter."

For a moment Gilroy wavered. Should he let him go? If Vere saw him, just as he was . . . well, he, Gilroy, would be under no necessity of sharing her with a ghost all their life together. When she saw Maurice Tisdale of today her dream would be scorched out of existence in the humiliation of the moment. He would be left without a rival.

But . . . what would it do to her? If her dream went would it not take with it something that was part of her charm? She would be nothing but a shamed, broken woman, all the fine aloofness and evasive frost of her smirched and draggled. Could he do this thing to her?

"I'm afraid it's no use your going up there," he said quietly. "The Maybees aren't home just now . . . off for a visit somewhere, I understand."

Maurice Tisdale shrugged his fat shoulders.

"Just my luck. However, maybe it's as well. Vere was the type that would make an awful skinny old maid. But she was one of the kind that sort of hang on to an idea. Just as well to let sleeping dogs lie. Guess I'll toddle down to the hotel and wait for my train. It's too darned hot to prowl about any longer."

Gilroy watched him out of sight . . . the fatuous sordid creature who still held sway in the deepest recesses of Vere Maybee's heart. He laughed . . . a little bitterly but unregretfully.

"I have saved her dream for her," he thought.

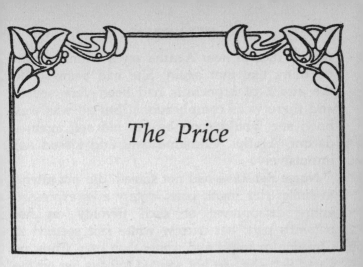

The Price

On the day when Dr. Lennox told Agatha North that she was out of danger and would soon be as well as ever, if she took proper care of herself, Agatha smiled her old, gallant smile up at him and Christine and Nurse Ransome.

"That's the most interesting thing you've said this long while," she told him. "I was beginning to think you were stupid—your conversation has been so dull. I'm glad I'm going to get better. I want to live. There are so many things I want to do yet. And, oh, I'd hate to die and leave all my nice dishes and my open fire—and that row of tulips I planted out the day I took sick."

Christine and Dr. Lennox laughed, the former with a note of heartfelt relief in her laughter. It

was so nice to hear Agatha say a whimsical little thing like that again. She had been so ill;
the attack of bronchitis had been very severe
and there were complications. But all was well
now; she would soon be her old self again—
darling Agatha. Christine bent and kissed her
impulsively.

Nurse Ransome had not smiled, did not intend
to smile. Her small, pale, watery eyes expressed
entire disapproval of such frivolity on her
patient's part; her narrow white face seemed to
Christine narrower and whiter than ever. Christine
hated her; she had not wanted to have her on the
case, but no other nurse could be had at the time,
and Miss Ransome was certainly competent.
Nurse Ransome could not hate—she had not
enough intensity for that—but she disliked Christine and pretended to herself that she disdained
her. She would have said that Christine was a
vain, proud, selfish, thoughtless, idle chatterbox.
All of this, and more, was true; but it was equally
true, though Nurse Ransome would never have
said it, that Christine was an exquisitely pretty,
loving, winsome, sensitive creature.

Dr. Lennox was thinking this, as he looked at
her across Agatha's bed. He was madly in love
with Christine, as all Harrowsdene knew. They
were not engaged yet, but everybody took it for
granted they soon would be. A good many people
thought Dr. Lennox was making a mistake. Of
course, Christine was a North and would eventually be the heiress of Agatha's not inconsiderable

estate, including "Whiteflowers"; but then she was such a wild, laughing thing, "a pretty butterfly," Dr. Lennox's aunt called her contemptuously. She thought, they said, of nothing but dress, dances and beaus, and "spinning street yarn." She laughed and talked too much and too freely—"you always heard her before you saw her." "A doctor's wife above all things should know how to hold her tongue—she would ruin his practice." She was far too intimate with Jen Keefe and her set; she was delicate; she was extravagant; she was, in short, thoroughly spoiled.

Ward Lennox had been told all these things at sundry times and by divers people, and they had made no impression on him at all. He had loved Christine from the moment of their first meeting, and he meant to ask her to marry him as soon as he could muster up the courage to do it. In his eyes she was all but perfection; her few faults were but the faults of petted youth; the only thing he seriously disapproved of in her was her intimacy with Jen Keefe, that lady of the pale gold hair and over-large dark eyes and free-and-easy ways. But once Christine was his wife she would see no more of the Keefes. Ward Lennox fondly believed that he could mould Christine to his views in all things; he had no idea of the strength of will that lay hidden under the soft curves and behind the coquettish eyes of her youth.

Agatha smiled up adoringly into Christine's face. They were cousins, but Agatha was the senior by twenty years. She had brought Christine

up, when the latter was orphaned by the death
of both father and mother in babyhood.
"Whiteflowers" was the only home Christine had
ever known. She loved it and she loved Agatha
passionately. But then everybody loved Agatha
North, that busy, kindly, charitable, broad-
minded, wonderful woman, who was always
helping somebody or something, always planning
and engineering and succeeding, always full of
life and interest and zest and wholesome laughter. Why, Harrowsdene could not get along without Agatha North. A sensation of relief and
gladness went over the whole town like a wave
when Dr. Lennox went away from "Whiteflowers" that day and spread the news that Agatha
was going to get better and would be about in a
few weeks. There had been anxiety; bronchitis so
easily ran to pneumonia, and Agatha had the
"North heart."

Before he went away Dr. Lennox explained
the change of medicines to Nurse Ransome and
Christine.

"She is listening to him, not to what he says,"
thought Nurse Ransome, watching Christine
covertly.

Christine was more aware of Ward Lennox than
of what he was saying. She thrilled with a delicious sense of his nearness; she was acutely conscious of his tall straightness, his glossy black
hair, his luminous dark blue eyes, and the passionate tenderness she sensed behind the aloofness of his professional manner. But she heard

what he said distinctly and remembered it perfectly for all this. She never forgot anything Ward said to her. In all the world there was no music like his voice.

"This is her regular medicine," said the doctor. "Give her four of these tablets every three hours. This," he held out another smaller bottle, "is only to be used if she has one of those restless attacks at night and cannot sleep. Give her one of these tablets—on no account more than one—every four hours if necessary. Two would be dangerous—three fatal. I'll set the bottle up on this little shelf by itself."

It was Christine's turn to sit up that night. Nurse Ransome repeated the caution about the tablets before she went to her room. Christine listened with a slightly mutinous, insolent expression; there was no need of Nurse Ransome's reminders. She had not forgotten what Ward had said; she was not a child. She sent a glance of pettish dislike after the spare figure of the nurse. She felt that Nurse Ransome insinuated doubts to the doctor as to her fitness for waiting on Agatha; it was agony to think he might have or acquire a poor opinion of her in this respect. Christine was vain and abnormally proud; she could not bear to be looked down upon by anybody for any reason. She hated Nurse Ransome because she felt that Nurse Ransome looked down upon her. Christine would have gone to the stake in olden days, not for her religion, but for dread of the contempt she would incur from her co-religionists if she proved

too weak for the test of martyrdom. The most
acute suffering of her childhood had been endured
when a schoolmate had publicly taunted her with
a distant cousin of the Norths who had been sent
to prison for forgery. She never forgot the shame
and humiliation and torture of that day.

Agatha was very restless that night. At the best
of times she was liable to sleeplessness—strangely
so for her type. At ten o'clock Christine gave her
one of the tablets and at two another. She was
very careful to set the bottle back on the bookshelf. She was afraid of it. She hoped Agatha
would not need it again.

When a week had passed Agatha was feeling
so well that she wanted to be allowed to sit up.
Dr. Lennox would not permit it. He told her her
heart was not yet fit for any exertion. "You must
lie here for another week yet. Then I may let you
sit up for a few minutes every day."

"You tyrant!" she said, smiling up at him. "He
is a tyrant, isn't he, Christine? My heart isn't
going to kill me. My grandmother had the same
kind of a heart and she lived for ninety-five years.
I'm going to live for ninety-five years—and enjoy
every minute of them, and do a thousand things
I want to do."

She laughed up at him and Christine. Dr. Lennox laughed back—dimples came out in his cheeks
when he laughed—said good-night, and went out
of the room.

Christine put the green shade over the light,
and sat down by the window. It was her night to

watch again, but the night vigils by now were little more than matters of form. Agatha had never required the sleeping tablets since that first night. She slept soundly, seldom waking until dawn. The sinister little bottle had never been taken down from the bookshelf.

Christine at the window began to dream, looking out into the chilly moonlit night of October. She was beginning to wish acutely that Agatha were quite well. She was getting tired of the sick room, tired of the monotonous existence which Agatha's illness had necessitated. She wanted to get back to her gay round of social doings again, the dances, the teas, the dinners, all the diversions of the little town. She wanted to wear her pretty dresses and jewels again—Christine loved jewels. Agatha had given her a string of tiny real pearls and a glittering Spanish hair comb for her last birthday. She had never had a chance to wear them yet. She wanted to flood "Whiteflowers" with music again. Next to her love for Ward, music was Christine's most intense passion, and she had not touched her piano since Agatha became ill. She wanted to get off for a weekend at Jen Keefe's Muskoka lodge for the deer-shooting. She knew Agatha wouldn't want her to go, but she meant to go for all that. It was nothing but sheer envy that made people talk about Mrs. Keefe and her set. There was nothing wrong with them; they were gay and up-to-date and not hidebound by silly old conventions.

Then she let herself think of Ward Lennox—

gave herself up to a vivid dream of their life together. She forgot her surroundings totally until she was recalled to them by a realization that Agatha was moving uneasily on her pillows.

Christine went to the bed. "Do you want anything?"

"I think I must have one of those tablets," said Agatha. "My restlessness has just returned—I thought perhaps it wouldn't—I've been doing so well lately. But for half an hour now I've just wanted to toss and scream."

Christine went over to the table, took down the bottle and returned with a tablet. She moved a little absently, for she was still partially in her dream of Ward.

After Agatha had taken her tablet she soon fell asleep. It was now eleven o'clock. Christine went back to the window and dreamed herself into a doze, leaning back in her big upholstered chair. She did not awaken until Agatha called her. It was the first time she had slept on guard.

"Would you like another tablet, dear?"

"No. The restlessness is gone. I think I'll sleep normally now—but since I'm awake, give me my regular dose. Ugh, when will I ever get square with Ward Lennox for all those hundreds of detestable little white tablets he's made me swallow? But after all they're preferable to the nauseous tablespoonfuls of liquid his father used to inflict on me."

Christine went over to the table rather stupidly. She yawned—she was not wholly awake yet. The clock in the parlour below was striking three. She counted the strokes absently as she took out the four tablets. Agatha sat up in bed to wash them down with a sip of water from the glass Christine held to her lips. She had been warned not to do this and now she slipped back with a sigh.

"I'm weaker than I thought I was."

"Is there anything else you'd like?" Christine asked, smothering another yawn.

"No, no, dear. I'm all right. It's only that I rather feel as if I were a dish of jelly and would all fall apart if violently jarred," said Agatha. "Go back to your chair and rest all you can. Sitting up like this is too hard on you—you're not strong. But you won't have to sit up many more nights. How glad I'll be when I'm well again. It will be so nice to keep my house again—and read my books—and eat just what I want—and be finally rid of that respectable female, Miss Ransome."

Christine went back, but she was thoroughly wakened up now and did not want to sleep. Agatha was soon asleep again. Moving softly, Christine turned on the light by the dressing table, screened it from the sick bed, and sat down before the mirror. Taking the pins out of the masses of her rich glossy black hair she began to experiment with various ways of hairdressing. Christine loved to do this. She was very proud and fond of her beautiful hair, and was in the habit of spending hours at her glass, sleeking and brushing it. After several experiments she got it up in a new way she liked exceedingly. She would wear it like that

to Jen Keefe's next dance—with her Spanish comb
in it. She slipped across the hall to her own room,
and returned with the comb, and put it in her
hair. How pretty she was! She leaned her elbows
on the table, cupped her chin in her hands, and
studied her reflected face earnestly. How very
white her skin was! What a delicate bloom was
on her round modelled cheeks. How golden-
brown her eyes were behind their long black
lashes; her forehead was rather high, but this new
way of doing her hair banished that defect. Her
neck and arms were lovely. She was the prettiest
girl in Harrowsdene, there was no doubt of that.
And the happiest. And she would be happier
yet—when she married Ward. Oh, she was
going to have a splendid, joyous life—ever so
much gayer than life at "Whiteflowers" had been.
Though Agatha was a darling, she did not care
much for social doings. But as young Mrs. Ward
Lennox, she could do as she liked. Ward adored
her—he would give her her own way in everything. No "settling down" for her into any poky
routine of married life, looking after babies and
pantry supplies. No, indeed—not for years to
come. She hated children anyhow, children and
housework. She was young and beautiful: she
would grasp at all youth and beauty could give
her. For years to come she would know the joy
of pleasing the eyes of men.

She would entertain: Harrowsdene should have
its eyes opened. And she would never give up
Jennie. Ward didn't like her, she knew, but he
would get over that. He would have to get over

his strict old-fashioned notions about things. She loved Jennie; Jennie was a dear thing, so gay and good-hearted. Of course, she wasn't an old Calvinistic prude like most of the Harrowsdene women—like all of them, except Agatha. She believed in living and letting live. So did Christine.

"I'm—going—to—do—exactly—as—I—please," she nodded with every word at the radiant face in the glass. "I'm—going—to—have—a—splendid—time."

She touched her lovely shoulders admiringly.

"How sorry I am for ugly women," she said. "What can they have to live for? But, of course, there must be some to do the stupid drudgery of life. We who are beautiful should be exempt from all that. It is just enough that we are beautiful."

She laughed softly again, softly, triumphantly, insolently, defiant of fate—the last laughter of her youth.

It was dawn now. Agatha still slept. Christine turned off the mirror light and went to the open window. The grounds of "Whiteflowers" were very lovely in the faint, pearly lustre. The wind was whistling rather eerily in the dead reeds of the little swampy hollow behind "Whiteflowers," but the sky was exquisite, with white clouds floating across it.

It was going to be a fine day. Christine was glad. She hated dull stormy days. She would go to see Jen in the afternoon. She hadn't been anywhere since Agatha took ill. But there was no need to mew herself up any longer.

She turned and went over to the bed. Agatha

was lying on the pillows, her face turned to the grey light. Something about it sent a strange, horrible dart of vague dismay to Christine's heart. She bent once and touched Agatha's cheek. Christine had never touched a dead person's cheek before—but she knew—she knew.

A shriek of terror broke from her lips. Nurse Ransome, who had just been coming across the hall, rushed through the doorway, followed by old Jean, the housekeeper, who had been on her way downstairs. Nurse Ransome saw at a glance what had happened, but she went promptly to work with all proper attempts at revival. Jean was dispatched downstairs to telephone for the doctor. White, shaking, useless, Christine was told to open the other window.

Christine went uncertainly toward the window. On her way she passed the table where the medicine bottle stood. Suddenly she stopped, looking at it. The bottle of sleeping tablets was on it. It had not been put up in its place at eleven o'clock. The bottle of regular tablets was back in the corner, half hidden by the window curtain, just as it had been at eleven o'clock.

What had she given to Agatha at three o'clock?

A hideous conviction suddenly took possession of her mind. She remembered—as if the whole incident rose out of subliminal depths into consciousness—she remembered feeling the raised letters of the poison bottle in her fingers as she counted out the four tablets. The regular medicine bottle was smooth. Her conscious mind, dulled

by sleep, had not been aware of what she was
doing—had retained no memory of it. But she
knew what she had done. At eleven o'clock, her
thoughts still tangled in the cobweb meshes of her
voluptuous dreaming, she had forgotten to put
the sleeping tablets safely back on the shelf. At
three o'clock she had picked up the bottle and
given Agatha four tablets from it. Four—and three
were fatal!

A sensation of deadly cold went over her from
head to foot—then nausea, horrible, beyond expression. She fought it off, and, blindly obeying
the dictates of an impulse that had no connection
with reason but rushed furiously up from the
deeps of being, she caught the poison bottle in
her icy hand and set it on the shelf, with one
wild, terrified look back at Nurse Ransome. Nurse
Ransome had not seen; she was busy with what
had been Agatha.

Christine felt herself falling—falling—falling—
into unimagined, unimaginable depths of horror. She slid down to the floor by the table,
unconscious.

Agatha North's death, coming when everyone
had supposed she was beyond all danger,
shocked Harrowsdene to its centre. She had died
in her sleep from heart failure, Dr. Lennox said.
He had known it was possible, but, as she herself
had said, her grandmother had lived to old age
with just the same kind of a heart, so he had not
been much afraid of it. There was no doubt—no

suspicion. Everybody was very sorry for Christine who seemed, it was said—for but few people saw her—to be dazed by the blow.

When Christine had recovered consciousness in her own room, Dr. Lennox and Nurse Ransome had tried to keep her there, but she broke away from them with unnatural strength and ran wildly to Agatha's room. Nurse Ransome was quite disgusted with her entire lack of self-control. She had screamed—laughed—implored Agatha to speak to her—look at her. Agatha had always answered her when she called before. Now she did not even open her eyes—her beautiful, large-lidded eyes. Christine had wrung her hands and torn her hair. Mingled with all her horror and agony was incredulity. This thing could not have happened. Agatha could not be dead—it was absurd—impossible. Why didn't they do something?

"Everything has been done—everything," said Ward Lennox compassionately. Even he did not like this frenzy of Christine's. But she was very young and this was her first sorrow. Agatha had been everything to her, mother, sister, comrade.

Under all Christine's agony was a horror of the discovery of what she had done, and a mad, unreasoning determination that it must not be discovered. She fainted again when she was forced to accept the fact that Agatha was dead; when she recovered she was calm, spent, quiet. She learned that Ward thought Agatha had died of heart failure; no one seemed to have the slightest inkling of the truth. Nurse Ransome questioned her concerning the events of the night, sharply enough, with a shrewish glint in her eyes, as was her way, but evidently without suspicion. Christine told her tale unhesitatingly, looking straight into Nurse Ransome's eyes as she told it. She was glad it was Nurse Ransome and not Ward Lennox who asked her. She could not, she thought, have told that story unshrinkingly to him.

Agatha had been very restless at eleven—she had given her one sleeping tablet and she had slept until three. Then she had asked for her usual medicine.

"I gave it to her," said Christine unquailingly, "and then she went to sleep again."

"Was there anything unusual about her?" asked Nurse Ransome. "Did she complain of anything?"

"I noticed nothing unusual." Christine's voice was steady and even. "She spoke of feeling her weakness—and she raised herself up to take her tablets before I could prevent her."

Nurse Ransome nodded.

"The exertion may have affected her heart a little. She must have died soon after three o'clock, Dr. Lennox says. It is strange you never noticed anything before morning."

"I was sitting over by the window—I never heard the slightest sound from her. I thought she was asleep."

"Did you doze off?" Nurse Ransome was a little contemptuous.

"No, I was wide awake all the time," said Christine deliberately.

She was tearless now, tearless, cunning, and terrified to the bottom of her soul. She shut herself up in her room when Nurse Ransome had gone and walked the floor.

No one must ever know. She would not confess. It could do Agatha no good now. And what harm might it not do to herself? She was wholly ignorant of what was or might be done in such cases and in her ignorance imagined the worst. They might not believe her—not now, at all events, after those instinctive lies of terror—they might think she had done it on purpose, that she might the sooner fall heir to Agatha's money. Sent to prison—tried—she, Christine North, on whom the winds of heaven had not dared to blow too roughly. And even at the best—even if they believed her—even if nothing could or would be done to her—what shame, what humiliation, what outrage to her pride! To have it known that she had poisoned Agatha, her virtual mother, through sheer carelessness, to be always pointed out as one who had been capable of such a deed, no, no, she could never face such a thing—never. Anything, any fate, would be better than that. And she knew what her fate must be. She could never marry Ward Lennox now. Confessed or unconfessed, this thing must always stand between them. But just now in her guilt and dismay and dread, this seemed of little moment. The soul can entertain but one overmastering passion at a time.

She stood before her mirror and looked at her changed face, her white, haggard face with its horror-filled eyes. It was as if in one hour she had passed from youth to middle age.

"I will not tell—it must never be known," she whispered, clenching her hands.

Her dread, and the unscrupulous determination caused by it, carried her through the funeral. People talked of her unnatural composure and her marble-white face. They pitied her, knowing what she had lost in Agatha. But in the back of their minds was the thought that she was a rich woman now, the mistress and owner of "Whiteflowers," and in due time would be wife of Ward Lennox. Back of this again was a thought, or rather a feeling, that giddy, shallow Christine was not worthy of such good fortune.

"She didn't shed a tear—too proud to cry before folks, North-like," said old Aunt Hetty Lawson. "She doesn't become her black. You'll see, she won't wear it longer than she has to. She'll make Agatha's money fly. Well, well, Harrowsdene will miss Agatha North. There aren't many women in the world like her."

Christine never forgot the agony of that hour. She had to sit still among the mourners. She had to look once more on Agatha's dead face—Agatha's lovely, placid face—and know that she had killed her, had cut her off in her gracious, beloved, useful prime. Agatha, who had loved her so entirely and whom she had loved so deeply in return. She had to endure the consolations of people who would despise and condemn her ruthlessly if they knew the truth. At moments it seemed to Christine that they must know it—that her horrible inward sense of guilt and remorse must be branded on her face for all to see. Her own realization of what she had done was so intense and vivid that it seemed as if it must radiate from her to the minds of all around her. Yet she sat on like a white statue, as motionless, as seemingly calm as the dead woman herself.

It was over; Agatha's beautiful soul, full of fancy and charm and love, had gone to its own place; her ripe, beautiful body was buried in Harrowsdene cemetery and covered speedily with a loose drift of autumn leaves. And Christine shut herself up at "Whiteflowers" alone, refusing to see anyone, even Ward Lennox.

Her dread of being found out was almost gone. Agatha was buried. Since there had been no suspicion before, there would be none now. She was safe. But now that terror was over, another emotion rose up and possessed her soul, horror of herself, passionate, unappeasable remorse. By sheer carelessness she had killed Agatha; she had preened and exulted before her mirror while Agatha was lying dead behind her—Agatha who wanted so much to live. She must atone for it, she must atone for it by lifelong penance. Sitting alone in her room, listening to the heavy rain that she knew was streaming down on Agatha's unprotected grave, she made her enduring vow.

"I have robbed her of life. I will not have life myself," said Christine.

* * *

At first people thought the change in Christine was merely the result of grief and trouble. It would soon wear off, they said. But it did not; then they began to talk and wonder and whisper again. They talked and wondered and whispered until they were tired of talking and wondering and whispering and lapsed into acceptance of a threadbare fact.

Christine cared nothing for their talking and wondering and whispering. She was bent only on atonement—bent on dulling the sting of remorse to a bearable degree by increasing penance. Within a month of Agatha's death she had organized her existence on the lines it was henceforth to follow, and nothing—entreaty, advice, blame—ever availed to move her one jot from her elected path, until people gave up blaming, entreating, advising; left her alone, and practically forgot her. Nobody could ever have believed that, much as Christine was known to have loved Agatha, her sorrow could have had such a lasting and revolutionary effect on her. But since it was undeniably so, they accepted it, concluding that Christine's mind had been affected by the shock of Agatha's death. After all, there had always been a strain of eccentricity in the Norths. Agatha herself had been eccentric in her very philosophy of living—so gay and tolerant and vivid at the years when other women had grown sober and hidebound and drab with the stress of existence.

Christine, with her own hands, put away all the things Agatha would never wear or use more, pretty things all of them, for Agatha had loved pretty things. She hung Agatha's picture in the room where Agatha had died, that she might not see it, and locked the door. But she took the brown bottle of sleeping tablets and set it on her own dressing table before her mirror, on the dressing table from which had been banished all the little implements of beauty she had been wont to use assiduously. She had no longer any use for them, but every night and every morning as she brushed her thick black hair straightly and unbecomingly off her face to its prim coil behind, she looked at the deadly reminder of her deed.

Ward Lennox respected her grief and desire for solitude as long as he could bear it. Then he went to her, told her his love, and asked her to marry him. Christine coldly refused. He was thunderstruck; he had been sure Christine loved him. Had he not seen her eyes change at sight of him, the revealing colour rise in her lovely face? Yet now she looked unblushingly at him and told him she could never marry him. He did not give up easily; he urged, entreated, reproached. Christine listened and said nothing.

"Don't you love me?" he asked.

"No," she said, with her eyes cast down.

Ward did not believe her. He went away at last, intending to return soon. But when he went back he rang the bell at "Whiteflowers" unavailingly; and no answer came to his letters. He tried at intervals for a year to see Christine; then he gave up, convinced that she did not care for him, never had cared. What he had mistaken for love had only been the coquettish allurement of a wild girl, who had been sobered by trouble into a realization that she should not so play with the great passion of life.

Christine loved him as she had always done. For one mad moment she was tempted to confess all and throw herself on his mercy. Surely if he loved her as he said he did he would overlook and forgive. But then, to feel always humiliated before him in his knowledge of her indefensible carelessness; she could not bear the thought. This one master dread held back the words. Without it she would not have been strong enough to put away love from her, even for atonement. All other joys she could sacrifice to her craving for remorse. But not this. If it had not been for the pride that could not brook the thought of shame she would have fallen at his feet and gasped out the truth. But that pride sealed her lips forever.

She put all her old friends out of her life. Most of them had been of the Keefe set. When Mrs. Keefe came to "Whiteflowers" old Jean Stewart told her ungraciously that Christine would not see her. Mrs. Keefe went away insulted and never made any further attempt to renew her intimacy with Christine. When, two years later, the scandal of the Keefe divorce case, with all its unsavoury details in the matter of a certain Muskoka house party, burst upon Harrowsdene, people said significantly that it was well Christine North was not mixed up in that. But by this time Harrowsdene had accepted and almost forgotten the new Christine.

Old Jean Stewart died three years after Agatha's death, and thenceforth Christine lived alone, keeping the big house herself in the immaculate fashion that Agatha had loved. She had always hated housework. She did it all now, down to the very scrubbing and stove-blacking, taking a fierce satisfaction in these hated tasks, glad when her beautiful white hands, on which never a jewel shone, grew rough and hardened. She had to have help outside, to keep the grounds as Agatha had liked them. For this purpose she employed half-witted old Dormy Woods, who pottered about all the lawns of Harrowsdene and liked to insinuate that he knew dark secrets about everybody. Sometimes the queer remarks he occasionally let fall gave Christine a start of dread; when he looked at her with his horrible filmy eyes and said leeringly, "I could tell strange tales o' some folks,"she grew cold to her very heart. Was it possible he knew and guessed her secret? No, it was not possible. But she was always uneasy in his presence, and it was for that very reason she employed him. It was part of her penance. Perhaps, too, old Dormy told her bits of unsolicited news now and then.

She gave largely and secretly to the charities that Agatha had always supported, but she never spent an unnecessary cent. When people called her miserly she said bitterly to herself, "That is better than being called a murderess." She never wore anything but severe black. She never went anywhere save to the stores, where she did her economical buying, and to church. Every Sunday she sat alone in the old North pew, reading her Bible until the service began, never lifting her eyes. She did this because she detested reading the Bible. For the same reason she read a chapter in it every night and every morning. One month, eight years after Agatha's death, she suffered from a slight but uncomfortable affection of the eyes that was epidemic in Harrowsdene, and could not read at all. Then she discovered that she missed her Bible, that she had come to enjoy it. From that time she never opened her Bible again. Yet she had read through it so often that it had become part of her, its philosophy, its poetry, its drama, its ageless, incredible wisdom, of earth and of spirit, its unexampled range of colourful human nature were hers inalienably, permeating her soul and intellect.

Her reading was all heavy and serious now. She never looked at one of the sentimental romances she had once revelled in. Now she read only the old histories and biographies and poems in the old North bookcases. This filled part of the time left over from her meticulous housekeeping; the rest she passed in knitting and sewing, making garments which she secretly sent to the poor of the nearest city.

She never touched her piano after Agatha's death; no one ever heard her sing again. She never spoke to anyone beyond a grave Good Day, and when people talked to her or strove to hold her in conversation she answered with brief gravity and went her way—she who had once been such a chatterbox. She had put all companionship out of her life. She would not even have a cat or dog at "Whiteflowers." She kept the flowers that Agatha had loved in her garden, but she never touched one. Moonlight was still a fair thing, but she would not look at it. She would not accept any enjoyment, and she never for one waking moment forgot that she had killed Agatha. The passing of years never dulled or dimmed the realization. Sometimes she dreamed that people knew of it and looked on her with horror and contempt. She would wake up with perspiration on her forehead and breathe a word of passionate relief that it was only a dream.

She did not wholly succeed in banishing all passion from her life. When old Dormy told her that he'd heard Dr. Lennox was going to marry Florence King, the high school teacher, she felt a sudden savage thrill of jealousy.

"Surely he will never marry that stiff, pedantic creature," she thought. Yet she knew Miss King was handsome and clever, and Dormy reported Harrowsdene as approving the match. That night Christine looked from her window through the gap in the pines to the light that burned in a house across the river. She knew the light was in Ward Lennox's office, and she kept an ugly vigil with pain and longing. But by dawn she had conquered it. Ward Lennox might marry Florence

King. It was naught to her. She had put all that
behind her.

But Dr. Lennox did not marry Florence King;
he did not marry anyone, though gossip linked
his name with this or that for many years before
it accepted the fact that Dr. Lennox meant to
remain a bachelor. He was a busy, friendly man,
with a large practice; everybody liked him and
trusted him. People got well of serious illnesses
just because they believed in him. His personality
cured more patients than his medicine. He was
no hermit. He went freely into society and enjoyed
life. He and Christine never met. At long intervals
they passed each other on the street. He would
bow courteously and Christine coldly; that was
all. People had forgotten that it had ever been
supposed they would marry.

After this fashion fourteen years passed. Christine
was thirty-four years old—if anybody had thought
about her age. Nobody did. Her own generation
were all married and gone. To the younger she
was what she had always seemed—a grave,
stately, middle-aged eccentric woman, considered
miserly, living her strange secluded life at old-
fashioned "Whiteflowers." She was always pale,
darkly and plainly dressed; yet there was a
haunting, tragic charm about her that made the
younger beauties seem cheap and common beside
her. Christine never thought about her appearance save when, looking into her unshaded mirror over the brown bottle on the table, she saw

the lines on her face and the slight hollows in the cheeks that had once been so round and delicately hued, and had a momentary impression that she was old and faded—much more so than her contemporaries. But that was part of her atonement. She had given up her beauty when she gave up love and life's fulfillment.

Her atonement was becoming easier—too easy, she thought. She had ceased to have wild longings of the things she had put away from her. She had ceased to dream of Ward—ceased to desire feverishly to fling open her silent piano and plunge her fingers into music. She was beginning to like her housework, her reading, even her sewing and knitting. When she realized this, she felt all the old sting of her guilt and remorse. She must not be happy. What could she do to make herself miserable?

The thought came to her that she would adopt a child. Nothing could be more distasteful to her. She had always disliked children. Most of all she disliked ugly children. She went to the orphan asylum in the city and brought home its ugliest inmate—a boy of eight, with a pitiful little face scarred by some inhuman attack of a drunken father. His name was Jacky Brent and he was a timid, silent little fellow—the very type which made Christine feel most uncomfortable. But she revelled in her discomfort and in all the annoyances which the care and upbringing of this child brought into her methodical existence. She left nothing undone that could contribute to his comfort and welfare. She studied dietetic tables and child welfare magazines, and vexed her soul with balanced meals and tables of weights. She helped him with his lessons; she invited his schoolmates to "Whiteflowers" to make it lively for him and watched over their games and their manners, and got up appropriate lunches for them. She got a dog for him and forced herself to tolerate muddy paw tracks; she played halma and dominoes with him—even ball in the backyard because she abhorred it. She helped him with his lessons, even, she remembered, as Agatha had once helped her. She helped him build a playhouse and picnicked with him in it. She forced herself to talk to him. She had lived so long with silence that she found it difficult to talk, and more difficult still to talk to a child. But she persevered, and eventually, as they gradually built up a little store of common interests, she found it easier and easier. Jacky learned to talk too, as his timidity wore off somewhat, and sometimes his quaint, unexpected remarks prompted in Christine a desire for laughter to which she had long been a stranger. She never let herself laugh. She did not even smile, but momentarily the eyes of her girlhood returned to her.

In spite of his delicacy of appearance Jacky was a healthy child, but one night, when he had been at "Whiteflowers" nearly a year, he was suddenly taken violently ill. Christine telephoned wildly for old Dr. Abbott. Dr. Abbott was away; there was nothing to do but send for Ward Lennox. Ward

Lennox crossed the threshold of "Whiteflowers" for the first time in fifteen years. He was cool, impersonal, professional; Christine was so upset about Jacky that she could think of nothing else. They met and talked like casual acquaintances.

Ward Lennox told her that Jacky had appendicitis and that an operation was imperative. No time must be lost. At dawn a trained nurse was in charge of the case, and the specialist from the city had come. Christine locked herself in her room and paced the floor until the operation was over. Then they told her that the abscess had broken before the operation and that Jacky's condition was very critical. Christine went back to her room.

She did not pray. She had never prayed since Agatha's death—she had never dared to. Always in the back of her mind was the feeling that she must not pray without confession—and she could not confess. She did not pray now; she looked at her drawn, anguished face in her glass and for the first time she was unconscious of the little brown bottle under it.

Jacky might die, and she loved Jacky!

"I cannot live without him," she said, wringing her hands. "I cannot."

She remembered with a stab of horrible compunction that she had rebuked him sharply the day before for something he had said. She recalled his grieved look, the look that always came into his poor little face when he displeased her. He had always tried so hard to please her. That very night before he went to bed, when he had seemed

so tired and dull, he had faithfully hung his
clothes up and set his shoes straight, and put all
his little treasures tidily away in his box, as her
rigid rules required. Christine went and looked at
them, his little tops and nails and balls and
engines, his new jack-knife and the old broken
one he still loved because it had been his only
prized possession in the asylum, his tin pail and
spade, and the dancing monkey which had
delighted him so. If Jacky died . . .

Jacky did not die. He recovered. And when he
was well again Christine sat down in her room
on the first day he went back to school and took
stock of her emotions.

She had taken Jacky for a penance. He had
ceased to be a penance; he had become her
delight. She loved him with all the intensity of
her passionate nature. She could not give him
up—she could not. Such a sacrifice she could not
make. She had once given her lover up in the
surge of a new horror and remorse. But that surge
had spent itself. She could not give Jacky up now;
neither could she keep him with her guilty secret.
One must be surrendered. She must make her
choice.

When Jacky came from school, running through
the hall calling gaily for "Aunty," who had moth-
ered and petted and spoiled him all through his
convalescence, her choice was made. She got
Jacky his supper, helped him with his lessons and
put him to bed, reconciling him to its unusual
earliness by the promise of a treat on the morrow.

Then she went out, bareheaded, into the autumn dusk—not realizing that she was bareheaded.

She had thought it all over. The tale must be told. She did not know what the result might be. Probably at this lapse of time nothing would be done to her. People would believe that it was merely carelessness and content themselves with gossip and wonder and condemnation. Christine's pride still cringed at thought of it. It would be horrible, horrible to open up the old wound, horrible to have her long-hidden secret proclaimed to her world. But it must be.

To whom could she tell it? Nurse Ransome had died five years ago. Ward Lennox? Yes, it should be to him. Her punishment must be as severe as it could possibly be. She would go and confess to him.

She walked steadily along the street. The world about her seemed weird and purple and shadowy, with great cold clouds piling up above a sharp yellow eastern sky.

Christine felt that it was in keeping with her terrible errand; when she passed a house through whose open windows came the sound of music and laughter and dancing, she shuddered. Tomorrow these people would be talking of her—of her, Christine North, who had poisoned Agatha. And yet they were dancing tonight as if there were no such things in the world as horrible carelessness and never-dying remorse and public shame. She struck her hands together in her misery but she went on.

Ward Lennox was sitting on his verandah when Christine came up the walk in the pale moonshine that was beginning to silver the October dusk. His amazement could not have been much greater if Agatha North herself had come up the walk—it almost made him speechless. But he contrived to murmur a few conventional words and asked Christine to come in.

"I would rather stay out here," said Christine, who felt that what she had come to say could not be said in a lighted room.

She sat down in the chair he drew forward for her. The light streaming out through the window of the room behind her made a primrose nimbus around her shapely head. In the dim light she looked very beautiful, a majestic creature with that subtly knowing, deep-eyed white face of hers in its frame of flat dark hair. The lovely line of cheek and throat rose above her black collar. Ward Lennox suddenly remembered the time he had dared to kiss that white throat—the only time he had ever kissed her. It seemed to him that he could almost hear her little, deprecating laugh as she escaped him. Surely it had been the laugh of a woman who loved the man who kissed her. No coquette could have laughed just like that.

Christine looked straight at him, sensing the vast reserve of strength that underlay his external courtesy and gaiety and charm. How strong he was! And she—she had been so weak and cowardly!

"I have come to tell you something," she said.

"Yes," he said gently.

Christine waited a moment. She must find very plain, direct words. Her hands, she found, were clammy and her mouth was dry.

"I killed Agatha fifteen years ago. I didn't mean to—but I killed her."

"Christine!"

It gave her a strange shock to hear her name again. It was so long since she had heard it. For years she had been Miss North to everyone. Even to Jacky she was only "Aunty." Under the shock she was also conscious of an enormous relief, as if some horrible darkness or weight had been suddenly lifted from her soul.

She hurried on, rather incoherently now.

"I gave her four of the sleeping tablets by mistake, through carelessness. My thoughts were wool-gathering. I hadn't put the tablets back in the right place when I gave her one at eleven— and I fell asleep—and was stupid when I went to give her the regular medicine—and then I—I— played with my hair at the glass for hours, and she was dead—I never knew it. And I could not confess. I knew I ought to—but I was afraid to. I thought they might put me in prison, or always point the finger of scorn at me. I couldn't face it, so I lied. But I am telling the truth now, and I've done penance—oh, I've done penance. But I can't give Jacky up—so I'm telling it all now. Oh, whatever they do to me, don't let them take Jacky from me.

Ward Lennox was moved profoundly, Everything was clear to him now and, oh, the pity of it! For it had all been so unnecessary.

"Christine," he said slowly. "You did not kill Agatha. The tablets you gave her were quite harmless."

Christine looked up, dazed, incredulous.

"The day before Agatha died Nurse Ransome told me that she did not think the sleeping tablets would be needed again and I took them away, wanting them for another patient, as my supply had run low. I left in their place a bottle of tablets to be used if Agatha had any return of certain annoying digestive symptoms. They were harmless—the whole bottleful wouldn't have hurt her. I remember it all distinctly. Nurse Ransome should have told you. I suppose she forgot. Agatha died of heart failure—there is absolutely no doubt of that. Oh, Christine, my poor darling, and this was why—if you had trusted me . . ."

"If" indeed! Christine was struggling with a whirlpool of emotion in which a still half-incredulous joy was uppermost. She had not killed Agatha—there was no blood on her hands—that was the only fact she could grasp clearly now. Later on would come bitter regret, for her folly and cowardice, for the lost, wasted years, for everything she had thrown away in insensate sacrifice to her pride and her vain hunger for atonement. Later yet again would come a wistful realization that, after all, the years had not been wasted. Vanity, selfishness, frivolity had been stripped from her soul as a garment. Strength, fineness, reserve, dignity, all she had lacked had been given unto her in those years of penance; even physically they had not been barren. In her regular, simple life the delicacy of her girlhood had vanished. She had become a perfectly healthy woman. All this had been bought with a great price, but she could never have purchased it in a cheaper market.

She stood up . . . and swayed unsteadily.

"I must go home—think this out. I can't—no, no, you must not come with me—I must be alone."

"Christine!" His voice was a sharp protest. "You are not going to shut me out of your life again—I love you. I've always loved you—we must . . ."

"Not yet—not yet," she besought him feverishly, pushing him away from her.

He stepped back and let her pass. He had waited long—he could wait a little longer.

Christine went blindly home to "Whiteflowers." She went to Agatha's room and knelt by Agatha's bed. For the first time in fifteen years she prayed—a prayer of thankfulness and humility. For the rest of the night she sat at Agatha's window looking out into the moonlit beauty of "Whiteflowers," or walked about the dim haunted room in a mingled intoxication of joy and regret. Under all the turmoil of her mind she felt curiously young again—as if life had suddenly folded back many of its pages. Through the gap in the pines she saw Ward's light in the house across the river. For the first time since Agatha's death she let herself think about him. A door of life she had thought shut forever seemed slowly opening before her.

A Golden Wedding

The land dropped abruptly down from the gate, and a thick, shrubby growth of young apple orchard almost hid the little weather-grey house from the road. This was why the young man who opened the sagging gate could not see that it was boarded up, and did not cease his cheerful whistling until he had pressed through the crowding trees and found himself almost on the sunken stone doorstep over which in olden days honeysuckle had been wont to arch. Now only a few straggling, uncared-for vines clung forlornly to the shingles, and the windows were, as has been said, all boarded up.

The whistle died on the young man's lips and an expression of blank astonishment and dismay settled down on his face—a good, kindly, honest face it was, although perhaps it did not betoken any pronounced mental gifts on the part of its owner.

"What can have happened?" he said to himself. "Uncle Tom and Aunt Sally can't be dead—I'd have seen their deaths in the paper if they was. And I'd a-thought if they'd moved away it'd been printed too. They can't have been gone long—that flower-bed must have been made up last spring. Well, this is a kind of setback for a fellow. Here I've been tramping all the way from the station, a-thinking how good it would be to see Aunt Sally's sweet old face again, and hear Uncle Tom's laugh, and all I find is a boarded-up house going to seed. S'pose I might as well toddle over to Stetsons' and inquire if they haven't disappeared, too."

He went through the old firs back of the lot and across the field to a rather shabby house beyond. A cheery-faced woman answered his knock and looked at him in a puzzled fashion. "Have you forgot me, Mrs. Stetson? Don't you remember Lovell Stevens and how you used to give him plum tarts when he'd bring your turkeys home?"

Mrs. Stetson caught both his hands in a hearty clasp.

"I guess I haven't forgotten!" she declared. "Well, well, and you're Lovell! I think I ought to know your face, though you've changed a lot. Fifteen years have made a big difference in you. Come right in. Pa, this is Lovell—you mind Lovell, the boy Aunt Sally and Uncle Tom had for years?"

"Reckon I do," drawled Jonah Stetson with a friendly grin. "Ain't likely to forget some of the capers you used to be cutting up. You've filled out considerable. Where have you been for the last ten years? Aunt Sally fretted a lot over you, thinking you was dead or gone to the bad."

Lovell's face clouded.

"I know I ought to have written," he said repentantly, "but you know I'm a terrible poor scholar, and I'd do most anything than try to write a letter. But where's Uncle Tom and Aunt Sally gone? Surely they ain't dead?"

"No," said Jonah Stetson slowly, "no—but I guess they'd rather be. They're in the poorhouse."

"The poorhouse! Aunt Sally in the poorhouse!" exclaimed Lovell.

"Yes, and it's a burning shame," declared Mrs. Stetson. "Aunt Sally's just breaking her heart from the disgrace of it. But it didn't seem as if it could be helped. Uncle Tom got so crippled with rheumatism he couldn't work and Aunt Sally was too frail to do anything. They hadn't any relations and there was a mortgage on the house."

"There wasn't any when I went away."

"No; they had to borrow money six years ago when Uncle Tom had his first spell of rheumatic fever. This spring it was clear that there was nothing for them but the poorhouse. They went three months ago and terrible hard they took it, especially Aunt Sally, I felt awful about it myself.

Jonah and I would have took them if we could, but we just couldn't—we've nothing but Jonah's wages and we have eight children and not a bit of spare room. I go over to see Aunt Sally as often as I can and take her some little thing, but I dunno's she wouldn't rather not see anybody than see them in the poorhouse."

Lovell weighed his hat in his hands and frowned over it reflectively.

"Who owns the house now?"

"Peter Townley. He held the mortgage. And all the old furniture was sold too, and that most killed Aunt Sally. But do you know what she's fretting over most of all? She and Uncle Tom will have been married fifty years in a fortnight's time and Aunt Sally thinks it's awful to have to spend their golden wedding anniversary in the poorhouse. She talks about it all the time. You're not going, Lovell"—for Lovell had risen—"you must stop with us, since your old home is closed up. We'll scare you up a shakedown to sleep on and you're welcome as welcome. I haven't forgot the time you caught Mary Ellen just as she was tumbling into the well."

"Thank you, I'll stay to tea," said Lovell, sitting down again, "but I guess I'll make my headquarters up at the station hotel as long as I stay round here. It's kind of more central."

"Got on pretty well out west, hey?" queried Jonah.

"Pretty well for a fellow who had nothing but his two hands to depend on when he went out," said Lovell cautiously. "I've only been a labouring man, of course, but I've saved up enough to start a little store when I go back. That's why I came east for a trip now—before I'd be tied down to business. I was hankering to see Aunt Sally and Uncle Tom once more. I'll never forget how kind and good they was to me. There I was, when Dad died, a little sinner of eleven, just heading for destruction. They give me a home and all the schooling I ever had and all the love I ever got. It was Aunt Sally's teachings made as much a man of me as I am. I never forgot 'em and I've tried to live up to 'em."

After tea Lovell said he thought he'd stroll up the road and pay Peter Townley a call. Jonah Stetson and his wife looked at each other when he had gone.

"Got something in his eye," nodded Jonah. "Him and Peter weren't never much of friends."

"Maybe Aunt Sally's bread is coming back to her after all," said his wife. "People used to be hard on Lovell. But I always liked him and I'm real glad he's turned out so well."

Lovell came back to the Stetsons' the next evening. In the interval he had seen Aunt Sally and Uncle Tom. The meeting had been both glad and sad. Lovell had also seen other people.

"I've bought Uncle Tom's old house from Peter Townley," he said quietly, "and I want you folks to help me out with my plans. Uncle Tom and Aunt Sally ain't going to spend their golden wedding in the poorhouse—no, sir. They'll spend it in their own home with their old friends about them. But they're not to know anything about it till the very night. Do you s'pose any of the old furniture could be got back?"

"I believe every stick of it could," said Mrs. Stetson excitedly. "Most of it was bought by folks living handy and I don't believe one of them would refuse to sell it back. Uncle Tom's old chair is here to begin with—Aunt Sally give me that herself. She said she couldn't bear to have it sold. Mrs. Isaac Appleby at the station bought the set of pink-sprigged china and James Parker bought the grandfather's clock and the whatnot is at the Stanton Grays'."

For the next fortnight Lovell and Mrs. Stetson did so much travelling round together that Jonah said genially he might as well be a bachelor as far as meals and buttons went. They visited every house where a bit of Aunt Sally's belongings could be found. Very successful they were too, and at the end of their jaunting the interior of the little house behind the apple trees looked very much as it had looked when Aunt Sally and Uncle Tom lived there.

Meanwhile, Mrs. Stetson had been revolving a design in her mind, and one afternoon she did some canvassing on her own account. The next time she saw Lovell she said:

"We ain't going to let you do it all. The women folks around here are going to furnish the refreshments for the golden wedding and the girls are going to decorate the house with golden rod."

The evening of the wedding anniversary came. Everybody in Blair was in the plot, including the matron of the poorhouse. That night Aunt Sally watched the sunset over the hills through bitter tears.

"I never thought I'd be celebrating my golden wedding in the poorhouse," she sobbed. Uncle Tom put his twisted hand on her shaking old shoulder, but before he could utter any words of comfort Lovell Stevens stood before them.

"Just get your bonnet on, Aunt Sally," he cried jovially, "and both of you come along with me. I've got a buggy here for you . . . and you might as well say goodbye to this place, for you're not coming back to it any more."

"Lovell, oh, what do you mean?" said Aunt Sally tremulously.

"I'll explain what I mean as we drive along. Hurry up—the folks are waiting."

When they reached the little old house, it was all aglow with light. Aunt Sally gave a cry as she entered it. All her old household goods were back in their places. There were some new ones too, for Lovell had supplied all that was lacking. The house was full of their old friends and neighbours. Mrs. Stetson welcomed them home again.

"Oh, Tom," whispered Aunt Sally, tears of happiness streaming down her old face, "oh, Tom, isn't God good?"

They had a right royal celebration, and a supper such as the Blair housewives could produce.

There were speeches and songs and tales. Lovell kept himself in the background and helped Mrs. Stetson cut cake in the pantry all the evening. But when the guests had gone, he went to Aunt Sally and Uncle Tom, who were sitting by the fire.

"Here's a little golden wedding present for you," he said awkwardly, putting a purse into Aunt Sally's hand. "I reckon there's enough there to keep you from ever having to go to the poorhouse again and if not, there'll be more where that comes from when it's done."

There were twenty-five bright twenty-dollar gold pieces in the purse.

"We can't take it, Lovell," protested Aunt Sally. "You can't afford it."

"Don't you worry about that," laughed Lovell. "Out west men don't think much of a little wad like that. I owe you far more than can be paid in cash, Aunt Sally. You must take it—I want to know there's a little home here for me and two kind hearts in it, no matter where I roam."

"God bless you, Lovell," said Uncle Tom huskily. "You don't know what you've done for Sally and me."

That night, when Lovell went to the little bedroom off the parlour—for Aunt Sally, rejoicing in the fact that she was again mistress of a spare room, would not hear of his going to the station hotel—he gazed at his reflection in the gilt-framed mirror soberly.

"You've just got enough left to pay your passage back west, old fellow," he said, "and then it's begin all over again just where you begun before. But Aunt Sally's face was worth it all— yes, sir. And you've got your two hands still and an old couple's prayers and blessings. Not such a bad capital, Lovell, not such a bad capital."

Mrs. March's
Revenge

"I declare, it is a real fall day," said Mrs. Stapp, dropping into a chair with a sigh of relief as Mrs. March ushered her into the cosy little sitting-room. "The wind would chill the marrow in your bones; winter'll be here before you know it."

"That's so," assented Mrs. March, bustling about to stir up the fire. "But I don't know as I mind it at all. Winter is real pleasant when it does come, but I must say, I don't fancy these betwixt-and-between days much. Sit up to the fire, Theodosia. You look real blue."

"I feel so too. Lawful heart, but this is comfort. This chimney-corner of yours, Anna, is the cosiest spot in the world."

"When did you get home from Maitland?"

asked Mrs. March. "Did you have a pleasant time? And how did you leave Emily and the children?"

Mrs. Stapp took this trio of interrogations in calm detail.

"I came home Saturday," she said, as she unrolled her knitting. "Nice wet day it was too! And as for my visit, yes, I enjoyed myself pretty well, not but what I worried over Peter's rheumatism a good deal. Emily is well, and the children ought to be, for such rampageous young ones I never saw! Emily can't do no more with them than an old hen with a brood of ducks. But, lawful heart, Anna, don't mind about my little affairs! The news Peter had for me about you when I got home fairly took my breath. He came down to the garden gate to shout it before I was out of the wagon. I couldn't believe but what he was joking at first. You should have seen Peter. He had an old red shawl tied round his rheumatic shoulder, and he was waving his arms like a crazy man. I declare, I thought the chimney was afire! 'Theodosia, Theodosia!' he shouted. 'Anna March has had a fortune left her by her brother in Australy, and she's bought the old Carroll place, and is going to move up there!' That was his salute when I got home. I'd have been over before this to hear all about it, but things were at such sixes and sevens in the house that I couldn't go visiting until I'd straightened them out a bit. Peter's real neat, as men go, but, lawful heart, such a mess as he makes of housekeeping! I didn't know you had a brother living."

"No more did I, Theodosia. I thought, as everyone else did, that poor Charles was at the bottom of the sea forty years ago. It's that long since he ran away from home. He had a quarrel with Father, and he was always dreadful high-spirited. He went to sea, and we heard that he had sailed for England in the *Helen Ray*. She was never heard of after, and we all supposed that my poor brother had perished with her. And four weeks ago I got a letter from a firm of lawyers in Melbourne, Australia, saying that my brother, Charles Bennett, had died and left all his fortune to me. I couldn't believe it at first, but they sent me some things of his that he had when he left home, and there was an old picture of myself among them with my name written on it in my own hand, so then I knew there was no mistake. But whether Charles did sail in the *Helen Ray*, or if he did, how he escaped from her and got to Australia, I don't know, and it isn't likely I ever will."

"Well, of all wonderful things!" commented Mrs. Stapp.

"I was glad to hear that I was heir to so much money," said Mrs. March firmly. "At first I felt as if it were awful of me to be glad when it came to me by my brother's death. But I mourned for poor Charles forty years ago, and I can't sense that he has only just died. Not but what I'd rather have seen him come home alive than have all the money in the world, but it has come about otherwise, and as the money is lawfully mine, I may as well feel pleased about it."

"And you've bought the Carroll place," said

Mrs. Stapp, with the freedom of a privileged friend. "Whatever made you do it? I'm sure you are as cosy here as need be, and nobody but yourself. Isn't this house big enough for you?"

"No, it isn't. All my life I've been hankering for a good, big, roomy house, and all my life I've had to put up with little boxes of places, not big enough to turn round in. I've been contented, and made the best of what I had, but now that I can afford it, I mean to have a house that will suit me. The Carroll house is just what I want, for all it is a little old-fashioned. I've always had a notion of that house, although I never expected to own it any more than the moon."

"It's a real handsome place," admitted Mrs. Stapp, "but I expect it will need a lot of fixing up. Nobody has lived in it for six years. When are you going to move in?"

"In about three weeks, if all goes well. I'm having it all painted and done over inside. The outside can wait until the spring."

"It's queer how things come about," said Mrs. Stapp meditatively. "I guess old Mrs. Carroll never imagined her home was going to pass into other folks' hands as it has. When you and I were girls, and Louise Carroll was giving herself such airs over us, you didn't much expect to ever stand in her shoes, did you? Do you remember Lou?"

"Yes, I do," said Mrs. March sharply. A change came over her sonsy, smiling face. It actually looked hard and revengeful, and a cruel light flickered in her dark brown eyes. "I'll not forget

Lou Carroll as long as I live. She is the only person in this world I ever hated. I suppose it is sinful to say it, but I hate her still, and always will."

"I never liked her myself," admitted Mrs. Stapp. "She thought herself above us all. Well, for that matter I suppose she was—but she needn't have rubbed it in so."

"Well, she might have been above me," said Mrs. March bitterly, "but she wasn't above twitting and snubbing me every chance she got. She always had a spite at me from the time we were children together at school. When we grew up it was worse. I couldn't begin to tell you all the times that girl insulted me. But there was once in particular—I'll never forgive her for it. I was at a party, and she was there too, and so was that young Trenham Manning, who was visiting the Ashleys. Do you remember him, Dosia? He was a handsome young fellow, and Lou had a liking for him, so all the girls said. But he never looked at her that night, and he kept by me the whole time. It made Lou furious, and at last she came up to me with a sneer on her face, and her black eyes just snapping, and said, 'Miss Bennett, Mother told me to tell you to tell your ma that if that plain sewing isn't done by tomorrow night she'll send for it and give it to somebody else; if people engage to have work done by a certain time and don't keep their word, they needn't expect to get it.' Oh, how badly I felt! Mother and I were poor, and had to work hard, but we had feelings just like other people, and to be insulted like that before Trenham Manning! I just burst out crying then and there, and ran away and hid. It was very silly of me, but I couldn't help it. That stings me yet. If I was ever to get a chance to pay Lou Carroll out for that, I'd take it without any compunction."

"Oh, but that is unchristian!" protested Mrs. Stapp feebly.

"Perhaps so, but it's the way I feel. Old Parson Jones used to say that people were marbled good and bad pretty even, but that in everybody there were one or two streaks just pure wicked. I guess Lou Carroll is my wicked streak. I haven't seen or heard of her for years—ever since she married that worthless Dency Baxter and went away. She may be dead for all I know. I don't expect ever to have a chance to pay her out. But mark what I say, Theodosia, if I ever have, I will."

Mrs. March snipped off her thread, as if she challenged the world. Mrs. Stapp felt uncomfortable over the unusual display of feeling she had evoked, and hastened to change the subject.

In three weeks' time Mrs. March was established in her new home, and the "old Carroll house" blossomed out into renewed splendour. Theodosia Stapp, who had dropped in to see it, was in a rapture of admiration.

"You have a lovely home now, Anna. I used to think it fine enough in the Carrolls' time, but it wasn't as grand as this. And that reminds me, I have something to tell you, but I don't want you to get as excited as you did the last time I mentioned her name. You remember the last day I was to see you we were talking of Lou Carroll? Well, next day I was downtown in a store, and who should sail in but Mrs. Joel Kent, from Oriental. You know Mrs. Joel—Sarah Chapple that was? She and her man keep a little hotel up at Oriental. They're not very well off. She is a cousin of old Mrs. Carroll, but, lawful heart, the Carrolls didn't used to make much of the relationship! Well, Mrs. Joel and I had a chat. She told me all her troubles—she always has lots of them. Sarah was always of a grumbling turn, and she had a brand-new stock of them this time. What do you think, Anna March? Lou Carroll—or Mrs. Baxter, I suppose I should say—is up there at Joel Kent's at Oriental, dying of consumption; leastwise, Mrs. Joel says she is."

"Lou Carroll dying at Oriental!" cried Mrs. March.

"Yes. She came there from goodness knows where, about a month ago—might as well have dropped from the clouds, Mrs. Joel says, for all she expected of it. Her husband is dead, and I guess he led her a life of it when he was alive, and she's as poor as second skimmings. She was aiming to come here, Mrs. Joel says, but when she got to Oriental she wasn't fit to stir a step further, and the Kents had to keep her. I gather from what Mrs. Joel said that she's rather touched in her mind too, and has an awful hankering to get home here—to this very house. She appears to have the idea that it is hers, and all just the same as it used to be. I guess she is a sight of trouble, and Mrs. Joel ain't the woman to like that. But there! She has to work most awful hard, and I suppose a sick person doesn't come handy in a hotel. I guess you've got your revenge, Anna, without lifting a finger to get it. Think of Lou Carroll coming to that!"

The next day was cold and raw. The ragged, bare trees in the old Carroll grounds shook and writhed in the gusts of wind. Now and then a drifting scud of rain dashed across the windows. Mrs. March looked out with a shiver, and turned thankfully to her own cosy fireside again.

Presently she thought she heard a low knock at the front door, and went to see. As she opened it a savage swirl of damp wind rushed in, and the shrinking figure leaning against one of the fluted columns of the Grecian porch seemed to cower before its fury. It was a woman who stood there, a woman whose emaciated face wore a piteous expression, as she lifted it to Mrs. March.

"You don't know me, of course," she said, with a feeble attempt at dignity. "I am Mrs. Baxter. I— I used to live here long ago. I thought I'd walk over today and see my old home."

A fit of coughing interrupted her words, and she trembled like a leaf.

"Gracious me!" exclaimed Mrs. March blankly. "You don't mean to tell me that you have walked over from Oriental today—and you a sick woman! For pity's sake, come in, quick. And if you're not wet to the skin!"

She fairly pulled her visitor into the hall, and led her to the sitting-room.

"Sit down. Take this big easy-chair right up to the fire—so. Let me take your bonnet and shawl. I must run right out to tell Hannah to get you a hot drink."

"You are very kind," whispered the other. "I don't know you, but you look like a woman I used to know when I was a girl. She was a Mrs. Bennett, and she had a daughter, Anna. Do you know what became of her? I forget. I forget everything now."

"My name is March," said Mrs. March briefly, ignoring the question. "I don't suppose you ever heard it before."

She wrapped her own warm shawl about the other woman's thin shoulders. Then she hastened to the kitchen and soon returned, carrying a tray of food and a steaming hot drink. She wheeled a small table up to her visitor's side and said, very kindly,

"Now, take a bite, my dear, and this raspberry vinegar will warm you right up. It is a dreadful day for you to be out. Why on earth didn't Joel Kent drive you over?"

"They didn't know I was coming," whispered Mrs. Baxter anxiously. "I—I ran away. Sarah wouldn't have let me come if she had known. But I wanted to come so much. It is so nice to be home again."

Mrs. March watched her guest as she ate and drank. It was plain enough that her mind, or rather her memory, was affected. She did not realize that this was no longer her home. At moments she seemed to fancy herself back in the past again. Once or twice she called Mrs. March "Mother."

Presently a sharp knock was heard at the hall door. Mrs. March excused herself and went out. In the porch stood Theodosia Stapp and a woman whom Mrs. March did not at first glance recognize—a tall, aggressive-looking person, whose sharp black eyes darted in past Mrs. March and searched every corner of the hall before anyone had time to speak.

"Lawful heart!" puffed Mrs. Stapp, as she stepped in out of the biting wind. "I'm right out of breath. Mrs. March, allow me to introduce Mrs. Kent. We're looking for Mrs. Baxter. She has run away, and we thought perhaps she came here. Did she?"

"She is in my sitting-room now," said Mrs. March quietly.

"Didn't I say so?" demanded Mrs. Kent, turning to Mrs. Stapp. She spoke in a sharp, high-pitched tone that grated on Mrs. March's nerves. "Doesn't she beat all! She slipped away this morning when I was busy in the kitchen. And to think of her walking six miles over here in this wind! I dunno how she did it. I don't believe she's half as sick as she pretends. Well, I've got my wagon out here, Mrs. March, and I'll be much obliged if you'll tell her I'm here to take her home. I s'pose we'll have a fearful scene."

"I don't see that there is any call for a scene,"

said Mrs. March firmly. "The poor woman has just got here, and she thinks she has got home. She might as well think so if it is of any comfort to her. You'd better leave her here."

Theodosia gave a stifled gasp of amazement, but Mrs. March went serenely on,

"I'll take care of the poor soul as long as she needs it—and that will not be very long in my opinion, for if ever I saw death in a woman's face, it is looking out of hers. I've plenty of time to look after her and make her comfortable."

Mrs. Joel Kent was voluble in her thanks. It was evident that she was delighted to get the sick woman off her hands. Mrs. March cut her short with an invitation to stay to tea, but Mrs. Kent declined.

"I've got to hurry home straight off and get the men's suppers. Such a scamper to have over that woman! I'm sure I'm thankful you're willing to let her stay, for she'd never be contented anywhere else. I'll send over what few things she has tomorrow."

When Mrs. Kent had gone, Mrs. March and Mrs. Stapp looked at each other.

"And so this is your revenge, Anna March?" said the latter solemnly. "Do you remember what you said to me about her?"

"Yes, I do, Theodosia, and I thought I meant every word of it. But I guess my wicked streak ran out just when I needed it to depend on. Besides, you see, I've thought of Lou Carroll all these years as she was when I knew her—handsome and saucy and proud. But that poor creature in there isn't any more like the Lou Carroll I knew than you are—not a mite. The old Lou Carroll is dead already, and my spite is dead with her. Will you come in and see her?"

"Well, no, not just now. She wouldn't know me, and Mrs. Joel says strangers kind of excite her—a pretty bad place the hotel would be for her at that rate, I should think. I must go and tell Peter about it, and I'll send up some of my black currant jam for her."

When Mrs. Stapp had gone, Mrs. March went back to her guest. Lou Baxter had fallen asleep with her head pillowed on the soft plush back of her chair. Mrs. March looked at the hollow, hectic cheeks and the changed, wasted features, and her bright brown eyes softened with tears.

"Poor Lou," she said softly, as she brushed a loose lock of grey hair back from the sleeping woman's brow.

An Unpremeditated Ceremony

Selwyn Grant sauntered in upon the assembled family at the homestead as if he were returning from an hour's absence instead of a western sojourn of ten years. Guided by the sound of voices on the still, pungent autumnal air, he went around to the door of the dining room which opened directly on the poppy walk in the garden.

Nobody noticed him for a moment and he stood in the doorway looking at them with a smile, wondering what was the reason of the festal air that hung about them all as visibly as a garment. His mother sat by the table, industriously polishing the best silver spoons, which, as he remembered, were only brought forth upon some great occasion. Her eyes were as bright, her form

as erect, her nose—the Carston nose—as pronounced and aristocratic as of yore.

Selwyn saw little change in her. But was it possible that the tall, handsome young lady with the
sleek brown pompadour and a nose unmistakably
and plebeianly Grant, who sat by the window
doing something to a heap of lace and organdy
in her lap, was the little curly-headed, sunburned
sister of thirteen whom he remembered? The
young man leaning against the sideboard must be
Leo, of course; a fine-looking, broad-shouldered
young fellow who made Selwyn think suddenly
that he must be growing old. And there was the
little, thin, grey father in the corner, peering at his
newspaper with nearsighted eyes. Selwyn's heart
gave a bound at the sight of him which not even
his mother had caused. Dear old Dad! The years
had been kind to him.

Mrs. Grant held up a glistening spoon and sur-
veyed it complacently. "There, I think that is
bright enough even to suit Margaret Graham. I
shall take over the whole two dozen teas and one
dozen desserts. I wish, Bertha, that you would tie
a red cord around each of the handles for me.
The Carmody spoons are the same pattern and I
shall always be convinced that Mrs. Carmody carried off two of ours the time that Jenny Graham
was married. I don't mean to take any more risks.
And, Father—"

Something made the mother look around, and
she saw her first-born!

When the commotion was over Selwyn asked
why the family spoons were being rubbed up.

"For the wedding, of course," said Mrs. Grant, polishing her gold-bowed spectacles and deciding that there was no more time for tears and sentiment just then. "And there, they're not half done—and we'll have to dress in another hour. Bertha is no earthly use—she is so taken up with her bridesmaid finery."

"Wedding? Whose wedding?" demanded Selwyn, in bewilderment.

"Why, Leo's, of course. Leo is to be married tonight. Didn't you get your invitation? Wasn't that what brought you home?"

"Hand me a chair, quick," implored Selwyn. "Leo, are *you* going to commit matrimony in this headlong fashion? Are you sure you're grown up?"

"Six feet is a pretty good imitation of it, isn't it?" grinned Leo. "Brace up, old fellow. It's not so bad as it might be. She's quite a respectable girl. We wrote you all about it three weeks ago and broke the news as gently as possible."

"I left for the East a month ago and have been wandering around preying on old college chums ever since. Haven't seen a letter. There, I'm better now. No, you needn't fan me, Sis. Well, no family can get through the world without its seasons of tribulations. Who is the party of the second part, little brother?"

"Alice Graham," replied Mrs. Grant, who had a habit of speaking for her children, none of whom had the Carston nose.

"Alice Graham! That child!" exclaimed Selwyn in astonishment.

Leo roared. "Come, come, Sel, perhaps we're not very progressive here in Croyden, but we don't actually stand still. Girls are apt to stretch out some between ten and twenty, you know. You old bachelors think nobody ever grows up. Why, Sel, you're grey around your temples."

"Too well I know it, but a man's own brother shouldn't be the first to cast such things up to him. I'll admit, since I come to think of it, that Alice has probably grown bigger. Is she any better-looking than she used to be?"

"Alice is a charming girl," said Mrs. Grant impressively. "She is a beauty and she is also sweet and sensible, which beauties are not always. We are all very much pleased with Leo's choice. But we have really no more time to spare just now. The wedding is at seven o'clock and it is four already."

"Is there anybody you can send to the station for my luggage?" asked Selwyn. "Luckily I have a new suit, otherwise I shouldn't have the face to go."

"Well, I must be off," said Mrs. Grant. "Father, take Selwyn away so that I shan't be tempted to waste time talking to him."

In the library father and son looked at each other affectionately.

"Dad, it's a blessing to see you just the same. I'm a little dizzy with all these changes. Bertha grown up and Leo within an inch of being married! To Alice Graham at that, whom I can't think of yet as anything else than the long-legged,

black-eyed imp of mischief she was when a kiddy.
To tell you the truth, Dad, I don't feel in a mood
for going to a wedding at Wish-ton-wish tonight.
I'm sure you don't either. You've always hated
fusses. Can't we shirk it?"

They smiled at each other with chummy remembrance of many a family festival they had
"shirked" together in the old days. But Mr. Grant
shook his head. "Not this time, sonny. There are
some things a decent man can't shirk and one of
them is his own boy's wedding. It's a nuisance,
but I must go through with it. You'll understand
how it is when you're a family man yourself. By
the way, why aren't you a family man by this
time? Why haven't I been put to the bother and
inconvenience of attending your wedding before
now, son?"

Selwyn laughed, with a little vibrant note of bitterness in the laughter, which the father's quick
ears detected. "I've been too busy with law books,
Dad, to find me a wife."

Mr. Grant shook his bushy grey head. "That's
not the real reason, son. 'The world has a wife
for every man'; if he hasn't found her by the time
he's thirty-five, there's some real reason for it.
Well, I don't want to pry into yours, but I hope
it's a sound one and not a mean, sneaking, selfish
sort of reason. Perhaps you'll choose a Madam
Selwyn some day yet. In case you should I'm
going to give you a small bit of good advice. Your
mother—now, she's a splendid woman, Selwyn,
a splendid woman. She can't be matched as a

housekeeper and she has improved my finances
until I don't know them when I meet them. She's
been a good wife and a good mother. If I were a
young man I'd court her and marry her over
again, that I would. But, son, when *you* pick a
wife pick one with a nice little commonplace nose,
not a family nose. Never marry a woman with a
family nose, son."

A woman with a family nose came into the
library at this juncture and beamed maternally
upon them both. "There's a bite for you in the
dining room. After you've eaten it you must
dress. Mind you brush your hair well down,
Father. The green room is ready for you, Selwyn.
Tomorrow I'll have a good talk with you, but
tonight I'll be too busy to remember you're
around. How are we all going to get over to Wish-
ton-wish? Leo and Bertha are going in the pony
carriage. It won't hold a third passenger. You'll
have to squeeze in with Father and me in the
buggy, Selwyn."

"By no means," replied Selwyn briskly. "I'll
walk over to Wish-ton-wish. It's only half a mile
across lots. I suppose the old way is still open?"

"It ought to be," answered Mr. Grant drily;
"Leo has kept it well trodden. If you've forgotten
how it runs he can tell you."

"I haven't forgotten," said Selwyn, a little
brusquely. He had his own reasons for remembering the wood path. Leo had not been the first
Grant to go courting to Wish-ton-wish.

When he started, the moon was rising round

and red and hazy in an eastern hill-gap. The autumn air was mild and spicy. Long shadows stretched across the fields on his right and silvery mosaics patterned the floor of the old beechwood lane. Selwyn walked slowly. He was thinking of Esme Graham or, rather, of the girl who had been Esme Graham, and wondering if he would see her at the wedding. It was probable, and he did not want to see her. In spite of ten years' effort, he did not think he could yet look upon Tom St. Clair's wife with the proper calm indifference. At the best, it would taint his own memory of her; he would never again be able to think of her as Esme Graham but only as Esme St. Clair.

The Grahams had come to Wish-ton-wish eleven years before. There was a big family of girls of whom the tall, brown-haired Esme was the oldest. There was one summer during which Selwyn Grant had haunted Wish-ton-wish, the merry comrade of the younger girls, the boyishly, silently devoted lover of Esme. Tom St. Clair had always been there too, in his right as second cousin, Selwyn had supposed. One day he found out that Tom and Esme had been engaged ever since she was sixteen; one of her sisters told him. That had been all. He had gone away soon after, and some time later a letter from home made casual mention of Tom St. Clair's marriage.

He narrowly missed being late for the wedding ceremony. The bridal party entered the parlour at Wish-ton-wish at the same moment as he slipped in by another door. Selwyn almost whistled with amazement at sight of the bride. *That* Alice Graham, that tall, stately, blushing young woman, with her masses of dead-black hair, frosted over by the film of wedding veil! Could that be the scrawny little tomboy of ten years ago? She looked not unlike Esme, with that subtle family resemblance that is quite independent of feature and colouring.

Where was Esme? Selwyn cast his eyes furtively over the assembled guests while the minister read the marriage ceremony. He recognized several of the Graham girls but he did not see Esme, although Tom St. Clair, stout and florid and prosperous-looking, was standing on a chair in a faraway corner, peering over the heads of the women.

After the turmoil of handshakings and congratulations, Selwyn fled to the cool, still outdoors, where the rosy glow of Chinese lanterns mingled with the waves of moonshine to make fairyland. And there he met her, as she came out of the house by a side door, a tall, slender woman in some glistening, clinging garment, with white flowers shining like stars in the coils of her brown hair. In the soft glow she looked even more beautiful than in the days of her girlhood, and Selwyn's heart throbbed dangerously at sight of her.

"Esme!" he said involuntarily.

She started, and he had an idea that she changed colour, although it was too dim to be sure. "Selwyn!" she exclaimed, putting out her hands. "Why, Selwyn Grant! Is it really you? Or are you such stuff as dreams are made of? I did not know you were here. I did not know you were home."

He caught her hands and held them tightly, drawing her a little closer to him, forgetting that she was Tom St. Clair's wife, remembering only that she was the woman to whom he had given all his love and life's devotion, to the entire beggaring of his heart.

"I reached home only four hours ago, and was haled straightway here to Leo's wedding. I'm dizzy, Esme. I can't adjust my old conceptions to this new state of affairs all at once. It seems ridiculous to think that Leo and Alice are married. I'm sure they can't be really grown up."

Esme laughed as she drew away her hands. "We are all ten years older," she said lightly.

"Not you. You are more beautiful than ever, Esme. That sunflower compliment is permissible in an old friend, isn't it?"

"This mellow glow is kinder to me than sunlight now. I am thirty, you know, Selwyn."

"And I have some grey hairs," he confessed. "I knew I had them but I had a sneaking hope that other folks didn't until Leo destroyed it today. These young brothers and sisters who won't stay children are nuisances. You'll be telling me next thing that 'Baby' is grown up."

" 'Baby' is eighteen and has a beau," laughed Esme. "And I give you fair warning that she insists on being called Laura now. Do you want to come for a walk with me—down under the

beeches to the old lane gate? I came out to see if
the fresh air would do my bit of a headache good.
I shall have to help with the supper later on."

They went slowly across the lawn and turned
into a dim, moonlight lane beyond, their old
favourite ramble. Selwyn felt like a man in a
dream, a pleasant dream from which he dreads
to awaken. The voices and laughter echoing out
from the house died away behind them and the
great silence of the night fell about them as they
came to the old gate, beyond which was a range
of shining, moonlight-misted fields.

For a little while neither of them spoke. The
woman looked out across the white spaces and
the man watched the glimmering curve of her
neck and the soft darkness of her rich hair. How
virginal, how sacred, she looked! The thought of
Tom St. Clair was a sacrilege.

"It's nice to see you again, Selwyn," said Esme
frankly at last. "There are so few of our old set
left, and so many of the babies grown up. Sometimes I don't know my own world, it has changed
so. It's an uncomfortable feeling. You give me a
pleasant sensation of really belonging here. I'd be
lonesome tonight if I dared. I'm going to miss
Alice so much. There will be only Mother and
Baby and I left now. Our family circle has dwindled woefully."

"Mother and Baby and you!" Selwyn felt his
head whirling again. "Why, where is Tom?"

He felt that it was an idiotic question, but it
slipped from his tongue before he could catch it.

Esme turned her head and looked at him wonderingly. He knew that in the sunlight her eyes were as mistily blue as early meadow violets, but here they looked dark and unfathomably tender.

"Tom?" she said perplexedly. "Do you mean Tom St. Clair? He is here, of course, he and his wife. Didn't you see her? That pretty woman in pale pink, Lil Meredith. Why, you used to know Lil, didn't you? One of the Uxbridge Merediths?"

To the day of his death Selwyn Grant will firmly believe that if he had not clutched fast hold of the top bar of the gate he would have tumbled down on the moss under the beeches in speechless astonishment. All the surprises of that surprising evening were as nothing to this. He had a swift conviction that there were no words in the English language that could fully express his feelings and that it would be a waste of time to try to find any. Therefore he laid hold of the first baldly commonplace ones that came handy and said tamely, "I thought you were married to Tom."

"You—thought—I—was—married—to—Tom!" repeated Esme slowly. "And have you thought *that* all these years, Selwyn Grant?"

"Yes, I have. Is it any wonder? You were engaged to Tom when I went away, Jenny told me you were. And a year later Bertha wrote me a letter in which she made some reference to Tom's marriage. She didn't say to *whom*, but hadn't I the right to suppose it was to you?"

"Oh!" The word was partly a sigh and partly a little cry of long-concealed, long-denied pain. "It's been all a funny misunderstanding. Tom and I *were* engaged once—a boy-and-girl affair in the beginning. Then we both found out that we had made a mistake—that what we had thought was love was merely the affection of good comrades. We broke our engagement shortly before you went away. All the older girls knew it was broken but I suppose nobody mentioned the matter to Jen. She was such a child, we never thought about her. And you've thought I was Tom's wife all this time? It's—funny."

"Funny. You mean tragic! Look here, Esme, I'm not going to risk any more misunderstanding. There's nothing for it but plain talk when matters get to such a state as this. I love you—and I've loved you ever since I met you. I went away because I could not stay here and see you married to another man. I've stayed away for the same reason. Esme, is it too late? Did you ever care anything for me?"

"Yes, I did," she said slowly.

"Do you care still?" he asked.

She hid her face against his shoulder. "Yes," she whispered.

"Then we'll go back to the house and be married," he said joyfully.

Esme broke away and stared at him. "Married!"

"Yes, married. We've wasted ten years and we're not going to waste another minute. We're *not*, I say."

"Selwyn! It's impossible."

"I have expurgated that word from my dictionary. It's the very simplest thing when you look at it in an unprejudiced way. Here is a ready-made wedding and decorations and assembled guests, a minister on the spot and a state where no licence is required. You have a very pretty new dress on and you love me. I have a plain gold ring on my little finger that will fit you. Aren't all the conditions fulfilled? Where is the sense of waiting and having another family upheaval in a few weeks' time?"

"I understand why you have made such a success of the law," said Esme, "but—"

"There are no buts. Come with me, Esme. I'm going to hunt up your mother and mine and talk to them."

Half an hour later an astonishing whisper went circulating among the guests. Before they could grasp its significance Tom St. Clair and Jen's husband, broadly smiling, were hustling scattered folk into the parlour again and making clear a passage in the hall. The minister came in with his blue book, and then Selwyn Grant and Esme Graham walked in hand in hand.

When the second ceremony was over, Mr. Grant shook his son's hand vigorously. "There's no need to wish you happiness, son; you've got it. And you've made one fuss and bother do for both weddings, that's what I call genius. And"—this in a careful whisper, while Esme was temporarily obliterated in Mrs. Grant's capacious embrace— "she's got the right sort of a nose. But your mother is a grand woman, son, a grand woman."

Missy's Room

Mrs. Falconer and Miss Bailey walked home together through the fine blue summer afternoon from the Ladies' Aid meeting at Mrs. Robinson's. They were talking earnestly; that is to say, Miss Bailey was talking earnestly and volubly, and Mrs. Falconer was listening. Mrs. Falconer had reduced the practice of listening to a fine art. She was a thin, wistful-faced mite of a woman, with sad brown eyes, and with snow-white hair that was a libel on her fifty-five years and girlish step. Nobody in Lindsay ever felt very well acquainted with Mrs. Falconer, in spite of the fact that she had lived among them forty years. She kept between her and her world a fine, baffling reserve which no one had ever been able to penetrate. It

was known that she had had a bitter sorrow in
her life, but she never made any reference to it,
and most people in Lindsay had forgotten it.
Some foolish ones even supposed that Mrs. Falconer had forgotten it.

"Well, I do not know what on earth is to be
done with Camilla Clark," said Miss Bailey, with
a prodigious sigh. "I suppose that we will simply
have to trust the whole matter to Providence."

Miss Bailey's tone and sigh really seemed to
intimate to the world at large that Providence was
a last resort and a very dubious one. Not that
Miss Bailey meant anything of the sort; her faith
was as substantial as her works, which were
many and praiseworthy and seasonable.

The case of Camilla Clark was agitating the
Ladies' Aid of one of the Lindsay churches. They
had talked about it through the whole of that
afternoon session while they sewed for their mis-
sionary box—talked about it, and come to no
conclusion.

In the preceding spring James Clark, one of the
hands in the lumber mill at Lindsay, had been
killed in an accident. The shock had proved
nearly fatal to his young wife. The next day
Camilla Clark's baby was born dead, and the poor
mother hovered for weeks between life and death.
Slowly, very slowly, life won the battle, and
Camilla came back from the valley of the shadow.
But she was still an invalid, and would be so for
a long time.

The Clarks had come to Lindsay only a short

time before the accident. They were boarding at
Mrs. Barry's when it happened, and Mrs. Barry
had shown every kindness and consideration to
the unhappy young widow. But now the Barrys
were very soon to leave Lindsay for the West,
and the question was, what was to be done with
Camilla Clark? She could not go west; she could
not even do work of any sort yet in Lindsay; she
had no relatives or friends in the world; and she
was absolutely penniless. As she and her husband
had joined the church to which the aforesaid
Ladies' Aid belonged, the members thereof felt
themselves bound to take up her case and see
what could be done for her.

The obvious solution was for some of them to
offer her a home until such time as she would be
able to go to work. But there did not seem to be
anyone who could offer to do this—unless it was
Mrs. Falconer. The church was small, and the
Ladies' Aid smaller. There were only twelve members in it; four of these were unmarried ladies
who boarded, and so were helpless in the matter;
of the remaining eight seven had large families,
or sick husbands, or something else that pre-
vented them from offering Camilla Clark an asylum. Their excuses were all valid; they were good,
sincere women who would have taken her in if
they could, but they could not see their way clear
to do so. However, it was probable they would
eventually manage it in some way if Mrs. Falconer
did not rise to the occasion.

Nobody liked to ask Mrs. Falconer outright to

take Camilla Clark in, yet everyone thought she might offer. She was comfortably off, and though her house was small, there was nobody to live in it except herself and her husband. But Mrs. Falconer sat silent through all the discussion of the Ladies' Aid, and never opened her lips on the subject of Camilla Clark despite the numerous hints which she received.

Miss Bailey made one more effort as aforesaid. When her despairing reference to Providence brought forth no results, she wished she dared ask Mrs. Falconer openly to take Camilla Clark, but somehow she did not dare. There were not many things that could daunt Miss Bailey, but Mrs. Falconer's reserve and gentle aloofness always could.

When Miss Bailey had gone on down the village street, Mrs. Falconer paused for a few moments at her gate, apparently lost in deep thought. She was perfectly well aware of all the hints that had been thrown out for her benefit that afternoon. She knew that the Aids, one and all, thought that she ought to take Camilla Clark. But she had no room to give her—for it was out of the question to think of putting her in Missy's room.

"I couldn't do such a thing," she said to herself piteously. "They don't understand—they can't understand—but I *couldn't* give her Missy's room. I'm sorry for poor Camilla, and I wish I could help her. But I can't give her Missy's room, and I have no other."

The little Falconer cottage, set back from the

road in the green seclusion of an apple orchard and thick, leafy maples, was a very tiny one. There were just two rooms downstairs and two upstairs. When Mrs. Falconer entered the kitchen an old-looking man with long white hair and mild blue eyes looked up with a smile from the bright-coloured blocks before him.

"Have you been lonely, Father?" said Mrs. Falconer tenderly.

He shook his head, still smiling.

"No, not lonely. These"—pointing to the blocks—"are so pretty. See my house, Mother."

This man was Mrs. Falconer's husband. Once he had been one of the smartest, most intelligent men in Lindsay, and one of the most trusted employees of the railroad company. Then there had been a train collision. Malcolm Falconer was taken out of the wreck fearfully injured. He eventually recovered physical health, but he was from that time forth merely a child in intellect—a harmless, kindly creature, docile and easily amused.

Mrs. Falconer tried to dismiss the thought of Camilla Clark from her mind, but it would not be dismissed. Her conscience reproached her continually. She tried to compromise with it by saying that she would go down and see Camilla that evening and take her some nice fresh Irish moss jelly. It was so good for delicate people.

She found Camilla alone in the Barry sitting-room, and noticed with a feeling that was almost like self-reproach how thin and frail and white the poor young creature looked. Why, she seemed lit-

tle more than a child! Her great dark eyes were
far too big for her wasted face, and her hands
were almost transparent.

"I'm not much better yet," said Camilla tremulously, in response to Mrs. Falconer's inquiries.
"Oh, I'm so slow getting well! And I know—I feel
that I'm a burden to everybody."

"But you mustn't think that, dear," said Mrs.
Falconer, feeling more uncomfortable than ever.
"We are all glad to do all we can for you."

Mrs. Falconer paused suddenly. She was a very
truthful woman and she instantly realized that
that last sentence was not true. She was not doing
all she could for Camilla—she would not be glad,
she feared, to do all she could.

"If I were only well enough to go to work,"
sighed Camilla. "Mr. Marks says I can have a
place in the shoe factory whenever I'm able to.
But it will be so long yet. Oh, I'm so tired and
discouraged!"

She put her hands over her face and sobbed.
Mrs. Falconer caught her breath. What if Missy
were somewhere alone in the world—ill, friend-
less, with never a soul to offer her a refuge or a
shelter? It was so very, very probable. Before she
could check herself Mrs. Falconer spoke. "My
dear, don't cry! I want you to come and stay with
me until you get perfectly well. You won't be a
speck of trouble, and I'll be glad to have you for
company."

Mrs. Falconer's Rubicon was crossed. She could
not draw back now if she wanted to. But she was

not at all sure that she did want to. By the time
she reached home she was sure she didn't want
to. And yet—to give Missy's room to Camilla! It
seemed a great sacrifice to Mrs. Falconer.

She went up to it the next morning with firmly
set lips to air and dust it. It was just the same as
when Missy had left it long ago. Nothing had ever
been moved or changed, but everything had
always been kept beautifully neat and clean.
Snow-white muslin curtains hung before the small
square window. In one corner was a little white
bed. Missy's pictures hung on the walls; Missy's
books and work-basket were lying on the square
stand; there was a bit of half-finished fancy work,
yellow from age, lying in the basket. On a small
bureau before the gilt-framed mirror were several
little girlish knick-knacks and boxes whose contents had never been disturbed since Missy went
away. One of Missy's gay pink ribbons—Missy
had been so fond of pink ribbons—hung over the
top of the mirror. On a chair lay Missy's hat,
bright with ribbons and roses, just as Missy had
laid it there on the night before she left her home.

Mrs. Falconer's lips quivered as she looked
about the room, and tears came to her eyes. Oh,
how could she put these things away and bring
a stranger here—here, where no one save herself
had entered for fifteen years, here in this room,
sacred to Missy's memory, waiting for her return
when she should be weary of wandering? It
almost seemed to the mother's vague fancy, dis-
torted by long, silent brooding, that her daugh-

ter's innocent girlhood had been kept here for her
and would be lost forever if the room were given
to another.

"I suppose it's dreadful foolishness," said Mrs.
Falconer, wiping her eyes. "I know it is, but I
can't help it. It just goes to my heart to think of
putting these things away. But I must do it.
Camilla is coming here today, and this room must
be got ready for her. Oh, Missy, my poor lost
child, it's for your sake I'm doing this—because
you may be suffering somewhere as Camilla is
now, and I'd wish the same kindness to be shown
to you."

She opened the window and put fresh linen on
the bed. One by one Missy's little belongings
were removed and packed carefully away. On the
gay, foolish little hat with its faded wreath of
roses the mother's tears fell as she put it in a box.
She remembered so plainly the first time Missy
had worn it. She could see the pretty, delicately
tinted face, the big shining brown eyes, and the
riotous golden curls under the drooping, lace-
edged brim. Oh, where was Missy now? What
roof sheltered her? Did she ever think of her
mother and the little white cottage under the
maples, and the low-ceilinged, dim room where
she had knelt to say her childhood's prayer?

Camilla Clark came that afternoon.

"Oh, it is lovely here," she said gratefully, looking out into the rustling shade of the maples. "I'm
sure I shall soon get well here. Mrs. Barry was so
kind to me—I shall never forget her kindness—
but the house is so close to the factory, and there

was such a whirring of wheels all the time, it seemed to get into my head and make me wild with nervousness. I'm so weak that sounds like that worry me. But it is so still and green and peaceful here. It just rests me."

When bedtime came, Mrs. Falconer took Camilla up to Missy's room. It was not as hard as she had expected it to be after all. The wrench was over with the putting away of Missy's things, and it did not hurt the mother to see the frail, girlish Camilla in her daughter's place.

"What a dear little room!" said Camilla, glancing around. "It is so white and sweet. Oh, I know I am going to sleep well here, and dream sweet dreams."

"It was my daughter's room," said Mrs. Falconer, sitting down on the chintz-covered seat by the open window.

Camilla looked surprised.

"I did not know you had a daughter," she said.

"Yes—I had just the one child," said Mrs. Falconer dreamily.

For fifteen years she had never spoken of Missy to a living soul except her husband. But now she felt a sudden impulse to tell Camilla about her, and about the room.

"Her name was Isabella, after her father's mother, but we never called her anything but Missy. That was the little name she gave herself when she began to talk. Oh, I've missed her so!"

"When did she die?" asked Camilla softly, sympathy shining, starlike, in her dark eyes.

"She—she didn't die," said Mrs. Falconer. "She

went away. She was a pretty girl and gay and
fond of fun—but such a good girl. Oh, Missy was
always a good girl! Her father and I were so proud
of her—too proud, I suppose. She had her little
faults—she was too fond of dress and gaiety, but
then she was so young, and we indulged her.
Then Bert Williams came to Lindsay to work in
the factory. He was a handsome fellow, with taking ways about him, but he was drunken and pro-
fane, and nobody knew anything about his past
life. He fascinated Missy. He kept coming to see
her until her father forbade him the house. Then
our poor, foolish child used to meet him elsewhere. We found this out afterwards. And at last
she ran away with him, and they were married
over at Peterboro and went there to live, for Bert
had got work there. We—we were too hard on
Missy. But her father was so dreadful hurt about
it. He'd been so fond and proud of her, and he
felt that she had disgraced him. He disowned her,
and sent her word never to show her face here
again, for he'd never forgive her. And I was angry
too. I didn't send her any word at all. Oh, how
I've wept over that! If I had just sent her one little
word of forgiveness, everything might have been
different. But Father forbade me to.

"Then in a little while there was a dreadful
trouble. A woman came to Peterboro and claimed
to be Bert Williams's wife—and she was—she
proved it. Bert cleared out and was never seen
again in these parts. As soon as we heard about
it Father relented, and I went right down to

Peterboro to see Missy and bring her home. But she wasn't there—she had gone, nobody knew where. I got a letter from her the next week. She said her heart was broken, and she knew we would never forgive her, and she couldn't face the disgrace, so she was going away where nobody would ever find her. We did everything we could to trace her, but we never could. We've never heard from her since, and it is fifteen years ago. Sometimes I am afraid she is dead, but then again I feel sure she isn't. Oh, Camilla, if I could only find my poor child and bring her home!

"This was her room. And when she went away I made up my mind I would keep it for her just as she left it, and I have up to now. Nobody has ever been inside the door but myself. I've always hoped that Missy would come home, and I would lead her up here and say, 'Missy, here is your room just as you left it, and here is your place in your mother's heart just as you left it.' But she never came. I'm afraid she never will."

Mrs. Falconer dropped her face in her hands and sobbed softly. Camilla came over to her and put her arms about her.

"I think she will," she said. "I think—I am sure your love and prayers will bring Missy home yet. And I understand how good you have been in giving me her room—oh, I know what it must have cost you! I will pray tonight that God will bring Missy back to you."

When Mrs. Falconer returned to the kitchen to close the house for the night, her husband being already sound asleep, she heard a low, timid knock at the door. Wondering who it could be so late, she opened it. The light fell on a shrinking, shabby figure on the step, and on a pale, pinched face in which only a mother could have recognized the features of her child. Mrs. Falconer gave a cry.

"Missy! Missy! Missy!"

She caught the poor wanderer to her heart and drew her in.

"Oh, Missy, Missy, have you come back at last? Thank God! Oh, thank God!"

"I *had* to come back. I was starving for a glimpse of your face and of the old home, Mother," sobbed Missy. "But I didn't mean you should know—I never meant to show myself to you. I've been sick, and just as soon as I got better I came here. I meant to creep home after dark and look at the dear old house, and perhaps get a glimpse of you and Father through the window if you were still here. I didn't know if you were. And then I meant to go right away on the night train. I was under the window and I heard you telling my story to someone. Oh, Mother, when I knew that you had forgiven me, that you loved me still and had always kept my room for me, I made up my mind that I'd show myself to you."

The mother had got her child into a rocking-chair and removed the shabby hat and cloak. How ill and worn and faded Missy looked! Yet her face was pure and fine, and there was in it something sweeter than had ever been there in her beautiful girlhood.

"I'm terribly changed, am I not, Mother?" said Missy, with a faint smile. "I've had a hard life— but an honest one, Mother. When I went away I was almost mad with the disgrace my wilfulness had brought on you and Father and myself. I went as far as I could get away from you, and I got work in a factory. I've worked there ever since, just making enough to keep body and soul together. Oh, I've starved for a word from you— the sight of your face! But I thought Father would spurn me from his door if I should ever dare to come back."

"Oh, Missy!" sobbed the mother. "Your poor father is just like a child. He got a terrible hurt ten years ago, and never got over it. I don't suppose he'll even know you—he's clean forgot everything. But he forgave you before it happened. You poor child, you're done right out. You're too weak to be travelling. But never mind, you're home now, and I'll soon nurse you up. I'll put on the kettle and get you a good cup of tea first thing. And you're not to do any more talking till the morning. But, oh, Missy, I can't take you to your own room after all. Camilla Clark has it, and she'll be asleep by now; we mustn't disturb her, for she's been real sick. I'll fix up a bed for you on the sofa, though. Missy, Missy, let us kneel down here and thank God for His mercy!"

Late that night, when Missy had fallen asleep in her improvised bed, the wakeful mother crept in to gloat over her.

"Just to think," she whispered, "if I hadn't taken Camilla Clark in, Missy wouldn't have heard me telling about the room, and she'd have gone away again and never have known. Oh, I don't deserve such a blessing when I was so unwilling to take Camilla! But I know one thing: this is going to be Camilla's home. There'll be no leaving it even' when she does get well. She shall be my daughter, and I'll love her next to Missy."

The Story of
Uncle Dick

I had two schools offered me that summer, one at Rocky Valley and one at Bayside. At first I inclined to Rocky Valley; it possessed a railway station and was nearer the centres of business and educational activity. But eventually I chose Bayside, thinking that its country quietude would be a good thing for a student who was making school-teaching the stepping-stone to a college course.

I had reason to be glad of my choice, for in Bayside I met Uncle Dick. Ever since it has seemed to me that not to have known Uncle Dick would have been to miss a great sweetness and inspiration from my life. He was one of those rare souls whose friendship is at once a pleasure and

a benediction, showering light from their own
crystal clearness into all the dark corners in the
souls of others until, for the time being at least,
they reflected his own simplicity and purity.
Uncle Dick could no more help bringing delight
into the lives of his associates than could the sunshine or the west wind or any other of the best
boons of nature.

I had been in Bayside three weeks before I met
him, although his farm adjoined the one where I
boarded and I passed at a little distance from his
house every day in my short cut across the fields
to school. I even passed his garden unsuspecting-
ly for a week, never dreaming that behind that
rank of leafy, rustling poplars lay a veritable
"God's acre" of loveliness and fragrance. But one
day as I went by, a whiff of something sweeter
than the odours of Araby brushed my face and,
following the wind that had blown it through the
poplars, I went up to the white paling and found
there a trellis of honeysuckle, and beyond it Uncle
Dick's garden. Thereafter I daily passed close by
the fence that I might have the privilege of looking over it.

It would be hard to define the charm of that
garden. It did not consist in order or system, for
there was no trace of either, except, perhaps, in
that prim row of poplars growing about the
whole domain and shutting it away from all idle
and curious eyes. For the rest, I think the real
charm must have been in its unexpectedness. At
every turn and in every nook you stumbled on

some miracle of which you had never dreamed. Or perhaps the charm was simply that the whole garden was an expression of Uncle Dick's personality.

In one corner a little green dory, filled with earth, overflowed in a wave of gay annuals. In the centre of the garden an old birch-bark canoe seemed sailing through a sea of blossoms, with a many-coloured freight of geraniums. Paths twisted and turned among flowering shrubs, and clumps of old-fashioned perennials were mingled with the latest fads of the floral catalogues. The mid-garden was a pool of sunshine, with finely sifted winds purring over it, but under the poplars there were shadows and growing things that loved the shadows, crowding about the old stone benches at each side. Somehow, my daily glimpse of Uncle Dick's garden soon came to symbolize for me a meaning easier to translate into life and soul than into words. It was a power for good within me, making its influence felt in many ways.

Finally I caught Uncle Dick in his garden. On my way home one evening I found him on his knees among the rosebushes, and as soon as he saw me he sprang up and came forward with outstretched hand. He was a tall man of about fifty, with grizzled hair, but not a thread of silver yet showed itself in the ripples of his long brown beard. Later I discovered that his splendid beard was Uncle Dick's only vanity. So fine and silky was it that it did not hide the candid, sensitive curves of his mouth, around which a mellow

smile, tinged with kindly, quizzical humour, always
lingered. His face was tanned even more deeply
than is usual among farmers, for he had an invet-
erate habit of going about hatless in the most mer-
ciless sunshine; but the line of forehead under his
hair was white as milk, and his eyes were darkly
blue and as tender as a woman's.

"How do you do, Master?" he said heartily.
(The Bayside pedagogue was invariably ad-
dressed as "Master" by young and old.) "I'm
glad to see you. Here I am, trying to save my
rosebushes. There are green bugs on 'em, Master—green bugs, and they're worrying the life
out of me."

I smiled, for Uncle Dick looked very unlike a
worrying man, even over such a serious accident
as green bugs.

"Your roses don't seem to mind, Mr. Oliver,"
I said. "They are the finest I have ever seen."

The compliment to his roses, well-deserved as
it was, did not at first engage his attention. He
pretended to frown at me.

"Don't get into any bad habit of mistering me,
Master," he said. "You'd better begin by calling
me Uncle Dick from the start and then you won't
have the trouble of changing. Because it would
come to that—it always does. But come in, come
in! There's a gate round here. I want to get
acquainted with you. I have a taste for schoolmas-
ters. I didn't possess it when I was a boy" (a glint
of fun appeared in his blue eyes). "It's an acquired
taste."

I accepted his invitation and went, not only into his garden but, as was proved later, into his confidence and affection. He linked his arm with mine and piloted me about to show me his pets.

"I potter about this garden considerable," he said. "It pleases the women folks to have lots of posies."

I laughed, for Uncle Dick was a bachelor and considered to be a hopeless one.

"Don't laugh, Master," he said, pressing my arm. "I've no woman folk of my own about me now, 'tis true. But all the girls in the district come to Uncle Dick when they want flowers for their little diversions. Besides—perhaps—sometimes—"

Uncle Dick broke off and stood in a brown study, looking at an old stump aflame with nasturtiums for fully three minutes. Later on I was to learn the significance of that pause and reverie.

I spent the whole evening with Uncle Dick. After we had explored the garden he took me into his house and into his "den." The house was a small white one and wonderfully neat inside, considering the fact that Uncle Dick was his own housekeeper. His "den" was a comfortable place, its one window so shadowed by a huge poplar that the room had a grotto-like effect of emerald gloom. I came to know it well, for, at Uncle Dick's invitation, I did my studying there and browsed at will among his classics. We soon became close friends. Uncle Dick had always "chummed with the masters," as he said, but our friendship went deeper. For my own part, I preferred his company to that of any young man I knew. There was a perennial spring of youth in Uncle Dick's soul that yet had all the fascinating flavour of ripe experience. He was clever, kindly, humorous and, withal, so crystal clear of mind and heart that an atmosphere partaking of childhood hung around him.

I knew Uncle Dick's outward history as the Bayside people knew it. It was not a very eventful one. He had lost his father in boyhood; before that there had been some idea of Dick's going to college. After his father's death he seemed quietly to have put all such hopes away and settled down to look after the farm and take care of his invalid stepmother. This woman, as I learned from others, but never from Uncle Dick, had been a peevish, fretful, exacting creature, and for nearly thirty years Uncle Dick had been a very slave to her whims and caprices.

"Nobody knows what he had to put up with, for he never complained," Mrs. Lindsay, my landlady, told me. "She was out of her mind once and she was liable to go out of it again if she was crossed in anything. He was that good and patient with her. She was dreadful fond of him too, for all she did almost worry his life out. No doubt she was the reason he never married. He couldn't leave her and he knew no woman would go in there. Uncle Dick never courted anyone, unless it was Rose Lawrence. She was a cousin of my man's. I've heard he had a kindness for her;

it was years ago, before I came to Bayside. But anyway, nothing came of it. Her father's health failed and he had to go out to California. Rose had to go with him, her mother being dead, and that was the end of Uncle Dick's love affair."

But that was not the end of it, as I discovered when Uncle Dick gave me his confidence. One evening I went over and, piloted by the sound of shrieks and laughter, found Uncle Dick careering about the garden, pursued by half a dozen school-girls who were pelting him with overblown roses. At sight of the master my pupils instantly became prim and demure and, gathering up their flowery spoil, they beat a hasty retreat down the lane.

"Those little girls are very sweet," said Uncle Dick abruptly. "Little blossoms of life! Have you ever wondered, Master, why I haven't some of my own blooming about the old place instead of just looking over the fence of other men's gardens, coveting their human roses?"

"Yes, I have," I answered frankly. "It has been a puzzle to me why you, Uncle Dick, who seem to me fitted above all men I have ever known for love and husbandhood and fatherhood, should have elected to live your life alone."

"It has not been a matter of choice," said Uncle Dick gently. "We can't always order our lives as we would, Master. I loved a woman once and she loved me. And we love each other still. Do you think I could bear life else? I've an interest in it that the Bayside folk know nothing of. It has kept youth in my heart and joy in my soul through long, lonely years. And it's not ended yet, Master—it's not ended yet! Some day I hope to bring a wife here to my old house—my wife, my rose of joy!"

He was silent for a space, gazing at the stars. I too kept silence, fearing to intrude into the holy places of his thought, although I was tingling with interest in this unsuspected outflowering of romance in Uncle Dick's life.

After a time he said gently,

"Shall I tell you about it, Master? I mean, do you care to know?"

"Yes," I answered, "I do care to know. And I shall respect your confidence, Uncle Dick."

"I know that. I couldn't tell you, otherwise," he said. "I don't want the Bayside folk to know—it would be a kind of desecration. They would laugh and joke me about it, as they tease other people, and I couldn't bear that. Nobody in Bayside knows or suspects, unless it's old Joe Hammond at the post office. And he has kept my secret, or what he knows of it, well. But somehow I feel that I'd like to tell you, Master.

"Twenty-five years ago I loved Rose Lawrence. The Lawrences lived where you are boarding now. There was just the father, a sickly man, and Rose, my "Rose of joy," as I called her, for I knew my Emerson pretty well even then. She was sweet and fair, like a white rose with just a hint of pink in its cup. We loved each other, but we couldn't marry then. My mother was an invalid, and one time, before I had learned to care for Rose, she, the mother, had asked me to promise her that I'd never marry as long as she lived. She didn't think then that she would live long, but she lived for twenty years, Master, and she held me to my promise all the time. Yes, it was hard"—for I had given an indignant exclamation—"but you see, Master, I had promised and I had to keep my word. Rose said I was right in doing it. She said she was willing to wait for me, but she didn't know, poor girl, how long the waiting was to be. Then her father's health failed completely, and the doctor ordered him to another climate. They went to California. That was a hard parting, Master. But we promised each other that we would be true, and we have been. I've never seen my Rose of joy since then, but I've had a letter from her every week. When the mother died, five years ago, I wanted to move to California and marry Rose. But she wrote that her father was so poorly she couldn't marry me yet. She has to wait on him every minute, and he's restless, and they move here and there—a hard life for my poor girl. So I had to take a new lease of patience, Master. One learns how to wait in twenty years. But I shall have her some day, God willing. Our love will be crowned yet. So I wait, Master, and try to keep my life and soul clean and wholesome and young for her.

"That's my story, Master, and we'll not say anything more about it just now, for I dare say you don't exactly know what to say. But at times I'll talk of her to you and that will be a rare plea-

sure to me. I think that was why I wanted you to
know about her."

He did talk often to me of her, and I soon came
to realize what this far-away woman meant in his
life. She was for him the centre of everything. His
love was strong, pure, and idyllic—the ideal love
of which the loftiest poets sing. It glorified his
whole inner life with a strange, unfailing radiance. I found that everything he did was done
with an eye single to what she would think of it
when she came. Especially did he put his love
into his garden.

"Every flower in it stands for a thought of her,
Master," he said. "It is a great joy to think that
she will walk in this garden with me some day.
It will be complete then—my Rose of joy will be
here to crown it."

That summer and winter passed away, and
when spring came again, lettering her footsteps
with violets in the meadows and waking all the
sleeping loveliness of old homestead gardens,
Uncle Dick's long deferred happiness came with
her. One evening when I was in our "den,"
mid-deep in study of old things that seemed
musty and unattractive enough in contrast with
the vivid, newborn, out-of-doors, Uncle Dick
came home from the post office with an open
letter in his hand. His big voice trembled as he
said,

"Master, she's coming home. Her father is dead
and she has nobody in the world now but me. In
a month she will be here. Don't talk to me of it

yet—I want to taste the joy of it in silence for a while."

He hastened away to his garden and walked there until darkness fell, with his face uplifted to the sky, and the love rapture of countless generations shining in his eyes. Later on, we sat on one of the old stone benches and Uncle Dick tried to talk practically.

Bayside people soon found out that Rose Lawrence was coming home to marry Uncle Dick. Uncle Dick was much teased, and suffered under it; it seemed, as he had said, desecration. But the real goodwill and kindly feeling in the banter redeemed it.

He went to the station to meet Rose Lawrence the day she came. When I went home from school Mrs. Lindsay told me she was in the parlour and took me in to be introduced. I was bitterly disappointed. Somehow, I had expected to meet, not indeed a young girl palpitating with youthful bloom, but a woman of ripe maturity, dowered with the beauty of harmonious middle-age—the feminine counterpart of Uncle Dick. Instead, I found in Rose Lawrence a small, faded woman of forty-five, gowned in shabby black. She had evidently been very pretty once, but bloom and grace were gone. Her face had a sweet and gentle expression, but was tired and worn, and her fair hair was plentifully streaked with grey. Alas, I thought compassionately, for Uncle Dick's dreams! What a shock the change to her must have given him! Could this be the woman on whom he had

lavished such a life-wealth of love and reverence?
I tried to talk to her, but I found her shy and
timid. She seemed to me uninteresting and commonplace. And this was Uncle Dick's Rose of joy!

I was so sorry for Uncle Dick that I shrank
from meeting him. Nevertheless, I went over
after tea, fearing that he might misunderstand,
nay, rather, understand, my absence. He was in
the garden, and he came down the path where
the buds were just showing. There was a smile
on his face and the glory in his eyes was quite
undimmed.

"Master, she's come. And she's not a bit changed.
I feared she would be, but she is just the same—
my sweet little Rose of joy!"

I looked at Uncle Dick in some amazement. He
was thoroughly sincere, there was no doubt of
that, and I felt a great throb of relief. He had
found no disillusioning change. I saw Rose Lawrence merely with the cold eyes of the stranger.
He saw her through the transfiguring medium of
a love that made her truly his Rose of joy. And
all was well.

They were married the next morning and walked
together over the clover meadow to their home.
In the evening I went over, as I had promised
Uncle Dick to do. They were in the garden, with a
great saffron sky over them and a glory of sunset
behind the poplars. I paused unseen at the gate.
Uncle Dick was big and splendid in his fine new
wedding suit, and his faded little bride was hanging on his arm. Her face was upturned to him; it

was a glorified face, so transformed by the tender
radiance of love shining through it that I saw her
then as Uncle Dick must always see her, and no
longer found it hard to understand how she could
be his Rose of joy. Happiness clothed them as a
garment; they were crowned king and queen in
the bridal realm of the springtime.

The Romance of
Aunt Beatrice

Margaret always maintains that it was a direct inspiration of Providence that took her across the street to see Aunt Beatrice that night. And Aunt Beatrice believes that it was too. But the truth of the matter is that Margaret was feeling very unhappy, and went over to talk to Aunt Beatrice as the only alternative to a fit of crying. Margaret's unhappiness has nothing further to do with this story, so it may be dismissed with the remark that it did not amount to much, in spite of Margaret's tragical attitude, and was dissipated at once and forever by the arrival of a certain missent letter the next day.

Aunt Beatrice was alone. Her brother and his wife had gone to the "at home" which Mrs. Cunningham was giving that night in honour of the Honourable John Reynolds, M.P. The children were upstairs in bed, and Aunt Beatrice was darning their stockings, a big basketful of which loomed up aggressively on the table beside her. Or, to speak more correctly, she had been darning them. Just when Margaret was sliding across the icy street Aunt Beatrice was bent forward in her chair, her hands over her face, while soft, shrinking little sobs shook her from head to foot.

When Margaret's imperative knock came at the front door, Aunt Beatrice started guiltily and wished earnestly that she had waited until she went to bed before crying, if cry she must. She knew Margaret's knock, and she did not want her gay young niece, of all people in the world, to suspect the fact or the cause of her tears.

"I hope she won't notice my eyes," she thought, as she hastily plumped a big ugly dark-green shade, with an almond-eyed oriental leering from it, over the lamp, before going out to let Margaret in.

Margaret did not notice at first. She was too deeply absorbed in her own troubles to think that anyone else in the world could be miserable too. She curled up in the deep easy-chair by the fire, and clasped her hands behind her curly head with a sigh of physical comfort and mental unhappiness, while Aunt Beatrice, warily sitting with her back to the light, took up her work again.

"You didn't go to Mrs. Cunningham's 'at home,' Auntie," said Margaret lazily, feeling that she must make some conversation to justify her appearance. "You were invited, weren't you?"

Aunt Beatrice nodded. The hole she was darning in the knee of Willie Hayden's stocking must be done very carefully. Mrs. George Hayden was particular about such matters. Perhaps this was why Aunt Beatrice did not speak.

"Why didn't you go?" asked Margaret absently, wondering why there had been no letter for her that morning—and this was the third day too! Could Gilbert be ill? Or was he flirting with some other girl and forgetting her? Margaret swallowed a big lump in her throat, and resolved that she would go home next week—no, she wouldn't, either—if he was as hateful and fickle as that— what was Aunt Beatrice saying?

"Well, I'm—I'm not used to going to parties now, my dear. And the truth is I have no dress fit to wear. At least Bella said so, because the party was to be a very fashionable affair. She said my old grey silk wouldn't do at all. Of course she knows. She had to have a new dress for it, and we couldn't both have that. George couldn't afford it these hard times. And, as Bella said, it would be very foolish of me to get an expensive dress that would be no use to me afterward. But it doesn't matter. And, of course, somebody had to stay with the children."

"Of course," assented Margaret dreamily. Mrs. Cunningham's "at home" was of no particular interest. The guests were all middle-aged people whom the M.P. had known in his boyhood and

Margaret, in her presumptuous youth, thought it
would be a very prosy affair, although it had
made quite a sensation in quiet little Murraybridge, where people still called an "at home" a
party plain and simple.

"I saw Mr. Reynolds in church Sunday afternoon," she went on. "He is very fine-looking, I
think. Did you ever meet him?"

"I used to know him very well long ago,"
answered Aunt Beatrice, bowing still lower over
her work. "He used to live down in Wentworth,
you know, and he visited his married sister here
very often. He was only a boy at that time.
Then—he went out to British Columbia and—
and —we never heard much more about him."

"He's very rich and owns dozens of mines and
railroads and things like that," said Margaret,
"and he's a member of the Dominion Parliament,
too. They say he's one of the foremost men in the
House and came very near getting a portfolio in
the new cabinet. I like men like that. They are
so interesting. Wouldn't it be awfully nice and
complimentary to have one of them in love with
you? Is he married?"

"I—I don't know," said Aunt Beatrice faintly.
"I have never heard that he was."

"There, you've run the needle into your finger," said Margaret sympathetically.

"It's of no consequence," said Aunt Beatrice
hastily.

She wiped away the drop of blood and went
on with her work. Margaret watched her dream-

ily. What lovely hair Aunt Beatrice had! It was so thick and glossy, with warm bronze tones where the lamp-light fell on it under that hideous weird old shade. But Aunt Beatrice wore it in such an unbecoming way. Margaret idly wondered if she would comb her hair straight back and prim when she was thirty-five. She thought it very probable if that letter did not come tomorrow.

From Aunt Beatrice's hair Margaret's eyes fell to Aunt Beatrice's face. She gave a little jump. Had Aunt Beatrice been crying? Margaret sat bolt upright.

"Aunt Beatrice, did you want to go to that party?" she demanded explosively. "Now tell me the truth."

"I did," said Aunt Beatrice weakly. Margaret's sudden attack fairly startled the truth out of her. "It is very silly of me, I know, but I did want to go. I didn't care about a new dress. I'd have been quite willing to wear my grey silk, and I could have fixed the sleeves. What difference would it have made? Nobody would ever have noticed me, but Bella thought it wouldn't do."

She paused long enough to give a little sob which she could not repress. Margaret made use of the opportunity to exclaim violently, "It's a shame!"

"I suppose you don't understand why I wanted to go to this particular party so much," went on Aunt Beatrice shyly. "I'll tell you why—if you won't laugh at me. I wanted to see John Reynolds—not to talk to him—oh, I dare say he

wouldn't remember me—but just to see him.
Long ago—fifteen years ago—we were engaged.
And—and—I loved him so much then, Margaret."

"You poor dear!" said Margaret sympathetically. She reached over and patted her aunt's
hand. She thought that this little bit of romance,
long hidden and unsuspected, blossoming out
under her eyes, was charming. In her interest she
quite forgot her own pet grievance.

"Yes—and then we quarrelled. It was a dreadful quarrel and it was about such a trifle. We
parted in anger and he went away. He never
came back. It was all my fault. Well, it is all over
long ago and everybody has forgotten. I—I don't
mind it now. But I just wanted to see him once
more and then come quietly away."

"Aunt Beatrice, you are going to that party
yet," said Margaret decisively.

"Oh, it is impossible, my dear."

"No, it isn't. Nothing is impossible when I
make up my mind. You must go. I'll drag you
there by main force if it comes to that. Oh, I have
such a jolly plan, Auntie. You know my black and
yellow dinner dress—no, you don't either, for I've
never worn it here. The folks at home all said it
was too severe for me—and so it is. Nothing suits
me but the fluffy, chuffy things with a tilt to
them. Gil—er—I mean—well, yes, Gilbert always
declared that dress made me look like a cross
between an unwilling nun and a ballet girl, so I
took a dislike to it. But it's as lovely as a dream.
Oh, when you see it your eyes will stick out. You

must wear it tonight. It's just your style, and I'm sure it will fit you, for our figures are so much alike."

"But it is too late."

" 'Tisn't. It's not more than half an hour since Uncle George and Aunt Bella went. I'll have you ready in a twinkling."

"But the fire—and the children!"

"I'll stay here and look after both. I won't burn the house down, and if the twins wake up I'll give them—what is it you give them—soothing syrup? So go at once and get you ready, while I fly over for the dress. I'll fix your hair up when I get back."

Margaret was gone before Aunt Beatrice could speak again. Her niece's excitement seized hold of her too. She flung the stockings into the basket and the basket into the closet.

"I will go—and I won't do another bit of darning tonight. I hate it—I hate it—I hate it! Oh, how much good it does me to say it!"

When Margaret came flying up the stairs Aunt Beatrice was ready save for hair and dress. Margaret cast the gown on the bed, revealing all its beauty of jetted lace and soft yellow silk with a dextrous sweep of her arm. Aunt Beatrice gave a little cry of admiration.

"Isn't it lovely?" demanded Margaret. "And I've brought you my opera cape and my fascinator and my black satin slippers with the cunningest gold buckles, and some sweet pale yellow roses that Uncle Ned gave me yesterday. Oh,

Aunt Beatrice! What magnificent arms and shoulders you have! They're like marble. Mine are so scrawny I'm just ashamed to have people know they belong to me."

Margaret's nimble fingers were keeping time with her tongue. Aunt Beatrice's hair went up as if by magic into soft puffs and waves and twists, and a golden rose was dropped among the bronze masses. Then the lovely dress was put on and pinned and looped and pulled until it fell into its simple, classical lines around the tall, curving figure. Margaret stepped back and clapped her hands admiringly.

"Oh, Auntie, you're beautiful! Now I'll pop down for the cloak and fascinator. I left them hanging by the fire."

When Margaret had gone Aunt Beatrice caught up the lamp and tiptoed shamefacedly across the hall to the icy-cold spare room. In the long mirror she saw herself reflected from top to toe—or was it herself! Could it be—that gracious woman with the sweet eyes and flushed cheeks, with rounded arms gleaming through their black laces and the cluster of roses nestling against the warm white flesh of the shoulder?

"I do look nice," she said aloud, with a little curtsey to the radiant reflection. "It is all the dress, I know. I feel like a queen in it—no, like a girl again—and that's better."

Margaret went to Mrs. Cunningham's door with her.

"How I wish I could go in and see the sensation you'll make, Aunt Beatrice," she whispered.

"You dear, silly child! It's just the purple and fine linen," laughed Aunt Beatrice. But she did not altogether think so, and she rang the doorbell unquailingly. In the hall Mrs. Cunningham herself came beamingly to greet her.

"My dear Beatrice! I'm so glad. Bella said you could not come because you had a headache."

"My headache got quite better after they left, and so I thought I would get ready and come, even if it were rather late," said Beatrice glibly, wondering if Sapphira had ever worn a black-and-yellow dress, and if so, might not her historic falsehood be traced to its influence?

When they came downstairs together, Beatrice, statuesque and erect in her trailing draperies, and Mrs. Cunningham secretly wondering where on earth Beatrice Hayden had got such a magnificent dress and what she had done to herself to make her look as she did—a man came through the hall. At the foot of the stairs they met. He put out his hand.

"Beatrice! It must be Beatrice! How little you have changed!"

Mrs. Cunningham was not particularly noted in Murraybridge for her tact, but she had a sudden visitation of the saving grace at that moment, and left the two alone.

Beatrice put her hand into the M.P.'s.

"I am glad to see you," she said simply, looking up at him.

She could not say that he had not changed, for there was little in this tall, broad-shouldered man of the world, with grey glints in his hair, to suggest the slim, boyish young lover whose image she had carried in her heart all the long years.

But the voice, though deeper and mellower, was the same, and the thin, clever mouth that went up at one corner and down at the other in a humorous twist; and one little curl of reddish hair fell over his forehead away from its orderly fellows, just as it used to when she had loved to poke her fingers through it; and, more than all, the deep-set grey eyes looking down into her blue ones were unchanged. Beatrice felt her heart beating to her fingertips.

"I thought you were not coming," he said. "I expected to meet you here and I was horribly disappointed. I thought the bitterness of that foolish old quarrel must be strong enough to sway you yet."

"Didn't Bella tell you I had a headache?" faltered Beatrice.

"Bella? Oh, your brother's wife! I wasn't talking to her. I've been sulking in corners ever since I concluded you were not coming. How beautiful you are, Beatrice! You'll let an old friend say that much, won't you?"

Beatrice laughed softly. She had forgotten for years that she was beautiful, but the sweet old knowledge had come back to her again. She could not help knowing that he spoke the simple truth, but she said mirthfully,

"You've learned to flatter since the old days, haven't you? Don't you remember you used to tell me I was too thin to be pretty? But I suppose a bit of blarney is a necessary ingredient in the composition of an M.P."

He was still holding her hand. With a glance of dissatisfaction at the open parlour door, he drew her away to the little room at the end of the hall, which Mrs. Cunningham, for reasons known only to herself, called her library.

"Come in here with me," he said masterfully. "I want to have a long talk with you before the other people get hold of you."

When Beatrice got home from the party ten minutes before her brother and his wife, Margaret was sitting Turk fashion in the big armchair, with her eyes very wide open and owlish.

"You dear girlie, were you asleep?" asked Aunt Beatrice indulgently.

Margaret nodded. "Yes, and I've let the fire go out. I hope you're not cold. I must run before Aunt Bella gets here, or she'll scold. Had a nice time?"

"Delightful. You were a dear to lend me this dress. It was so funny to see Bella staring at it."

When Margaret had put on her hat and jacket she went as far as the street door, and then tip-toed back to the sitting-room. Aunt Beatrice was leaning back in the armchair, with a drooping rose held softly against her lips, gazing dreamily into the dull red embers.

"Auntie," said Margaret contritely, "I can't go home without confessing, although I know it is a heinous offence to interrupt the kind of musing that goes with dying embers and faded roses in the small hours. But it would weigh on my conscience all night if I didn't. I was asleep, but I wakened up just before you came in and went to the window. I didn't mean to spy upon anyone— but that street was bright as day! And if you will let an M.P. kiss you on the doorstep in glaring moonlight, you must expect to be seen."

"I wouldn't have cared if there had been a dozen onlookers," said Aunt Beatrice frankly, "and I don't believe he would either."

Margaret threw up her hands. "Well, my conscience is clear, at least. And remember, Aunt Beatrice, I'm to be bridesmaid—I insist upon that. And, oh, won't you ask me to visit you when you go down to Ottawa next winter? I'm told it's such a jolly place when the House is in session. And you'll need somebody to help you entertain, you know. The wife of a cabinet minister has to do lots of that. But I forgot—he isn't a cabinet minister yet. But he will be, of course. Promise that you'll have me, Aunt Beatrice, promise quick. I hear Uncle George and Aunt Bella coming."

Aunt Beatrice promised. Margaret flew to the door.

"You'd better keep that dress," she called back softly, as she opened it.

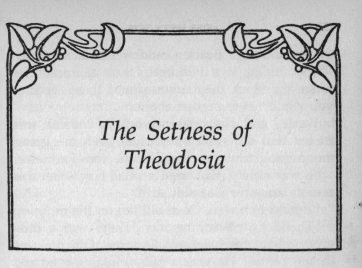

The Setness of
Theodosia

When Theodosia Ford married Wesley Brooke
after a courtship of three years, everybody concerned was satisfied. There was nothing particularly romantic in either the courtship or marriage.
Wesley was a steady, well-meaning, rather slow
fellow, comfortably off. He was not at all handsome. But Theodosia was a very pretty girl with
the milky colouring of an auburn blonde and large
china-blue eyes. She looked mild and Madonna-
like and was known to be sweet-tempered. Wesley's older brother, Irving Brooke, had married a
woman who kept him in hot water all the time,
so Heatherton folks said, but they thought there
was no fear of that with Wesley and Theodosia.
They would get along together all right.

223

Only old Jim Parmelee shook his head and said,
"They might, and then again they mightn't"; he
knew the stock they came of and it was a kind
you could never predict about.

Wesley and Theodosia were third cousins; this
meant that old Henry Ford had been the great-
great-grandfather of them both. Jim Parmelee,
who was ninety, had been a small boy when this
remote ancestor was still alive.

"I mind him well," said old Jim on the morning
of Theodosia's wedding day. There was a little
group about the blacksmith's forge. Old Jim was
in the centre. He was a fat, twinkling-eyed old
man, fresh and ruddy in spite of his ninety years.
"And," he went on, "he was about the settest
man you'd ever see or want to see. When old
Henry Ford made up his mind on any p'int a
cyclone wouldn't turn him a hairsbreadth—no,
nor an earthquake neither. Didn't matter a mite
how much he suffered for it—he'd stick to it if it
broke his heart. There was always some story or
other going round about old Henry's setness. The
family weren't quite so bad—only Tom. He was
Dosia's great-grandfather, and a regular chip of
the old block. Since then it's cropped out now
and again all through the different branches of
the family. I mistrust if Dosia hasn't got a spice
of it, and Wes Brooke too, but mebbe not."

Old Jim was the only croaker. Wesley and
Theodosia were married, in the golden prime of
the Indian summer, and settled down on their
snug little farm. Dosia was a beautiful bride, and

Wesley's pride in her was amusingly apparent. He thought nothing too good for her, the Heatherton people said. It was a sight to make an old heart young to see him march up the aisle of the church on Sunday in all the glossy splendour of his wedding suit, his curly black head held high and his round boyish face shining with happiness, stopping and turning proudly at his pew to show Theodosia in.

They always sat alone together in the big pew, and Alma Spencer, who sat behind them, declared that they held each other's hands all through the service. This lasted until spring; then came a sensation and scandal, such as decorous Heatherton had not known since the time Isaac Allen got drunk at Centreville Fair and came home and kicked his wife.

One evening in early April Wesley came home from the store at "the Corner," where he had lingered to talk over politics and farming methods with his cronies. This evening he was later than usual, and Theodosia had his supper kept warm for him. She met him on the porch and kissed him. He kissed her in return, and held her to him for a minute, with her bright head on his shoulder. The frogs were singing down in the south meadow swamp, and there was a splendour of silvery moonrise over the wooded Heatherton hills. Theodosia always remembered that moment.

When they went in, Wesley, full of excitement, began to talk of what he had heard at the store. Ogden Greene and Tom Cary were going to sell out and go to Manitoba. There were better chances for a man out there, he said; in Heatherton he might slave all his life and never make more than a bare living. Out west he might make a fortune.

Wesley talked on in this strain for some time, rehashing all the arguments he had heard Greene and Cary use. He had always been rather disposed to grumble at his limited chances in Heatherton, and now the great West seemed to stretch before him, full of alluring prospects and visions. Ogden and Tom wanted him to go too, he said. He had half a notion to. Heatherton was a stick-in-the-mud sort of place anyhow.

"What say, Dosia?"

He looked across the table at her, his eyes bright and questioning. Theodosia had listened in silence, as she poured his tea and passed him her hot, flaky biscuits. There was a little perpendicular wrinkle between her straight eyebrows.

"I think Ogden and Tom are fools," she said crisply. "They have good farms here. What do they want to go west for, or you, either? Don't get silly notions in your head, Wes."

Wesley flushed.

"Wouldn't you go with me, Dosia?" he said, trying to speak lightly.

"No, I wouldn't," said Theodosia, in her calm, sweet voice. Her face was serene, but the little wrinkle had grown deeper. Old Jim Parmelee would have known what it meant. He had seen the same expression on old Henry Ford's face many a time.

Wesley laughed good-humouredly, as if at a child. His heart was suddenly set on going west, and he was sure he could soon bring Theodosia around. He did not say anything more about it just then. Wesley thought he knew how to manage women.

When he broached the subject again, two days later, Theodosia told him plainly that it was no use. She would never consent to leave Heatherton and all her friends and go out to the prairies. The idea was just rank foolishness, and he would soon see that himself.

All this Theodosia said calmly and sweetly, without any trace of temper or irritation. Wesley still believed that he could persuade her and he tried perseveringly for a fortnight. By the end of that time he discovered that Theodosia was not a great-great-granddaughter of old Henry Ford for nothing.

Not that Theodosia ever got angry. Neither did she laugh at him. She met his arguments and pleadings seriously enough, but she never wavered.

"If you go to Manitoba, Wes, you'll go alone," she said. "I'll never go, so there is no use in any more talking."

Wesley was a descendant of old Henry Ford too. Theodosia's unexpected opposition roused all the latent stubbornness of his nature. He went over to Centreville oftener, and kept his blood at

fever heat talking to Greene and Cary, who
wanted him to go with them and spared no pains
at inducement.

The matter was gossiped about in Heatherton,
of course. People knew that Wesley Brooke had
caught "the western fever," and wanted to sell
out and go to Manitoba, while Theodosia was
opposed to it. They thought Dosia would have to
give in in the end, but said it was a pity Wes
Brooke couldn't be contented to stay where he
was well off.

Theodosia's family naturally sided with her and
tried to dissuade Wesley. But he was mastered
by that resentful irritation, roused in a man by
opposition where he thinks he should be master,
which will drive him into any cause.

One day he told Theodosia that he was going.
She was working her butter in her little, snowy-
clean dairy under the great willows by the well.
Wesley was standing in the doorway, his stout,
broad-shouldered figure filling up the sunlit space.
He was frowning and sullen.

"I'm going west in two weeks' time with the
boys, Dosia," he said stubbornly. "You can come
with me or stay here—just exactly as you please.
But I'm going."

Theodosia went on spatting her balls of golden
butter on the print in silence. She was looking
very neat and pretty in her big white apron, her
sleeves rolled up high above her plump, dimpled
elbows, and her ruddy hair curling about her face
and her white throat. She looked as pliable as her
butter.

Her silence angered her husband. He shuffled impatiently.

"Well, what have you to say, Dosia?"

"Nothing," said Theodosia. "If you have made up your mind to go, go you will, I suppose. But I will not. There is no use in talking. We've been over the ground often enough, Wes. The matter is settled."

Up to that moment Wesley had always believed that his wife would yield at last, when she saw that he was determined. Now he realized that she never would. Under that exterior of milky, dimpled flesh and calm blue eyes was all the iron will of old dead and forgotten Henry Ford. This mildest and meekest of girls and wives was not to be moved a hairsbreadth by all argument or entreaty, or insistence on a husband's rights.

A great, sudden anger came over the man. He lifted his hand and for one moment it seemed to Theodosia as if he meant to strike her. Then he dropped it with the first oath that had ever crossed his lips.

"You listen to me," he said thickly. "If you won't go with me I'll never come back here—never. When you want to do your duty as a wife you can come to me. But I'll never come back."

He turned on his heel and strode away. Theodosia kept on spatting her butter. The little perpendicular wrinkle had come between her brows again. At that moment an odd, almost uncanny resemblance to the old portrait of her great-great-grandfather, which hung on the parlour wall at home, came out on her girlish face.

The fortnight passed by. Wesley was silent and sullen, never speaking to his wife when he could avoid it. Theodosia was as sweet and serene as ever. She made an extra supply of shirts and socks for him, put up his lunch basket, and packed his trunk carefully. But she never spoke of his journey.

He did not sell his farm. Irving Brooke rented it. Theodosia was to live in the house. The business arrangements were simple and soon concluded.

Heatherton folks gossiped a great deal. They all condemned Theodosia. Even her own people sided against her now. They hated to be mixed up in a local scandal, and since Wes was bound to go they told Theodosia that it was her duty to go with him, no matter how much she disliked it. It would be disgraceful not to. They might as well have talked to the four winds. Theodosia was immoveable. They coaxed and argued and blamed—it all came to the same thing. Even those of them who could be "set" enough themselves on occasion could not understand Theodosia, who had always been so tractable. They finally gave up, as Wesley had done, baffled. Time would bring her to her senses, they said; you just had to leave that still, stubborn kind alone.

On the morning of Wesley's departure Theodosia arose at sunrise and prepared a tempting breakfast. Irving Brooke's oldest son, Stanley, who was to drive Wesley to the station, came over early with his express wagon. Wesley's trunk, corded and labelled, stood on the back platform.

The breakfast was a very silent meal. When it was over Wesley put on his hat and overcoat and went to the door, around which Theodosia's morning-glory vines were beginning to twine. The sun was not yet above the trees and the long shadows lay on the dewy grass. The wet leaves were flickering on the old maples that grew along the fence between the yard and the clover field beyond. The skies were all pearly blue, cleanswept of clouds. From the little farmhouse the green meadows sloped down to the valley, where a blue haze wound in and out like a glistening ribbon.

Theodosia went out and stood looking inscrutably on, while Wesley and Irving hoisted the trunk into the wagon and tied it. Then Wesley came up the porch steps and looked at her.

"Dosia," he said a little huskily, "I said I wouldn't ask you to go again, but I will. Will you come with me yet?"

"No," said Theodosia gently.

He held out his hand. He did not offer to kiss her.

"Goodbye, Dosia."

"Goodbye, Wes."

There was no tremor of an eyelash with her. Wesley smiled bitterly and turned away. When the wagon reached the end of the little lane he turned and looked back for the last time. Through all the years that followed he carried with him the picture of his wife as he saw her then, standing amid the airy shadows and wavering golden lights of the morning, the wind blowing the skirt

of her pale blue wrapper about her feet and ruf-
fling the locks of her bright hair into a delicate
golden cloud. Then the wagon disappeared around
a curve in the road, and Theodosia turned and
went back into her desolate home.

For a time there was a great buzz of gossip over
the affair. People wondered over it. Old Jim Parmelee understood better than the others. When
he met Theodosia he looked at her with a curious
twinkle in his keen old eyes.

"Looks as if a man could bend her any way
he'd a mind to, doesn't she?" he said. "Looks is
deceiving. It'll come out in her face by and by—
she's too young yet, but it's there. It does seem
unnatteral to see a woman so stubborn—you'd
kinder look for it more in a man."

Wesley wrote a brief letter to Theodosia when
he reached his destination. He said he was well
and was looking about for the best place to settle.
He liked the country fine. He was at a place called
Red Butte and guessed he'd locate there.

Two weeks later he wrote again. He had taken
up a claim of three hundred acres. Greene and
Cary had done the same. They were his nearest
neighbours and were three miles away. He had
knocked up a little shack, was learning to cook
his own meals, and was very busy. He thought
the country was a grand one and the prospects
good.

Theodosia answered his letter and told him all
the Heatherton news. She signed herself "Theodosia Brooke," but otherwise there was nothing

in the letter to indicate that it was written by a wife to her husband.

At the end of a year Wesley wrote and once more asked her to go out to him. He was getting on well, and was sure she would like the place. It was a little rough, to be sure, but time would improve that.

"Won't you let bygones be bygones, Dosia?" he wrote, "and come out to me. Do, my dear wife."

Theodosia wrote back, refusing to go. She never got any reply, nor did she write again.

People had given up talking about the matter and asking Theodosia when she was going out to Wes. Heatherton had grown used to the chronic scandal within its decorous borders. Theodosia never spoke of her husband to anyone, and it was known that they did not correspond. She took her youngest sister to live with her. She had her garden and hens and a cow. The farm brought her enough to live on, and she was always busy.

When fifteen years had gone by there were naturally some changes in Heatherton, sleepy and unprogressive as it was. Most of the old people were in the little hillside burying-ground that fronted the sunrise. Old Jim Parmelee was there with his recollections of four generations. Men and women who had been in their prime when Wesley went away were old now and the children were grown up and married.

Theodosia was thirty-five and was nothing like the slim, dimpled girl who had stood on the porch

steps and watched her husband drive away that
morning fifteen years ago. She was stout and
comely; the auburn hair was darker and arched
away from her face in smooth, shining waves
instead of the old-time curls. Her face was unlined
and fresh-coloured, but no woman could live in
subjection to her own unbending will for so many
years and not show it. Nobody, looking at Theodosia now, would have found it hard to believe
that a woman with such a determined, immoveable face could stick to a course of conduct in
defiance of circumstances.

Wesley Brooke was almost forgotten. People
knew, through correspondents of Greene and
Cary, that he had prospered and grown rich. The
curious old story had crystallized into accepted
history.

A life may go on without ripple or disturbance
for so many years that it may seem to have settled
into a lasting calm; then a sudden wind of passion
may sweep over it and leave behind a wake of
tempestuous waters. Such a time came at last to
Theodosia.

One day in August Mrs. Emory Merritt dropped
in. Emory Merritt's sister was Ogden Greene's
wife, and the Merritts kept up an occasional corre-
spondence with her. Hence, Cecilia Merritt
always knew what was to be known about Wesley Brooke, and always told Theodosia because
she had never been expressly forbidden to do
so.

Today she looked slightly excited. Secretly she

was wondering if the news she brought would have any effect whatever on Theodosia's impassive calm.

"Do you know, Dosia, Wesley's real sick? In fact, Phoebe Greene says they have very poor hopes of him. He was kind of ailing all the spring, it seems, and about a month ago he was took down with some kind of slow fever they have out there. Phoebe says they have a hired nurse from the nearest town and a good doctor, but she reckons he won't get over it. That fever goes awful hard with a man of his years."

Cecilia Merritt, who was the fastest talker in Heatherton, had got this out before she was brought up by a queer sound, half gasp, half cry, from Theodosia. The latter looked as if someone had struck her a physical blow.

"Mercy, Dosia, you ain't going to faint! I didn't suppose you'd care. You never seemed to care."

"Did you say," asked Theodosia thickly, "that Wesley was sick—dying?"

"Well, that's what Phoebe said. She may be mistaken. Dosia Brooke, you're a queer woman. I never could make you out and I never expect to. I guess only the Lord who made you can translate you."

Theodosia stood up. The sun was getting low, and the valley beneath them, ripening to harvest, was like a river of gold. She folded up her sewing with a steady hand.

"It's five o'clock, so I'll ask you to excuse me, Cecilia. I have a good deal to attend to. You can ask Emory if he'll drive me to the station in the morning. I'm going out to Wes."

"Well, for the land's sake," said Cecilia Merritt feebly, as she tied on her gingham sunbonnet. She got up and went home in a daze.

Theodosia packed her trunk and worked all night, dry-eyed, with agony and fear tearing at her heart. The iron will had snapped at last, like a broken reed, and fierce self-condemnation seized on her. "I've been a wicked woman," she moaned.

A week from that day Theodosia climbed down from the dusty stage that had brought her from the station over the prairies to the unpretentious little house where Wesley Brooke lived. A young girl, so like what Ogden Greene's wife had been fifteen years before that Theodosia involuntarily exclaimed, "Phoebe," came to the door. Beyond her, Theodosia saw the white-capped nurse.

Her voice trembled.

"Does—does Wesley Brooke live here?" she asked.

The girl nodded.

"Yes. But he is very ill at present. Nobody is allowed to see him."

Theodosia put up her hand and loosened her bonnet strings as if they were choking her. She had been sick with the fear that Wesley would be dead before she got to him. The relief was almost overwhelming.

"But I must see him," she cried hysterically— she, the calm, easy-going Dosia, hysterical—"I am his wife—and oh, if he had died before I got here!"

The nurse came forward.

"In that case I suppose you must," she conceded. "But he does not expect you. I must prepare him for the surprise."

She turned to the door of a room opening off the kitchen, but Theodosia, who had hardly heard her, was before her. She was inside the room before the nurse could prevent her. Then she stood, afraid and trembling, her eyes searching the dim apartment hungrily.

When they fell on the occupant of the bed Theodosia started in bitter surprise. All unconsciously she had been expecting to find Wesley as he had been when they parted. Could this gaunt, haggard creature, with the unkempt beard and prematurely grey hair and the hollow, beseeching eyes, be the ruddy, boyish-faced husband of her youth? She gave a choking cry of pain and shame, and the sick man turned his head. Their eyes met.

Amazement, incredulity, hope, dread, all flashed in succession over Wesley Brooke's lined face. He raised himself feebly up.

"Dosia," he murmured.

Theodosia staggered across the room and fell on her knees by the bed. She clasped his head to her breast and kissed him again and again.

"Oh, Wes, Wes, can you forgive me? I've been a wicked, stubborn woman—and I've spoiled our lives. Forgive me."

He held his thin trembling arms around her and devoured her face with his eyes.

"Dosia, when did you come? Did you know I was sick?"

"Wes, I can't talk till you say you've forgiven me."

"Oh, Dosia, you have just as much to forgive. We were both too set. I should have been more considerate."

"Just say, 'I forgive you, Dosia,' " she entreated.

"I forgive you, Dosia," he said gently, "and oh, it's so good to see you once more, darling. There hasn't been an hour since I left you that I haven't longed for your sweet face. If I had thought you really cared I'd have gone back. But I thought you didn't. It broke my heart. You did though, didn't you?"

"Oh, yes, yes, yes," she said, holding him more closely, with her tears falling.

When the young doctor from Red Butte came that evening he found a great improvement in his patient. Joy and happiness, those world-old physicians, had done what drugs and medicines had failed to do.

"I'm going to get better, Doc," said Wesley. "My wife has come and she's going to stay. You didn't know I was married, did you? I'll tell you the story some day. I proposed going back east, but Dosia says she'd rather stay here. I'm the happiest man in Red Butte, Doc."

He squeezed Theodosia's hand as he had used to do long ago in Heatherton church, and Dosia smiled down at him. There were no dimples now, but her smile was very sweet. The ghostly finger of old Henry Ford, pointing down through the generations, had lost its power to brand with its malediction the life of these, his descendants. Wesley and Theodosia had joined hands with their long-lost happiness.

quite admirable. So he came to beg me to go to

Between the Hill
and the Valley

It was one of the moist, pleasantly odorous nights of early spring. There was a chill in the evening air, but the grass was growing green in sheltered spots, and Jeffrey Miller had found purple-petalled violets and pink arbutus on the hill that day. Across a valley filled with beech and fir, there was a sunset afterglow, creamy yellow and pale red, with a new moon swung above it. It was a night for a man to walk alone and dream of his love, which was perhaps why Jeffrey Miller came so loiteringly across the springy hill pasture, with his hands full of the mayflowers.

He was a tall, broad-shouldered man of forty, and looking no younger, with dark grey eyes and a tanned, clean-cut face, clean-shaven save for a drooping moustache. Jeffrey Miller was considered a handsome man, and Bayside people had periodical fits of wondering why he had never married. They pitied him for the lonely life he must lead alone there at the Valley Farm, with only a deaf old housekeeper as a companion, for it did not occur to the Bayside people in general that a couple of shaggy dogs could be called companions, and they did not know that books make very excellent comrades for people who know how to treat them.

One of Jeffrey's dogs was with him now—the oldest one, with white breast and paws and a tawny coat. He was so old that he was half-blind and rather deaf, but, with one exception, he was the dearest of living creatures to Jeffrey Miller, for Sara Stuart had given him the sprawly, chubby little pup years ago.

They came down the hill together. A group of men were standing on the bridge in the hollow, discussing Colonel Stuart's funeral of the day before. Jeffrey caught Sara's name and paused on the outskirts of the group to listen. Sometimes he thought that if he were lying dead under six feet of turf and Sara Stuart's name were pronounced above him, his heart would give a bound of life.

"Yes, the old kunnel's gone at last," Christopher Jackson was saying. "He took his time dyin', that's sartain. Must be a kind of relief for Sara—she's had to wait on him, hand and foot, for years. But no doubt she'll feel pretty lonesome. Wonder what she'll do?"

"Is there any particular reason for her to do anything?" asked Alec Churchill.

"Well, she'll have to leave Pinehurst. The estate's entailed and goes to her cousin, Charles Stuart."

There were exclamations of surprise from the other men on hearing this. Jeffrey drew nearer, absently patting his dog's head. He had not known it either.

"Oh, yes," said Christopher, enjoying all the importance of exclusive information. "I thought everybody knew that. Pinehurst goes to the oldest male heir. The old kunnel felt it keen that he hadn't a son. Of course, there's plenty of money and Sara'll get that. But I guess she'll feel pretty bad at leaving her old home. Sara ain't as young as she used to be, neither. Let me see—she must be thirty-eight. Well, she's left pretty lonesome."

"Maybe she'll stay on at Pinehurst," said Job Crowe. "It'd only be right for her cousin to give her a home there."

Christopher shook his head.

"No, I understand they're not on very good terms. Sara don't like Charles Stuart or his wife— and I don't blame her. She won't stay there, not likely. Probably she'll go and live in town. Strange she never married. She was reckoned handsome, and had plenty of beaus at one time."

Jeffrey swung out of the group and started homeward with his dog. To stand by and hear Sara Stuart discussed after this fashion was more than he could endure. The men idly watched his tall, erect figure as he went along the valley.

"Queer chap, Jeff," said Alec Churchill reflectively.

"Jeff's all right," said Christopher in a patronizing way. "There ain't a better man or neighbour alive. I've lived next farm to him for thirty years, so I ought to know. But he's queer sartainly—not like other people—kind of unsociable. He don't care for a thing 'cept dogs and reading and mooning round woods and fields. That ain't natural, you know. But I must say he's a good farmer. He's got the best farm in Bayside, and that's a real nice house he put up on it. Ain't it an odd thing he never married? Never seemed to have no notion of it. I can't recollect of Jeff Miller's ever courting anybody. That's another unnatural thing about him."

"I've always thought that Jeff thought himself a cut or two above the rest of us," said Tom Scovel with a sneer. "Maybe he thinks the Bayside girls ain't good enough for him."

"There ain't no such dirty pride about Jeff," pronounced Christopher conclusively. "And the Millers *are* the best family hereabouts, leaving the kunnel's out. And Jeff's well off—nobody knows how well, I reckon, but I can guess, being his land neighbour. Jeff ain't no fool nor loafer, if he is a bit queer."

Meanwhile, the object of these remarks was striding homeward and thinking, not of the men behind him, but of Sara Stuart. He must go to her at once. He had not intruded on her since her father's death, thinking her sorrow too great for him to meddle with. But this was different. Perhaps she needed the advice or assistance only he could give. To whom else in Bayside could she turn for it but to him, her old friend? Was it possible that she must leave Pinehurst? The thought struck cold dismay to his soul. How could he bear his life if she went away?

He had loved Sara Stuart from childhood. He remembered vividly the day he had first seen her—a spring day, much like this one had been; he, a boy of eight, had gone with his father to the big, sunshiny hill field and he had searched for birds' nests in the little fir copses along the crest while his father plowed. He had so come upon her, sitting on the fence under the pines at the back of Pinehurst—a child of six in a dress of purple cloth. Her long, light brown curls fell over her shoulders and rippled sleekly back from her calm little brow; her eyes were large and greyish blue, straight-gazing and steadfast. To the end of his life the boy was to carry in his heart the picture she made there under the pines.

"Little boy," she had said, with a friendly smile, "will you show me where the mayflowers grow?"

Shyly enough he had assented, and they set out together for the barrens beyond the field, where the arbutus trailed its stars of sweetness under the dusty dead grasses and withered leaves of the old year. The boy was thrilled with delight. She was a fairy queen who thus graciously smiled on him and chattered blithely as they searched for mayflowers in the fresh spring sunshine. He thought it a wonderful thing that it had so chanced. It overjoyed him to give the choicest clusters he found into her slim, waxen little fingers, and watch her eyes grow round with pleasure in them. When the sun began to lower over the beeches she had gone home with her arms full of arbutus, but she had turned at the edge of the pineland and waved her hand at him.

That night, when he told his mother of the little girl he had met on the hill, she had hoped anxiously that he had been "very polite," for the little girl was a daughter of Colonel Stuart, newly come to Pinehurst. Jeffrey, reflecting, had not been certain that he had been polite; "But I am sure she liked me," he said gravely.

A few days later a message came from Mrs. Stuart on the hill to Mrs. Miller in the valley. Would she let her little boy go up now and then to play with Sara? Sara was very lonely because she had no playmates. So Jeff, overjoyed, had gone to his divinity's very home, where the two children played together many a day. All through their childhood they had been fast friends. Sara's parents placed no bar to their intimacy. They had soon concluded that little Jeff Miller was a very good playmate for Sara. He was gentle, well-behaved, and manly.

Sara never went to the district school which Jeff attended; she had her governess at home. With no other boy or girl in Bayside did she form any friendship, but her loyalty to Jeff never wavered.

As for Jeff, he worshipped her and would have done anything she commanded. He belonged to her from the day they had hunted arbutus on the hill.

When Sara was fifteen she had gone away to school. Jeff had missed her sorely. For four years he saw her only in the summers, and each year she had seemed taller, statelier, further from him. When she graduated her father took her abroad for two years; then she came home, a lovely, high-bred girl, dimpling on the threshold of womanhood; and Jeffrey Miller was face to face with two bitter facts. One was that he loved her—not with the boy-and-girl love of long ago, but with the love of a man for the one woman in the world; and the other was that she was as far beyond his reach as one of those sunset stars of which she had always reminded him in her pure, clear-shining loveliness.

He looked these facts unflinchingly in the face until he had grown used to them, and then he laid down his course for himself. He loved Sara—and he did not wish to conquer his love, even if it had been possible. It were better to love her, whom he could never win, than to love and be loved by any other woman. His great office in life was to be her friend, humble and unexpectant; to be at hand if she should need him for ever so trifling a service; never to presume, always to be faithful.

Sara had not forgotten her old friend. But their former comradeship was now impossible; they

could be friends, but never again companions.
Sara's life was full and gay; she had interests in
which he had no share; her social world was
utterly apart from his; she was of the hill and its
traditions, he was of the valley and its people.
The democracy of childhood past, there was no
common ground on which they might meet. Only
one thing Jeffrey had found it impossible to con-
template calmly. Some day Sara would marry—a
man who was her equal, who sat at her father's
table as a guest. In spite of himself, Jeffrey's heart
filled with hot rebellion at the thought; it was like
a desecration and a robbery.

But, as the years went by, this thing he dreaded
did not happen. Sara did not marry, although
gossip assigned her many suitors not unworthy
of her. She and Jeffrey were always friends,
although they met but seldom. Sometimes she
sent him a book; it was his custom to search for
the earliest mayflowers and take them to her; once
in a long while they met and talked of many
things. Jeffrey's calendar from year to year was
red-lettered by these small happenings, of which
nobody knew, or, knowing, would have cared.

So he and Sara drifted out of youth, together
yet apart. Her mother had died, and Sara was
the gracious, stately mistress of Pinehurst, which
grew quieter as the time went on; the lovers
ceased to come, and holiday friends grew few;
with the old colonel's failing health the gaieties
and lavish entertaining ceased. Jeffrey thought
that Sara must often be lonely, but she never said

so; she remained sweet, serene, calm-eyed, like
the child he had met on the hill. Only, now and
then, Jeffrey fancied he saw a shadow on her
face—a shadow so faint and fleeting that only the
eye of an unselfish, abiding love, made clear-
sighted by patient years, could have seen it. It
hurt him, that shadow; he would have given anything in his power to have banished it.

And now this long friendship was to be broken.
Sara was going away, At first he had thought only
of her pain, but now his own filled his heart. How
could he live without her? How could he dwell in
the valley knowing that she had gone from the
hill? Never to see her light shine down on him
through the northern gap in the pines at night!
Never to feel that perhaps her eyes rested on him
now and then as he went about his work in the
valley fields! Never to stoop with a glad thrill over
the first spring flowers because it was his privilege
to take them to her! Jeffrey groaned aloud. No,
he could not go up to see her that night; he must
wait—he must strengthen himself.

Then his heart rebuked him. This was selfishness; this was putting his own feelings before
hers—a thing he had sworn never to do. Perhaps
she needed him—perhaps she had wondered why
he had not come to offer her such poor service as
might be in his power. He turned and went down
through the orchard lane, taking the old field-path
across the valley and up the hill, which he had
traversed so often and so joyfully in boyhood. It
was dark now, and a few stars were shining in

the silvery sky. The wind sighed among the pines as he walked under them. Sometimes he felt that he must turn back—that his pain was going to master him; then he forced himself to go on.

The old grey house where Sara lived seemed bleak and stricken in the dull light, with its leafless vines clinging to it. There were no lights in it. It looked like a home left soulless.

Jeffrey went around to the garden door and knocked. He had expected the maid to open it, but Sara herself came.

"Why, Jeff," she said, with pleasure in her tones. "I am so glad to see you. I have been wondering why you had not come before."

"I did not think you would want to see me yet," he said hurriedly. "I have thought about you every hour—but I feared to intrude."

"*You* couldn't intrude," she said gently. "Yes, I have wanted to see you, Jeff. Come into the library."

He followed her into the room where they had always sat in his rare calls. Sara lighted the lamp on the table. As the light shot up she stood clearly revealed in it—a tall, slender woman in a trailing gown of grey. Even a stranger, not knowing her age, would have guessed it to be what it was, yet it would have been hard to say what gave the impression of maturity. Her face was quite unlined—a little pale, perhaps, with more finely cut outlines than those of youth. Her eyes were clear and bright; her abundant brown hair waved back from her face in the same curves that Jeffrey had noted in the purple-gowned child of six, under the pines. Perhaps it was the fine patience and serenity in her face that told her tale of years. Youth can never acquire it.

Her eyes brightened when she saw the mayflowers he carried. She came and took them from him, and her hands touched his, sending a little thrill of joy through him.

"How lovely they are! And the first I have seen this spring. You always bring me the first, don't you, Jeff? Do you remember the first day we spent picking mayflowers together?"

Jeff smiled. Could he forget? But something held him back from speech.

Sara put the flowers in a vase on the table, but slipped one starry pink cluster into the lace on her breast. She came and sat down beside Jeffrey; he saw that her beautiful eyes had been weeping, and that there were lines of pain around her lips. Some impulse that would not be denied made him lean over and take her hand. She left it unresistingly in his clasp.

"I am very lonely now, Jeff," she said sadly. "Father has gone. I have no friends left."

"You have me," said Jeffrey quietly.

"Yes. I shouldn't have said that. You are my friend, I know, Jeff. But, but—I must leave Pinehurst, you know."

"I learned that tonight for the first time," he answered.

"Did you ever come to a place where *everything* seemed ended—where it seemed that there was

nothing—simply nothing—left, Jeff?" she said
wistfully. "But, no, it couldn't seem so to a man.
Only a woman could fully understand what I
mean. That is how I feel now. While I had Father
to live for it wasn't so hard. But now there is
nothing. And I must go away."

"Is there anything I can do?" muttered Jeffrey
miserably. He knew now that he had made a
mistake in coming tonight; he could not help
her. His own pain had unmanned him. Presently he would say something foolish or selfish
in spite of himself.

Sara turned her eyes on him.

"There is nothing anybody can do, Jeff," she
said piteously. Her eyes, those clear child-eyes,
filled with tears. "I shall be braver—stronger—
after a while. But just now I have no strength left.
I feel like a lost, helpless child. Oh, Jeff!"

She put her slender hands over her face and
sobbed. Every sob cut Jeffrey to the heart.

"Don't—don't, Sara," he said huskily. "I can't
bear to see you suffer so. I'd die for you if it
would do you any good. I love you—I love you!
I never meant to tell you so, but it is the truth. I
oughtn't to tell you now. Don't think that I'm trying to take any advantage of your loneliness and
sorrow. I know—I have always known—that you
are far above me. But that couldn't prevent my
loving you—just humbly loving you, asking nothing else. You may be angry with my presumption,
but I can't help telling you that I love you. That's
all. I just want you to know it."

Sara had turned away her head. Jeffrey was overcome with contrition. Ah, he had no business to speak so—he had spoiled the devotion of years. Who was he that he should have dared to love her? Silence alone had justified his love, and now he had lost that justification. She would despise him. He had forfeited her friendship for ever.

"Are you angry, Sara?" he questioned sadly, after a silence.

"I think I am," said Sara. She kept her stately head averted. "If—if you have loved me, Jeff, why did you never tell me so before?"

"How could I dare?" he said gravely. "I knew I could never win you—that I had no right to dream of you so. Oh, Sara, don't be angry! My love has been reverent and humble. I have asked nothing. I ask nothing now but your friendship. Don't take that from me, Sara. Don't be angry with me."

"I *am* angry," repeated Sara, "and I think I have a right to be."

"Perhaps so," he said simply, "but not because I have loved you. Such love as mine ought to anger no woman, Sara. But you have a right to be angry with me for presuming to put it into words. I should not have done so—but I could not help it. It rushed to my lips in spite of me. Forgive me."

"I don't know whether I can forgive you for not telling me before," said Sara steadily. "*That* is what I have to forgive—not your speaking at last, even if it was dragged from you against your will.

Did you think I would make you such a very poor wife, Jeff, that you would not ask me to marry you?"

"Sara!" he said, aghast. "I—I—you were as far above me as a star in the sky—I never dreamed—I never hoped—"

"That I could care for you?" said Sara, looking round at last. "Then you were more modest than a man ought to be, Jeff. I did not know that you loved me, or I should have found some way to make you speak out long ago. I should not have let you waste all these years. I've loved you—ever since we picked mayflowers on the hill, I think—ever since I came home from school, I know. I never cared for anyone else—although I tried to, when I thought you didn't care for me. It mattered nothing to me that the world may have thought there was some social difference between us. There, Jeff, you cannot accuse me of not making my meaning plain."

"Sara," he whispered, wondering, bewildered, half-afraid to believe this unbelievable joy. "I'm not half worthy of you—but—but"—he bent forward and put his arm around her, looking straight into her clear, unshrinking eyes. "Sara, will you be my wife?"

"Yes." She said the word clearly and truly. "And I will think myself a proud and happy and honoured woman to be so, Jeff. Oh, I don't shrink from telling you the truth, you see. You mean too much to me for me to dissemble it. I've hidden it for eighteen years because I didn't think you wanted to hear it, but I'll give myself the delight of saying it frankly now."

She lifted her delicate, high-bred face, fearless love shining in every lineament, to his, and they exchanged their first kiss.

The Man
Who Forgot

I knew them all well . . . I had been minister in Claremont for ten years when it happened. In fact, it was I who preached the fatal sermon that shut the door of the past behind Gordon Mitchell. Not that I so much as thought of Gordon Mitchell when I preached it.

If a minister preaches a sermon that hits home to some particular individual, people always suppose he meant it for that very person. Ninety-nine times out of a hundred he never thought of him. A hand-me-down cap is bound to fit somebody's head, but it doesn't follow that it was made for him.

Dr. Stirling—"Old Doc" as he was affectionately called by everybody in Claremont—and his daughter, Gertrude, were particular friends of mine. They were not the kind of people to whom a minister dare not say anything until he has said it over to himself first to make sure it is a safe thing to say. Old Doc was one of my elders and we fought continually over church problems, but that did not interfere with our friendship. By a tacit agreement we never spoke of church affairs when I went to his house. We left that for the session room.

The Stirling house was at the extreme west of Claremont. It was an old house—the doctor's father, who had been a lawyer, and his grandfather, who had been a merchant, had lived their long lives out in it before him. Moreover, it was the ugliest house, not only in Claremont, but in the whole world—there is no doubt about that. It was more like a huge red brick box than anything else, too high for its breadth, and made still higher by a bulbous glass cupola on top.

But the doctor would never have it altered; he loved it as it was. The fine old trees around it veiled its ugliness somewhat, and inside—oh, there was nothing the matter with it there.

Internally it was a house of delightful personality. And the living room was the most delightful room in it. There the doctor and Gertrude always entertained their guests. It was a spacious, beautiful, dignified, friendly old room. The chairs clamoured to be sat upon; the mirrors had so often reflected beautiful women that they lent a certain charm to every face. In that room, it seemed to me, there were always in winter warm fires, old books, comfort, safety from storm, odours of pine; and in summer, coolness and shadows and wine-hues of flowers.

And Jigglesqueak! Jigglesqueak was always there winter and summer. It seemed to me he must always have been there, though Old Doc said he was a mere pup of fourteen. He was as ugly as the house and, like the house, had a beautiful soul.

Everybody loved Jigglesqueak. The sole point Old Doc and Anthony Fairweather had in common was their love of Jigglesqueak. They both agreed that Jigglesqueak was the only dog on earth that deserved to be a dog.

Old Doc was a character in his way. Claremont people believed that he could raise the dead to life if he wanted to and only refrained because it would be crossing the purposes of the Almighty.

He had done it once, they said. I have been solemnly assured by many sane people that Dan Hewlett was dead when Old Doc brought him to. You can believe that or not as you like.

But when living people saw Old Doc's long, lean face, with its big bushy white moustache and twinkling brown eyes, at their bedside and heard him growling, "There's nothing the matter with you" . . . why, they believed it until it was true.

He was a brusque old fellow and, older and all as he was, it didn't prevent him from rapping out a good round "d———n" when occasion offered, even before the cloth. Outside of Gertrude, his work, and Jigglesqueak, the only thing he cared for was golf. Our Claremont links are good in their way, and Old Doc was the best golfer in the burg—unless it was Anthony Fairweather. Nothing made Old Doc so furious as a hint that Anthony Fairweather could rival him in golf. But then, Old Doc did not like Anthony.

And Gertrude did!

Gertrude was about twenty at this time, a tall girl so stately that at school she had always been nicknamed "The Princess." As a child she had been rather plain, but now she was beautiful—with a beauty you never tired of. Hair as black as the proverbial raven's wing, eyes as blue as eyes could be, lips as softly red as the queen of roses. She was restrained and subtle, with exquisite taste, a wonderful laugh, and a personality that shone through her beautiful flesh like a lamp through alabaster.

Naturally she had some faults. She was a shade too fond of jewels and wore too many—it was the sole flaw in her taste. Some people said she overdressed, but I never thought it. Rich as her clothes were they were always subordinate to her. Her father liked to see her beautifully gowned.

And she was impatient. It could not be said that she suffered fools gladly. Also, she was stubborn, and I think if she had lived with other women those women would have had to play second fiddle in most things. But there was no other woman except a little maid in the house—never had been, since Gertrude's mother had died at her birth. That was one time Old Doc could not bring back the dead.

He had brought Gertrude up by himself without assistance from any woman and was a little over-proud of it—and of her. Yet she justified his pride—beautiful, gracious, humorous, companionable, tolerant, loyal. If I had been a young man instead of an old bachelor minister I would have been mad about her.

All the Claremont young men were, but the only two who mattered were Anthony Fairweather and Gordon Mitchell. Only one of them mattered to Gertrude—Anthony Fairweather.

But Old Doc, who would rather have liked her to marry Gordon if marry she must, was determined she shouldn't marry Anthony.

"Because of his Italian blood," he said.

But in my heart I always believed that it was because he wouldn't have a son-in-law who could rival him in golf.

To be sure, Old Doc had always detested Anthony. Everybody else in Claremont liked him and distrusted him, with the exception of Gordon Mitchell and myself. Gordon didn't like him and I didn't distrust him.

Captain Fairweather some twenty-two years before had married an Italian girl and brought her home to Claremont. It was before my time, but I gathered that Claremont had not taken Mrs. Fairweather to its bosom. She died when Anthony was four years old. Captain Fairweather broke his

heart and followed her three years later, leaving
Anthony to the care of a grim old aunt who
brought him up rigorously and always believed he
was just watching for a chance to do something
dreadful.

If he had inherited his father's plump, rosy face
and big blue eyes he would have stood a better
chance. But Anthony had his handsome mother's
dark eyes, smooth olive skin, and glossy, night-
black hair. He "looked foreign"—old Margaret
Grimes asserted it when she bathed him in the
first hour of his life.

Certainly he always had a grace and fire and
charm that no other Claremont boy possessed.
And, from the day of his christening when he had
pummelled the nose of the officiating minister,
Anthony was always in the limelight by reason of
some graceless exploit or other. He stole apples,
he put up a placard of measles where there were
none, he dropped a lump of ice down the Reverend John Arnold's neck at a church supper, he
stuck pins in the other boys in Sunday School, he
took an alarm clock to church, he wrote a false
but truthful obituary of a prominent citizen and
sent it to the Croyden papers, he put a plateful
of soap instead of cheese on the table at my induc-
tion festivities, and he was accused of shutting
the skunk up in the classroom.

In any other boy all this would just have been
considered natural boy-devilment, but in poor
Anthony it was, of course, "that Italian blood."

Everything that was a mystery was pinned to

him. But nobody except Old Doc really believed that Anthony started the fire that burned half the village down when he was about fifteen—the fire in which he almost lost his life saving the horses in Alex Peasley's stable.

That act won him approval in Claremont eyes, and public opinion was beginning to veer in his favour when a silly anonymous "poem" was published in the *Claremont Weekly*, making fun of all our prominent folks. Anthony was put down for the author, in spite of all his denials, and was never forgiven for it, since nobody ever forgives ridicule.

I knew he never wrote it. If he had, it wouldn't have been such insane trash—it would have cut to the bone. For Anthony had brains, though people were loath to admit it. They couldn't see how it was possible when he was "so fond of fiddling."

There was one thing they couldn't blame on his Italian blood—his gift for swimming. Captain Fairweather had been a star swimmer. Anthony swam across the Claremont river when he was eight years old and people bragged of the exploit to strangers for years in spite of Anthony's disrepute. Swimming, golfing, and fiddling were Anthony's hobbies, and he rode them so devotedly that he had no time to get into any serious scrapes. But people expected he would some day, and Old Doc both expected and hoped it.

Anthony and Gertrude had been playfellows in childhood, his home being across the street from hers. Once Anthony inveigled Gertrude away to the shore and they got caught in the quicksand and nearly swallowed up. That gave Old Doc his first scunner of Anthony. And when Gertrude fell off the stilts on which Anthony was teaching her to walk and hurt her back so that she was laid up for weeks, Old Doc was his enemy for life, although Gertrude always insisted that it wasn't Anthony's fault at all.

Her father forbade her ever playing with Anthony again, and she had nothing more to do with him until they met one night at a dance nine years later and loved each other—loved deeply, passionately, incurably. Naturally I was not at the dance, but I soon heard all about it. Old Doc himself told me.

He was furious—had forbidden Anthony the house, and had told Gertrude she was a fool. Gertrude had merely smiled and settled down to wait. She worshipped her father and wouldn't have disobeyed or hurt him, even for Anthony. But she knew time was on her side; she knew her father would come round in due course.

She and Anthony couldn't be married for a few years anyway. He had to get through college— he was attending the university in Croyden and coming home for weekends. Gertrude took it all with a fair degree of philosophy, except that she was horribly annoyed with Gordon Mitchell, who lived next door to the Stirlings and had long ago made up his mind to marry Gertrude. It did not discourage him at all to know that she had an understanding with Anthony Fairweather. Gordon knew that Old Doc was on his side and he had, besides, quite a bit of confidence in his own powers of attraction.

I ought to have liked Gordon: he was the most faithful member of my adult Bible class. He had always been what is called "religiously inclined," which shouldn't have been a count against him in a minister's eyes. Anthony once called him a "smug little hypocrite," but he was nothing of the sort. He was sincere and always impressed me as being morbidly conscientious. His mother told me that once, when a boy, he had stolen a jar of marmalade from the pantry and after a week of torment had confessed to her and done penance by crawling on bare hands and knees across the thistly meadow behind their lot. She seemed rather proud of this and of some similar things.

Gordon was likable enough in a superficial way and was popular in Claremont society. He was quite good-looking, with regular features, thick fair hair parted in the middle, and small, well-kept hands of which he was said to be very vain. In boyhood he was reputed to be a "sissy" owing to the fact or belief that at seven years of age he had pieced a quilt. His mother was foolish enough to mention it with pride. But he had lived this down.

He sang fairly well—though Gertrude said his voice was "muddy," whatever she meant by that—and was a member of the choir. His reputation was immaculate, and he took care people should know it. Besides being, as I have said, morbidly conscientious, he was abnormally sensitive to the opinions of other people. He was intelligent but had no sense of humour whatever—even Old Doc admitted that. But in every other respect Old Doc thought him a model and was exasperated because Gertrude didn't fancy him.

Gertrude admitted that he had an immense number of points.

"But he doesn't add up right," she said.

"What fault can you find in him?" challenged Old Doc angrily.

"None. But he tastes flat. He has all the virtues, but the pinch of salt was left out," said Gertrude, with her nose in the air.

Old Doc snorted and kicked a chair across the room.

"I can't see why you don't like him."

"But I do like him," asseverated Gertrude. "I like fully half the young men in Claremont. What then? I can't marry half the young men in Claremont, can I?"

"What can you do with a girl like that?" he demanded.

"Nothing," I said, "but let her marry Anthony."

"Never," said Old Doc, punishing his left hand with his right. "If you back Anthony up, Crandall, I swear I'll leave your church and go over to the Baptists."

I kept silence thereafter, not because I was afraid of Old Doc going over to the Baptists—who wouldn't have taken him as a gift—but because I knew I would only do Anthony harm by sticking up for him.

Gordon had a good position in his uncle's store and would eventually be head man and his uncle's heir. He was kind and obliging, but I always thought he was selfish. Certainly his mother spoiled him. His father was dead and she doted on Gordon. She was not in the least like him—she was a tall, austere, reserved woman who, for some reason I never could fathom, was a tremendous favourite with Old Doc.

Anthony and Gordon had always hated each other, even long before they set their fancy on the same woman. They were enemies when they were boys. Gordon aggravated Anthony by sneering at his Italian mother one day, and Anthony took off Gordon's trousers and made him go home through Claremont in his poor little shirt-tail. Then Gordon poisoned Anthony's dog.

To be sure, he always asserted that he meant the poison for a mongrel from over the river that was always snooping around, stealing. I believed him, for I knew Gordon would never have flouted public opinion by poisoning respectable village dogs. But Anthony didn't. From that day he hated Gordon with an indescribable intensity—the Italian blood did come out there. Yet I thought Gordon's hatred the deadlier thing of the two.

I think Gordon was quite sure he would win Gertrude. He couldn't believe that any girl would remain persistently indifferent to him. Anthony had cast some bewitchment over her, but that would pass—especially when Anthony, having got through college, suddenly shot off to Montreal to attend the School of Mines. He had sold his old Strad for nine hundred dollars to get board money. Nobody in Claremont but myself—not even Gertrude, I believe—realized what selling it meant to him. He walked the floor o' nights for a week afterwards. He told me he felt as if he had sold his own flesh and blood.

I went down to the Stirlings the night after Anthony had gone away and found Old Doc nearly speechless with rage. Anthony, it seemed, had come boldly there the previous evening to say goodbye to Gertrude, and Gertrude had insisted on seeing him and seeing him alone. But this wasn't what had maddened Old Doc.

It was the fact that Anthony had deliberately and wantonly—and apparently with Gertrude's toleration—adorned with horns and a tail a photograph of Gordon Mitchell that was standing on the piano. If Anthony had actually transmogrified Gordon into a devil Old Doc couldn't have been more worked up about it. He called Anthony all the names he could lay his tongue to—Old Doc's vocabulary of abuse was peculiarly rich—and prophesied a violent end for him.

"I hope not," I said mildly. "I shouldn't like to see your son-in-law hanged."

"Son-in-law! He'll never be a son-in-law of mine. No, thank God, I've fixed that. Gertrude has solemnly promised me that she'll never marry

Anthony Fairweather without my consent. You know how likely she is to get that."

Yes, I knew. I knew quite well that after Old Doc had fumed for a year or two, while Gertrude sat tight, he would suddenly give in and tell her to marry the Old Boy if she wanted to. I suppose Old Doc sensed something of this in my fece, for he roared,

"What are you chuckling inside about, Crandall? Do you think she won't keep her promise? I tell you she will."

I knew that too. Old Doc had brought Gertrude up to keep a promise. It was one of the few things he had put immense insistence upon. There was a sore spot somewhere in Old Doc—he had suffered horribly once because of someone's broken promise—I never heard the rights of the story—and he was determined that Gertrude should have it grained into her never to break a promise once given.

I knew she never would but I wasn't much worried over it. In spite of that promise I knew that Gordon Mitchell, hanging around more persistently than ever now that Anthony was gone, had just about as good a chance of marrying Gertrude Stirling as I had. Gertrude smiled and went to dances and flirted a wee bit with nice boys and wore delightful clothes and petted her father and thoroughly enjoyed herself.

And Old Doc left that bedizened photograph of Gordon on his desk and swore unholy oaths over it every day. Sometimes he raged at Ger-

trude because she wouldn't look on Gordon
with favour.

"You forget that I've promised Anthony that I
will never marry any man but him," she would
say sweetly. "I have to keep that promise as well
as the other. You've always told me I must never
break a promise."

Old Doc would glare.

"Anthony . . . Anthony . . . the man who said
he had only to ask you to get you!"

"He never said it," Gertrude would smile mad-
deningly. "But if he did . . . it would have been
true."

This rendered Old Doc speechless.

Gordon really had very little sense about his
courting. He had, of course, no chance with Gertrude, no matter what he did or didn't do, but
with some women he might have had a chance if
he had kept away for a time and left them alone.
Instead, he exasperated her by haunting the place
and forcing his attentions upon her everywhere.
She grew to hate the sight of him. Old Doc had
less sense also in the matter than I should have
expected of him. He had become quite chummy
with Gordon and even tried to teach him to play
golf. He would never have tried it if he had
thought Gordon would make a golfer, but there
was no danger. Gordon couldn't see anything in
it.

Two years went by like this. Anthony hadn't
been home. He went out with survey parties on
his vacations. I don't know whether he ever wrote

Gertrude. She never talked of him, and Old Doc thought she had forgotten him. I knew better.

Then a medical powwow came off in Croyden. Old Doc went to it, and Gordon Mitchell went down on the same train. It was in early spring—the frost was coming out—the rails had spread in one place—the engine jumped the track. Only one person was killed . . . Old Doc.

Gordon got to him just before he died. He hadn't been able to speak. Just smiled . . . pressed Gordon's hand . . . tried to say something . . . shut his eyes. That was all. Gertrude hadn't even a farewell word of love for her comforting.

She was heartbroken over it all. She and her father had been such chums.

"Father and I liked each other as well as loved each other," she had said to me once.

But a healthy grief heals in due time, no matter what its intensity. The day came when I heard her laugh again, though with something gained and something lost in her laughter.

I thought all would be plain sailing for her and Anthony now. She was her own mistress—a rich woman too, as Claremont standards went. But one autumn evening a year later Anthony came to me white to the lips with despair.

He told me the whole story, rushing up and down my study like a madman. Gertrude had told him she could never marry him; she had promised her father she would never marry Anthony "without his consent" and that consent could never now be obtained. Anthony had found her

quite immoveable. So he came to beg me to go to
Gertrude and use my influence on his behalf.

I went . . . though I had a feeling that it
wouldn't be any use. It was a cold, windy, autumn-
nal evening, and I found Gertrude by the open
fire in the living room, with Jigglesqueak snoring
beside her. She sat in the old wing chair and
looked so beautiful that I did not wonder at
Anthony's madness. She was not in black. Old
Doc had decreed in his will that she should not
follow "the barbarous survival" of mourning. She
wore a gown of golden-brown velvet, a little too
old and rich for a girl, I thought, but vastly
becoming. She had a rope of dull beads about her
slim white neck, and her black hair was pinned
close to her head with rich pins. On the middle
finger of her rather large firm white hand she
wore a ring her father had always worn—a ring
with some odd, flat, pale green stone in it. His
wife, I believe, had given it to him on their honey-
moon. It had been taken off Old Doc's dead hand.

"It's a fine evening," said Gertrude brilliantly.

"I haven't come to discuss the weather," I said.

"No," said Gertrude. "I know exactly what you
have come to say. So say it and ease your conscience. But it won't make any difference."

I said it . . . and it made no difference.

"You know," I said, for a final shot, "that your
father would have given in if he had lived."

Yes, she knew that.

"Then why the . . . the . . . the . . ."

"The devil," said Gertrude calmly. "That's what

you want to say, you know. Your cloth wouldn't let you say it so I say it for you. Go on from there."

"The mischief," I said, because I wasn't going to let a chit like Gertrude put a thing like that over on me. If she had no respect for my cloth she should have had some for my grey hairs. "Why the mischief can't you be sensible?"

"It isn't a matter of sense at all," said Gertrude. "I promised. I shall keep that promise to my father dead as I would have kept it to him living. Don't worry me with arguments, Mr. Crandall. Do you think you can move me when Anthony couldn't?"

"No. I'm not so conceited as that," I said. "But are you going to ruin Anthony's life and your own by such Quixotic nonsense?"

"Oh, it won't ruin our lives . . . Anthony's anyway. He'll get over it in time and marry somebody else. I may get over it myself . . . but I can never marry anyone else because I promised Anthony I wouldn't."

"Likely he will release you from that promise," I said drily.

"I shall never ask him to," she said. "Now, have a cup of tea with me, Mr. Crandall, and promise me that you'll help me to become a delightful old maid. There's nothing else for me, you see."

She poured my tea beautifully. She made an art of pouring tea. Then she sat and looked into the fire while I sipped it, the lovely line of her chin and neck melting into the red-gold glow of the flames behind it. And this was the woman who talked of being an old maid!

I told Anthony I had done my best and failed. I told him he must bear it like a man.

"How can you bear unbearable things?" he flung back at me as he rushed out, leaving all the doors open. I did not see him again for ten years.

Gertrude made short work of Gordon. She told me that since her father's death she simply detested him.

"I don't know why. I used to like him well enough before. Now I can't bear the sight of him. I've told him that I will never, under any circumstances, marry him and that he must stop plaguing my life out about it."

Gordon stopped. That winter he flung himself into business and church work with feverish activity. In the latter I saw a great deal of him and I thought him much changed in some indefinable way. He acted like a person desperately anxious to forget something . . . drug something . . . which was understandable enough in a man who had been refused by Gertrude Stirling.

He did not go as much into society as he had formerly done, and when he did people said he was subject to spells of moodiness, when he seemed to be brooding over something that worried him desperately. I felt that I ought to be very sorry for him.

One Sunday in early spring I preached a certain

sermon. I did mean it for somebody. A certain clique of people in the church, entirely unconnected with the Mitchells or the Stirlings, had been doing their best to worry my life out that winter with their spats and squabbles . . . all springing, as I knew perfectly well, from old Madam Ridgwood's deceit and mischief-making. I meant that sermon for her; it wasn't a hand-me-down, it was cut to fit. And everybody pinned it on to Gordon, a man whom nobody ever thought of as lying before that sermon. But I must say that they would not probably have done so if it had not been for his own behaviour.

My text was, "Deliver my soul, oh Lord, from lying lips and a deceitful tongue," and I made my sermon pretty strong, for I was considerably annoyed over the trouble I had encountered. Gordon was not in the choir that day. He was hoarse from a bad cold and he sat with his mother in the centre of the church.

Near the end of my discourse I happened to glance at Gordon and was struck by the expression on his face. I never saw such agony on a human countenance. I was sure he must be ill. Suddenly he stood up, turned round, looked foolishly about him, and sat down again . . . or was pulled down by his mother. I finished my sermon, leaving some few things I had intended to say unsaid, and the concluding hymn was sung. I did not see Gordon or his mother again.

But that evening Mrs. Mitchell sent for me. She met me at the door and told me that Gordon had gone out of his mind. She was in a distracted state, poor woman. But after I had seen Gordon and talked to him I knew that he was as sane as I was. He had simply forgotten everything—everything. He didn't even remember his own name. If he had just been born he couldn't have known less about his past.

Nowadays newspaper reports and popular books on neurasthenia have made us tolerably familiar with cases of this sort. But at that time, in Claremont, nobody had ever known anything like it. Most people persisted in believing that Gordon had gone insane—his grandfather, they said, had been "queer." His mother had every great alienist she could get, and they all agreed that he was perfectly sane and rational. They were quite helpless, but they said that his memory might return just as suddenly as it had gone. Meanwhile there was nothing to do but wait. His friends and his mother persisted in believing and asserting that my sermon was responsible for it all. When anyone said this to me I retorted, testily,

"Do you mean to say that Gordon was of lying lips and a deceitful tongue?"

That always posed everyone but Mrs. Mitchell. She said,

"Gordon was so conscientious. Some little evasion that nobody else would have thought a lie would worry him . . . and then your terrible sermon . . ."

She never forgave me.

A new doctor had come to town—a young fel-

low who knew a good bit, though people were
loath to admit that anyone knew anything but Old
Doc. I used to talk Gordon's case over with him.
He had some ideas about it that were so new-
fangled then that I couldn't accept them at all,
though I believe they are pretty well established
now.

"Mitchell has forgotten because he wanted to
forget," he said.

"Nonsense," I said. "Who would want to forget
his whole past life?"

"Oh, not his whole life . . . no, just one particular, unbearable thing. And when his torture
reached a certain point . . . perhaps your sermon
was the last turn of the rack . . . perhaps it had
nothing to do with it . . . he found relief from
his agony by forgetting what was torturing him.
Only," added Dr. Mills, who was fresh enough
from college to have a weakness for classical allu-
sions, "he who drinks of Lethe must forget his
good as well as his evil."

"I don't believe my sermon had anything to do
with it," I said.

And I couldn't see how it had. It was quite possible that Gordon's suffering over Gertrude's decision was unbearable and that he wanted to forget
it—but there could be no earthly connection
between it and my sermon. I believed he hadn't
been listening to it at all. He had been sitting
there, thinking wretchedly of Gertrude who sat
just across from him, looking unbelievably lovely,
and he couldn't endure it any longer. Something

gave way; in the pithy old vernacular, a screw got loose.

For a few weeks nothing was talked of but Gordon. Then Mary Curtis eloped and gossip switched to her. By the autumn everybody had accepted the new Gordon. He had accepted himself. After all, it was not correct to say that he had forgotten everything. He had not forgotten how to talk, read, write, behave in society, run his business. Of course he had forgotten everything and everybody connected with the business and had to get acquainted with it all over from the ground up. But he wasn't long in doing that. By spring he was going ahead full blast again, and a stranger would never have suspected that there was anything wrong with him. Only those who knew him well realized certain changes in him.

For one thing, he had forgotten all his loves and hates. In that respect his emotional life was a clean slate. He didn't love his mother . . . he, who had been so devoted to her. He didn't even like her; she knew it and it broke her heart, especially as the time went by and she realized that he never would like her. He cared nothing for any of his old friends. In a few cases he built up new friendships with some of them; to others he always remained indifferent. He had no interest in church work and wouldn't, I believe, have attended church at all if it hadn't been for public opinion which, in Claremont, was very hard on a man who flouted the church.

The greatest change in him, or what seemed so

to me, was in regard to Gertrude. She had gone
into limbo with everything else. I even thought
he seemed rather ill at ease in her presence, but
that may only have been my imagination. Anyhow, he cared nothing for her. He even tried to
go with other Claremont girls, but nobody would
have anything to do with him because he was
"queer" and he soon gave up trying. There was
a barrier between him and his kind.

I noticed one thing about him . . . I don't know
whether anyone else did or not. Sometimes he
would suddenly glance over his shoulder in a way
I didn't like. And it made him uncomfortable to
shake hands with anyone. That could be plainly
seen, but I never saw him absolutely refuse to
shake hands save once.

That was when Gertrude came home from a
long visit in Croyden, met him at a garden party
and offered him her hand. He looked . . . not at
her . . . not at her hand . . . but at the big ring
with the pale green stone. He turned death-white
and put his hands behind him. Gertrude thought
it odd, but then, one must expect poor Gordon to
be odd.

This was years after the fatal sermon. Time had
gone on. Everybody had given up expecting Gordon Mitchell's memory to come back . . . everybody but his mother, who nursed a feverish hope
and lived on it. Plenty of newcomers didn't know
he had forgotten. He was our most successful
businessman and was piling up a fortune. But he
was nothing like as rich as Anthony Fairweather.

Anthony had got through his School of Mines

and had gone surveying up in Cobalt at a dollar and a half a day. There he found the famous Lucia silver mine—named after his mother—and became, as you might say, a millionaire overnight. Even that didn't spoil him. He kept on working hard and soon was at the top of his profession, and a recognized expert on all questions of engineering. He had a hobby for collecting violins—his collection, headed by his old Strad, which he had hunted up and bought back, was the finest in America. He had all the good luck in the world . . . except the one bit he really wanted.

Claremont people referred to him with pride as the "most distinguished of all our boys," and served up the tales of his youthful pranks with an entirely different sauce. One would have supposed, from the way they talked, that there was some vital connection between offering soap for cheese and discovering silver mines and that they'd always known it. If Anthony had ever come home he would have been met at the station with a brass band and a torchlight procession.

But he never did come home. He never wrote to Gertrude, but now and then he sent her something rare and beautiful in the way of curios. It was always something that belonged to her—something which must have made Anthony say, the moment his eyes lighted on it, "That is Gertrude's . . . it couldn't be anybody else's." And on every one of her birthdays came a great sheaf of crimson roses from the Croyden florist. Anthony never forgot a birthday.

Gertrude seemed to be enjoying her life. She had a good time. Travelled a bit . . . entertained a bit . . . organized and ran some good clubs and societies . . . was a Regent of the Claremont Chapter of the I.O.D.E. and President of the Women's Canadian Club and the backbone of the Hypatia Circle. Her home was a thing of beauty, and the talks she and I had by her fireside, in the days of her maturity, were sometimes all that kept me sane amid the distracting problems of a minister's daily life.

"Drop in whenever you like," Gertrude had said to me. "You'll always find a chair by the fire and a cat on the rug."

Cats! I should say so. When Jigglesqueak had finally gone where good dogs go, lamented by all who had the privilege of knowing him, Gertrude went in for cats, being bound, so she said, to have all the prescriptive rights of old maidenhood. She wasn't really particularly fond of cats but she admired their general effect.

"Cats give atmosphere . . . charm . . . suggestion," she averred.

She had a big blue Persian that Anthony had sent her and four inky black toms. The Persian had some high-falutin name I've forgotten, but Gertrude called all the toms "Soot"—Soot I, II, III, and IV. They used to sit about looking so uncannily knowing, with their insolent green eyes, that their very expression would have sent Gertrude to the stake three hundred years ago. I am reasonably fond of cats, but those four black demons of

Gertrude's always gave me a slightly weird sensation.

Well, there she was. I groaned inwardly when I looked at her—beautiful, desirable, a king's daughter, glorious without and within, but—I was certain of it in spite of her jokes and her philosophy—a lonely, empty-hearted, starved woman.

Ten years after Old Doc's death Anthony came home. He was home for a week, staying with his old aunt, before anyone else—unless it was Gertrude—knew of it. He said he had come to Claremont for a good rest and meant to stay a month. Most people believed and said that he had come back to warm up the cold soup with Gertrude Stirling. Myself, I thought he had too. I wished he could and I knew he couldn't.

He was a splendid-looking fellow, fit as a fiddle, strong, distinguished, and graceful. There was an air of immortal, unquenchable youth about him. Beside him Gordon Mitchell looked tubby and middle-aged. Gordon had forgotten his hate of Anthony along with everything else and was prepared to be quite cordial to him. But Anthony had forgotten nothing. He believed that Gordon had poisoned Old Doc's mind in regard to him at the very beginning and he hated him with as much intensity as ever.

"Sneaking cad!" he said bitterly to me. "If it hadn't been for him . . . but it maddens me to think of it!"

"Isn't there any chance, Anthony?" I asked,

although I knew there wasn't. "Have you said anything to Gertrude?"

"Said anything! Said anything! Is there anything I haven't said? I've prayed and stormed and raged and threatened and grovelled . . . man, I've even cried! I came back . . . I had to come back . . . I thought perhaps she'd have changed her mind in those ten infernal years. She hasn't . . . she never will. Unless Old Doc comes back out of his grave to set her free she'll never marry me . . . never!"

Anthony groaned, and then said, in his old whimsical way, as if he wanted to camouflage the intensity of his feelings,

"And we would make such a darn good-looking couple, wouldn't we, Mr. Crandall?"

"I'm a bit out of patience with Gertrude," I said. "I think the whole thing is absolute nonsense."

"I won't have Gertrude abused," said Anthony. "Thank God there's one woman in the world anyhow that will keep her word. I don't blame her. It's all Gordon's doings. He told Old Doc lies about me years ago . . . I know he did. Hound! I tell you that if Gordon Mitchell were in deadly danger of his life and I could save him by lifting a finger I wouldn't lift it!"

It was rather funny that the very next day Gordon Mitchell should fall out of his canoe in the middle of the Claremont river and that Anthony Fairweather should rescue him!

Gordon was a member of the Canoe Club, but the only wonder was he hadn't drowned himself long before. His Maker had never meant him for canoes. On this day he was right out on the middle of the river when he upset. Only three people saw it: Anthony and myself and little Stan Baird.

In Anthony went, clothes and all, as quick as a flash.

There wasn't another man in Claremont—or out of it, as I believe—who could have swum that distance to Gordon Mitchell in time. As it was he was almost too late. Gordon had gone down for the last time, but Anthony dived, got him and brought him back to the wharf. Old Captain Fairweather had taught Anthony to swim when he was a lad of five, and if his soul were hovering anywhere around that day he must have been proud of his pupil. It was a splendid piece of work, as even I, dancing around on the wharf in a senile frenzy of horror and suspense, fully understood.

Anthony sent Stan Baird for Dr. Mills and fell to work with Gordon after the most scientific fashion. I helped as best I could, and by the time the doctor got there, with a crowd of folks pelting after him, Gordon had come back to life. They got him into a cab and took him home before he could speak coherently.

"So that's that," said Anthony. "Well, I'd better go home myself and get something dry. And I think I'll start back to Montreal tomorrow. There's no chance of me getting what I came for . . . and they'll heroize me for this stunt in the usual sickening way. I can't stand it . . . especially as I'm good and sorry I didn't let the brute drown!''

That evening Mrs. Mitchell sent for me again. She met me at the door with such a transfigured face that I hardly knew her.

"Oh, Mr. Crandall, Gordon has come back!" she exclaimed. "He remembers everything. And he knows me . . . he knows I'm his mother."

She was weeping with joy as she took me up to Gordon's room. He was in bed, shouldered up on the pillows. He greeted me kindly but he looked past me.

"Haven't they come yet?" he said.

"They'll be here soon," said Mrs. Mitchell soothingly.

"They" came almost on her words—"they" were Gertrude and Anthony, both looking puzzled. Evidently neither of them understood just why they had been thus summoned to take part in Gordon Mitchell's resurrection.

"Sit down. I have something to tell you," said Gordon. "I have Mr. Crandall here for a witness. Mother, please go out."

She went, too thankful for the old affection in his eyes and voice to resent being thus shut out. Anthony and Gertrude did not sit down. They continued standing just inside the door, where the pale lilac light of sunset fell on them through the window.

Gertrude was dressed in some rich, cream-hued stuff, with gold touches here and there and a heavy gold girdle. She looked like a brocaded moth. The years had not dimmed her beauty. Anthony as usual looked dark and royal.

They were, as Anthony had said a . . . ahem . . . an exceedingly good-looking pair of people.

Gordon began:

"I did not tell you the truth about your father's death, Gertrude. He lived a few minutes after I reached him. He said, 'I'm dying, Gordon. Give Gertrude my love and tell her she can marry whom she darn well pleases.' "

What odd thoughts come into one's mind at times. I looked at Gertrude and saw the miracle of her face, but all I really thought just then was, "Gordon has softened down Old Doc's expression a bit. Gordon wouldn't say even a second-hand damn."

"Your father," went on Gordon, "made me promise I would tell you. 'Shake hands on it,' he said, holding out his right hand with that big green stone on it. I shook . . . although even then I knew I wasn't going to tell you. Then he said, 'She's had the best golfer in town for a father; now she'll have to put up with the second-best as a husband. But when I'm dead Anthony will be the best, confound him.' Those were his last words . . . then he died.

"I didn't tell you," continued Gordon. "I couldn't. It would have been like cutting my heart out. But I lived in hell for that year . . . a hell I made for myself. I knew I ought to tell. I used to think, when at times it seemed I couldn't bear it any longer, 'Oh, if I could only forget what Old

Doc said!' Then you preached that sermon"—
Gordon flung me a glance—"and I knew I
couldn't bear it any longer. I stood up . . . I don't
know what I meant to say . . . and everything
went from me. You know all about that. But
today, just as I was drowning, I remembered
everything . . . everything! It was like the judg-
ment day."

Gordon shuddered.

"You'd better not talk any more just now, Gordon," I said soothingly.

"There's something else I want to confess," said
Gordon pathetically. "It was I told Old Doc that
Anthony said he could have Gertrude for the asking. That was a lie. And I shut the skunk up in
the classroom. I did it for a joke . . . and people
made such a fuss about it I was ashamed to confess. That's all."

He didn't ask to be forgiven, but Gertrude took
his hand and pressed it before she went out with
Anthony. They had the decency to hide their rapture until they got out of Gordon's sight. Gordon's eyes followed Gertrude starvingly. Yes,
everything had come back, even his love for her.
He groaned as she went out, hidden from him by
Anthony's broad shoulders.

But his mother slipped in past them, and he
turned to her and held out his hands like a child
seeking for comfort. I got up and went out. Neither of them heard me go.

I thought it all over as I walked up the street.
I could not be as hard on Gordon as he deserved.

Editorial Note

The stories in this collection were originally published in the following magazines and newspapers, and are listed here in alphabetical order. Obvious typographical errors have been corrected, spelling and punctuation normalized.

After Many Days, *Ram's Horn*, March 1903.

Between the Hill and the Valley, *Springfield Republican*, August 1905 (and as The Hill and the Valley, *Maclean's*, April 1915).

The Bride Roses, *Christian Endeavor World*, October 1903.

Elizabeth's Child, *Young People*, December 1904.

For a Dream's Sake, *Family Herald*, January 1935

A Golden Wedding, *American Messenger*, June 1909.

In the Old Valley, *American Agriculturist*, September 1906; and as The Old Valley, *Holland's Magazine*, March 1910.

The Man Who Forgot, *Family Herald*, January 1932.

Missy's Room, *Lion's Herald*, July 1907.

Mrs. March's Revenge, *Western Christian Advocate*, February 1904.

The Price, *Chatelaine*, March 1930.

The Prodigal Brother, *Ram's Horn*, May 1906; also *Holland's Magazine*, March 1914.

Robert Turner's Revenge, *Springfield Republican*, May 1909.

The Romance of Aunt Beatrice, *Springfield Republican*, April 1902.

The Romance of Jedediah, *Housewife*, September 1912.

The Setness of Theodosia, *Springfield Republican*, October 1901; also *Westminster*, January 1910.

The Story of Uncle Dick, *American Agriculturist*, July 1906.

An Unpremeditated Ceremony, *Gunter's Magazine*, May 1907; also *Canadian Courier*, February 1910.

Acknowledgements

The late Dr. Stuart Macdonald gave me permission to begin the research that culminated in my collection of Montgomery's stories; Professors Mary Rubio and Elizabeth Waterston encouraged and advised me; C. Anderson Silber gave his constant support. Librarians were unfailingly helpful.

ABOUT THE AUTHOR

L. M. MONTGOMERY'S fascinating accounts of the lives and romances of Anne, Emily, and other well-loved characters have achieved long-lasting popularity the world over. Born in 1874 in Prince Edward Island, Canada, Lucy Maud showed an early flair for storytelling. She soon began to have her writing published in papers and magazines, and when she died in Toronto in 1942 she had written more than twenty novels and a large number of short stories. Most of her books are set in Prince Edward Island, which she loved very much and wrote of most beautifully. *Anne of Green Gables*, her most popular work, has been translated into thirty-six languages, made into a film twice, and has had continuing success as a stage play. Lucy Maud Montgomery's early home in Cavendish, P.E.I., where she is buried, is a much-visited historic site.